GOT IT OUT DA MUD: This is a work of fiction and this statement is included to inform the reader that any celebrity name(s), business name(s), location(s), product(s), and organizations that are stated in the content of this book are real. However, they are used in a way that is purely fictional.

GOT IT OUT DA MUD

Written by: Andre McDougal

Illistrations: LeRoy Grayson
Published by: Jazzy Kitty Publications

Got It Out Da Mud

By Andre McDougal

Cover Art Created by LeRoy Grayson

Logo Design by Justin Ackerman and Angel Jones

Editor: Anelda L. Attaway

Co-editor: Andre McDougal

© 2023 Andre McDougal

ISBN 978-1-954425-68-2

Library of Congress Control Number: 2023900008

All rights reserved. This book is protected under the copyright laws of the United States of America. This book may not be copied or reprinted for commercial gain or profit. The use of short quotations or occasional page copying for personal or group study is permitted and encouraged. Permission will be granted upon request for Worldwide Distribution, available in Paperback. Printed in the United States of America. Published by Jazzy Kitty Greetings Marketing & Publishing, LLC. Dba Jazzy Kitty Publications utilizing Microsoft Publishing Software. Please be advised this book has strong language and content. Parental Advisory is suggested due to mature content. Disclaimer: This is a work of fiction and any celebrity name(s), business name(s), location(s), product(s), and organizations, while real are used in a way that is purely fictional.

DEDICATION

This book is dedicated to Jerome Boomer Green, Barry Cabber Wilson, and Wayne Reeves.

These are some of the realist dudes to ever grace the face of this earth. I know you're watching; I know y'all got my back until I reach the other side. I'm gonna stay a real nigga.

TABLE OF CONTENTS

TABLE OF CONTENTS

INTRODUCTION

Welcome to the main streets of Wilmington, Delaware, a.k.a. Hellaware, a.k.a. Murdertown, USA, where either you slangin' crack rock, or you got a wicked jump shot. Options are limited in the inter-city; role models are drug dealers, pimps and hustlers, and all niggas care about is money, cash, hoes, respect, and loyalty are rare.

This tale I'm about to spin is about two inner-city youths searching for a come up somehow; someway, a lot of shit comes with the game and they will soon find out, but will they rise to the occasion or die trying?

Well, buckle up because you're in for a treat. One of the best Urban Fiction Hood novels in quite some time. Follow Saleem and Scooby on their journey through the trenches of Wilmington, Delaware; you won't be disappointed.

CHAPTER 1

Show Me the Blueprint

Where I ask you to try your best to reach a verdict. If you still can't, I will be forced to declare a mistrial. The court will remain in recess until the jury is ready to be heard.

"Wow!!!" exclaims El-Jefe's attorney Tod Henry out of Philadelphia.

"This is good for us. How are you feeling?"

"Mr. Parker, you already know I am cool as a fan on in the wintertime." Using one of his many lines that he is known for…

Look at 'em now they/even fuckin scared of us/callin' the city/ for help 'cause they can't maintain/man shit done change. Biggie Smalls

"Boy, turn the damn music down; I can't hear myself think. All that damn boombty-bop shit in here all early in the morning and you need to take ya ass to school or find a job or somethin'. You ain't goin' be satisfied til ya ass in jail again. I ain't goin' come see ya ass neither. Since you think you so grown, I know you been smokin' weed and sellin' drugs. You better not have no police runnin' up in my house lookin' for ya ass neither."

"Mom! Mom! Chill!!! You buggin' with all that!"

"Boy, who the hell you think you talking to? You ain't too old to get back slapped. You might got them cowards in the street scared of you, but I ain't. I brought you in this world and I'll take you out!" shouts Ms. Betty, "Saleem, I love you and I just want you to be safe. Little boys your age are dying out there every day. Look at little Howie from down the projects, he was 14 years old. I don't want that for you. Do you understand?"

"Yeah, mom I feel you."

"Alright, now give me a hug."

Boom, Boom, Boom!

"Who the fuck is that bangin' on my door like they the mothafuckin' police. If it ain't, they goin' need 'em 'cause Imma put my foot in somebody ass. Who is it?!" yells Ms. Betty.

"It's me, Mom Betty."

"Me who!" she yells, snatchin' the door open, "Scooby boy, hey baby, I ain't no that was you; baby, you don't be knocking like the police next time. Saleem upstairs in his room."

"A'ight, Mom Betty."

My mom always did love herself some Scooby. She swears that nigga is an angel; that nigga smokes more weed and sells more drugs than me.

"Whats up nigga?" exclaims Scooby.

"Man, you already know I'm cool as a fan on in the wintertime." They both burst out laughin'

"Nigga you think you the shit."

"Nah nigga, I know I'm the shit."

"It's a difference, but you wouldn't know that being though you got shit for brains."

"All nigga fuck you. Nah, on some real shit, whats good for the day? I know you got a come-up lick for us or somethin'," said Scooby.

"Ma nigga, you already know what it is wit me. Don't a day go by I don't get high, get money, fuck bitches or commit a homicide."

"Yeah, Yeah, I heard that fly Shit."

"Whats the look?" (meaning the plan) said Scooby.

"Well, if you shut ya thirsty ass up, I can tell you," Saleem said with a smirk on his face, "but Nah, on some shit ma Nigga I've been watchin' them Jamaicans heavy. They fuckin' it up on Vandiver Avenue and now they got a nerve to be coming around the way fuckin' with our flow; them curry goat eatin' Mafuckas gotta go."

"Word, I feel you on that. You already know I'm down; ma nigga just show me the blueprint."

CHAPTER 2

Ayonna

"Ring, Ring, Ring!"

"Hello."

"Bitch, what chu' doing?" asked Tameka Ayonna's bestie.

Ayonna replied, "Sitting here thinking bout my boo."

"Bitch Stop the press; what the fuck else is new," said Tameka, with sarcasm dripping from every word.

"Hoe you just mad 'cause ya trifling ass can't keep a man," replied Ayonna.

"No Bitch I choose to be single; it's too many dicks out here to be sucked and fucked dry for me to playhouse with just one nigga," said Tameka. Both burst out laughin.'

"Bitch, you are so crazy wit cha nasty ass self," said Ayonna, "but no girl, I'm about to get dressed. I am not trying to hear my mom's mouth. I can hear her now; I don't worry, lazy bitches get your ass up for school!!!" Ayonna replied, imitating her mother.

"Well, girl, Imma let you get yourself together; I'll see you at school."

"A'ight, bye."

As Ayonna gets out of bed, she stretches her thick young legs and her arms as high as she can to the sky, then looks at herself in the mirror.

"Yeah, Imma bad young bitch."

And that she is at 15 years old, she's built like a grown ass woman, 5'2, caramel complexed, petite waist, nice bubble ass, some not too big, not too small perky titties and pretty shoulder length hair. She stays fly thanks to her dad Naheem, an O.G. from the hood that used to sell big coke back in the day but got out and went legit. He owns a lot of property; some say he still hustles on the low, but hey, to each his own.

Ayonna takes a shower, brushes her teeth, and gets dressed in her DKNY sweatsuit and some 5411 Reeboks to match. She then eats a bowl of cereal and heads for school.

CHAPTER 3

Omega is Gone

Nigga, you ain't gotta explain shit/I've been robbing motherfuckas since the slave ships/With the same clip and the same .45," by Biggie Smalls

"Man turn that shit down," said Saleem, "you got to be the dumbest robber ever playin' loud ass music outside a nigga crib. You bout to rob him."

"Man, you right," said Scooby, "but I use Biggie Shit as motivation."

"Yeah, I feel all that," said Saleem, "but the only motivation you and I both need is in them Dreadz spot ma nigga."

"True, True," replied Scooby.

"Now listen, you remember what I told you at the house, right?" asked Saleem.

"Yeah nigga, I ain't slow."

"Well, let's get this party started then ma nigga."

Saleem and Scooby both exit the sloop ride that they got from a junkie earlier for some coke. Both carrying handguns, Saleem keeps a .38 revolver on him; he said he likes them because they don't leave shells behind. Scooby carries a black nine; his motto is dead men can't tell no tales. Saleem looks all around, scanning the area before he creeps through the alley way blending in with the night in an all-black dickie suit, all-black gloves and black-on-black Reebok classics in case he has to take flight. On the other hand, Scooby is dressed as a Pizza Bellboy from Season's Pizza on Market Street. See, the plan is to get the front door open and 'cause a scene to make everyone come to the front door while Saleem climbs through the open kitchen window. He peeped days before that it's always open; this way, he has the element of surprise on his side. So as Scooby knocks on the front door, you can hear the music get turned down low and footsteps approach the door.

"OOW Dere?" a Jamaican with a strong accent asked.

"It's Season Pizza, Sir," said Scooby.

"Me no order no pizza!" the Jamaican yells through the door.

"Well, somebody here did and I'm not leaving until somebody pays for this shit. I ain't come here for nothing."

The Jamaican swings the door open fast, "OOW the fuck you tink talk to like dat?"

"I'm talkin' to you, you ugly Shabba Ranks-looking Mafucka!" said Scooby.

"Blood clot!" exclaims the Jamaican, followed by, "you don't know OOW ya fuck wit, do you? You little pussy clot madda fucker."

By now, two more Jamaicans approach the door; one with a shotgun and the other with a Rambo-style hunting knife in hand and a blunt dangling from his mouth. He's known in the street as Omega a big-time weed and coke dealer.

He said, blunt still dangling from his mouth in a heavy accent, "What dem boy want Max?"

The Jamaican that opened the door said, "'Em must want death comin' 'round 'ere talkin' like 'em killer."

Meanwhile, Saleem has successfully climbed through the kitchen window and is now creeping toward the front of the house, where everyone is distracted by Scooby. Saleem observes the situation. He sees one Jamaican has a shotgun and the other a knife.

He cases up on the one with the shotgun and whispers, "Don't move or I'll put your thoughts all over your comrades."

Omega turns slowly, "What the blood clot?"

Scooby pulls out his gun and now everyone realizes they've been set up. Scooby ushers everyone into the house and closes and locks the door behind them.

Saleem begins to speak, "I know you motherfuckers may look dumb, but I'm pretty sure y'all smart enough to know this is a robbery. The faster you cooperate the faster me and homeboy can blow this joint. Now it's on y'all; we can do this the easy way or the hard way; it really don't matter to me. So, what is going to be?" asked Saleem.

No one speaks, so Saleem smacks Omega upside the head sending him crashing to the floor with his head bleeding profusely.

"Dumba clot! What da fuck you do dat for!" exclaims Omega.

"Now, the next time, I'm putting hot shit in everybody! What de fuck it's going to be! Where the money and the drugs? All of it!!!" yells Saleem.

He makes eye contact with Scooby and then tells him to watch them as he heads for the kitchen. As he made his way through the window when he first came in, he noticed a bag of potatoes sitting by the refrigerator. He grabs one out of the bag and twists it on his .38 revolver to use it as a makeshift silencer. He then walks back into the front room and turns up the Island music they've been listening to. Then puts the gun to Max's head and squeezes the trigger.

"What Fuck!" Scooby said out loud.

Saleem replied, "It was too many of them, 3 on 2; I didn't like those odds. Now it's even and I also want these fake ass Rude boys to know we mean business. So, as I said earlier, where's the money and the drugs?" With no hesitation, Omega rises to his feet and leads Saleem down to the basement. As soon as you hit the bottom steps, you can smell the weed.

Omega said, "Ova dere." Pointing to a door towards the back.

"Nah mafucker, you open that shit and do it slowly or catch this hot shit," Saleem said.

"Me no want no problem, my yout everything is in dere, drugs, money, one hundred pounds of Ganja, 10 bricks of cocaine, and a hundred and eighty-five thousand dollars. Dats everything, I swear."

"Okay," replied Saleem, "now open the door."

Omega does as told and just like Omega said, everything is there stacked up real nice. Without warning, Saleem cuts Omega's throat with the Rambo-style knife he took from the other Jamaican upstairs. Omega clutches his throat, wide eyes and drops to his knees. He coughs up blood, shakes violently, and dies. Saleem Looks around in search of something to carry everything in. In the corner of the basement by the heater, he notices bags of what appear to be clothes and a set of old-looking suitcases.

"Bingo!" he exclaims.

Immediately he starts to fill the suitcases and once they are full, he grabs two and carries them into the kitchen, then goes back down the basement and retrieves the others.

He stops and sighs, "Damn them shits heavy," then wipes sweat from his brow as he walks back into the front room.

He makes eye contact with Scooby, who notices he's by his self and knowing Saleem, the Jamaican once known as Omega is gone. Saleem passes Scooby the already bloody knife and nods toward the remaining Jamaican; with no words spoken, Scooby knows it's time to handle business. He slits the Jamaican's throat with ease, the Jamaican dies silently.

"Yo, come help grab all this shit. We up ma nigga!" exclaims Saleem with excitement.

CHAPTER 4

Biggie at Pulsations

24th and Jessup Street, located on the Northside of Wilmington, Delaware.

"Yo Que did you hear from Saleem and Scooby," asked Cousin Wayne.

"Nah, not since yesterday and that was early in the day. They said they was on a mission; I told 'em be careful and haven't heard from them Lil' niggas since," replied Que.

"Well, I hope them niggas good. I wanted to take them niggas to see Biggie Smalls up Pulsations in PA," said Cousin Wayne.

"Yeah, I forgot Big was comin' up there to perform his hit "One More Chance" them Lil' niggas love Big, they goin' be hype," replied Que.

So, whats up wit you and the broad Carmen?" asked Cousin Wayne.

"Man, what you mean, whats up? I fucked, that's it, nothing more nothing less," replied Que.

"I heard that," responds cousin Wayne, "I was askin' 'cause you know that's the boy Ali's baby mom over Westside," said Cousin Wayne.

"And you say that to say what?" asked Que.

"Nah Nigga, it ain't bout nothin'. I was just seeing if you knew 'cause I don't trust these bitches. She could be on some setup shit; you feel me? I was just trying to make sure ma nigga was on point; that's all replied," Cousin Wayne.

"Oh, Okay, that's whats up," responds Que.

"Yeah, I know it's whats up, you tender dick ass nigga. I was makin' sure you ain't fall in love," cracks cousin Wayne.

"Fuck you Nigga," responds Que. And they both burst out laughin'.

"Yo wake up nigga," said Saleem to Scooby, who stayed the night.

"Man, whats up dog? Everything alright," replied Scooby, still half sleep.

"Yeah, ma nigga everything good, but we got to get all this work up outta ma moms crib; also, we got to holler at Cousin Wayne and Que. They'll definitely be able to give us some good advice on how to move all this work smart," said Saleem.

"Man, I don't think we should tell nobody; we smart ma nigga. You before ya time, you the smartest nigga I know. We can do this ourselves," replied Scooby.

"Ma nigga, I'm glad you believe in me like you do, but you and I both know that we ain't never had this much work and we some Lil' niggas we need some advice from somebody that's older and wiser. Don't never think you too old to take advice from nobody, remember that," said Saleem to a now more focused Scooby, "besides, we goin' break them off anyway. They our ol' heads them niggas make sure we good always, so now it's our turn to show our appreciation."

"You right," responds Scooby.

"Now let's go break some of this shit down, then go holler at cousin and them."

"A'ight," replied Scooby.

Just before they get started the phone rings.

CHAPTER 5

Ayonna and Saleem

"Argh!!!" exclaims Ayonna, "I know this boy betta answer the phone."

"Yo, who dis," a voice booms through her line.

"Boy, if you don't take all that bass out of your voice tryin' to sound grown." They both begin to laugh.

"Nah baby, whats up with chu'?" asked Saleem.

"Nothin' just sittin' here wonderin' why I haven't heard from you lately or seen you in school," replied Ayonna.

"Babe, I been busy, shit been hectic. A lot of shit been going on, but I promise things are about to change," responds Saleem.

"Yeah, yeah I hear you."

"Nah, real shit, babe," said Saleem.

"Babe, if it's someone else just tell me 'cause I'm too pretty to be getting played. Niggas be on my top daily and I shoot all of them lames down because I love you Saleem."

"Whoa, whoa, whoa, Sweetheart, I don't know where all this comin' from but pump ya breaks with all that somebody else shit. I'm out here in the streets tryin' to get this money, so me and mines don't have to struggle. I don't have time for no bitches; you my lady, that's it that's all and as far as the next nigga tryin' to get at chu' that's the least of my worries. If the next nigga can get you just like that then I never had you in the first place," replied Saleem, "baby, I know I haven't been the best boyfriend, but things are about to change, trust me. Give me some time, I love you, Sweetheart, I'll talk to you later."

"I love you more Saleem; I'm sorry for trippin'."

"Whoa, what I tell you about sorry."

"My bad, I apologize," Ayonna replied, remembering that Saleem told her never to say sorry unless you're a sorry person, so say you apologize. Ayonna smiles to herself as she remembers his words; as she snaps out of her reverie, she notices Saleem has hung up.

"Hello, Hello, argh!!! I hate when he does that."

She lays back and hugs her pillow wishing it was Saleem.

CHAPTER 6

Cousin Wayne

Saleem and Scooby bend the corner of 23rd and Jessup Street on their way up to 24th and Jessup in search of they old heads Cousin Wayne and Que. as they near the corner, they notice a big crowd.

"Saleem, what the fuck is going on up there?" asked Scooby.

"It looks like a riot or a crap game; knowing Cousin Wayne and Que, it's probably a crap game," responds Saleem.

As they get closer, they realize it's a crap game. Cousin Wayne got the dice, piles of money on the ground, everybody was screaming out bets, and the smell of weed is in the air heavy. Somebody got the car system blasting Biggie's new single "Juicy" the block live as always. Bitches everywhere, young bitches, old bitches, bad bitches, ugly bitches, light skin, dark skin, whatever the flavor the hood got 'em all. As we approach, Cousin Wayne sees us.

"All shit y'all know I am bout to break all you dumb bastards; now my youngins just popped up," said Cousin Wayne causing the whole crowd to turn in, look at us, then right back to the game.

Cousin Wayne rolls the dice and they land on eight.

"Nobody move; who bet six – eight? Gimme the loot, gimme the loot!" he yells like the Biggie song off of his Ready to Die album, "I told y'all I was goin' break you dumb bastards; now bet back if you can," replied Cousin Wayne.

A couple of niggas do, but the rest don't. Cousin shakes and rolls the dice again.

As he releases them, he yells, "Six bitches!"

And as if the dice heard him and understood they stopped on two - four. The bitches scream, niggas that lost yell fuck!!!

"Gimme the loot, gimme the loot!" Cousin Wayne yells.

Niggas pass off except for one dumb nigga that thinks he's exempt from paying.

Cousin Wayne looked at him and said, "Pay up your broke ass nigga, you ain't special. Point was six points seen money lost. You know how the game go," exclaims Cousin Wayne, "what you thought I wasn't goin' throw two - four on two-four?" The crowd burst out laughin', especially the bitches all on Cousin Wayne's dick.

The nigga that's holdin' out is none other than Gangstar nigga from the projects that gets a dollar but always try to chump niggas just because. He tells Cousin Wayne he beat and to suck his dick, get it like Tyson's pussy; with that being said, I reach for my .38 revolver. Scooby follows suit and grips his nine double M. Cousin Wayne looks at us 'cause he already knows how we play, but instead of giving us the okay, he smiles and winks at us and shakes his head no, so we fall back.

Our other ol' head Que spoke up and said, "Yo Star give Cousin his money before this shit go too far."

Gangstar replied, "Man, I ain't trying to hear that bullshit you talkin' bout nigga. I ain't never like you fake ass pretty boy wanna be as niggas any way. So, it's whatever with me," states Gangstar.

But now the couple niggas Gangstar brought wit 'em are looking like they wanna buck as well. I give Cousin Wayne another look like whats up, but he still shakes his head no.

He stepped up to Gangstar and said, "Get it like Tyson, huh?"

Then just like that he punches Star square on the chin punching him out cold, then goes in his pocket and takes what he won and throws the rest in the air and a frenzy breaks out. Everybody's trying to pick up as many bills as they can. The niggas that come with Gangstar pick him up and put him in one of the cars they come in, then pull off.

When they get to the end of the block, one of them gets out and shoots up in the air and shouts, "Riverside Mafuckers!" Then jumps back in the car.

Of course, everybody scatters and takes cover, not knowing that the shots were fired into the sky.

Que tells Wayne, "You know you may have just started a war, so stay strapped and on point."

Cousin Wayne, cocky as usual, replied, "I don't give a fuck about no war and I go where I want when I want. Fuck them niggas; they know what it is."

Que replied, "Let's get the fuck from round here plus, Saleem and Scooby said they need to talk to us about some things. So, let's go around my spot and chill for a while.

CHAPTER 7

The News

"Damn Cousin Wayne, you still got it too!" exclaims Saleem.

"It ain't going nowhere no time soon Lil' nigga," replied Cousin Wayne.

"I heard that ol' head," Saleem states in response.

"Yo Que turn that up," said Saleem.

"Youngin' you don't know nothin' about this here," replied Que as he turned up the volume and started rappin' the song out loud with the artist known as Scarface. *"Money in the power money in the power, I ain't fallin' short 'cause I get money in the power."*

"Yeah, yeah, yeah, that's my shit!" exclaims Saleem all hype, "that's what I'm talkin' bout y'all money in the power. Yo turn it down Que, so I can tell you what that look is," said Saleem.

"Okay, Okay, calm down, Lil' nigga; whats on ya mind. Cousin pass the weed baby sittin' ass nigga," said Que.

"Yo, this is what it is, said Saleem, "me and my brother from another done came into some work and I mean a lot of work and being though y'all our ol' heads we goin' break bread."

"Lil' nigga, what you talkin' about?" said Que.

"I'm talkin' bout me and Scooby goin' give you and Cousin Wayne two bricks and 10 pounds of weed just because we fucks with y'all."

"Hold up, Lil' niggas, who the fuck y'all done killed?" Cousin Wayne asked.

"Ol' head all that's irrelevant. Do you want it or not?"

"Hell yeah, we want it," exclaims Que.

"Where is it at?" asked Cousin Wayne.

"That's also irrelevant," replied Saleem.

"You right," Que and Cousin Wayne respond in unison.

"Well, I need one of y'all to get me and Scooby an apartment in one of y'all bitches names. Also, we both want a couple of whips; nothing too flashy, maybe some tinted-out Honda Accords with some systems in 'em."

"Damn, you niggas must've really hit a nice lick," said Que.

"A Lil somethin' somethin'," replied Saleem, "well we bout to fuck the city up. Northside on the rise; either you with us or against us. It's our time to shine," said Saleem.

"Well, we got a surprise for y'all too. We was really planning it but y'all nigga was M.I.A., so we couldn't tell y'all," said Cousin Wayne.

"So, whats the news?" Saleem and Scooby both asked.

"Well, Biggie Smalls is going to be at Pulsations tomorrow night and we was goin' take y'all that's if y'all wanted to go."

"Oh, Shit are y'all serious," exclaims Saleem.

"Of course, we are," said Que.

"Yo Leem we gotta get fly dog," states Scooby.

"You already know what it is ma nigga; yo Cousin Wayne call ya peoples so we can get our cars done up today," said Saleem.

"Damn, y'all got the money for that right now?" asked Cousin Wayne.

"Yeah," replied Saleem.

"Well, that's all it is then; they should be ready by the end of the day," said Cousin Wayne.

"Okay," said Saleem and Scooby.

"Yo, Imma holler at cha'll. I'm bout to holler at my girl take her shoppin' or somethin'," said Saleem.

"Okay, Lil' nigga," said Cousin Wayne and Que.

"Yo Scoob, you good," asked Leem.

"Yeah, I'm cool I'm a chill with the ol' heads a Lil' while longer than Imma go shoppin' myself," replied Scooby.

"A'ight y'all peace."

CHAPTER 8

Saleem Stops the Foreclosure

Before Saleem went to meet his girlfriend Ayonna at her bus stop, he went home to pick up some money. When he enters his house, he sees his mom crying in the living room, holding papers in her hand. So, he goes over to her and asks her what's wrong. She has him the papers and he starts to read them out loud.

Dear Ms. Parker

We're sad to tell you that if you don't pay the back mortgage on your home, we will have to Foreclose it and you will have to find housing elsewhere. You have until the end of this week to pay the amount due, which is $28,846.32

Thank you for your time.

Sincerely,

Susan Clark

PS. My contact number is 302-555-0086

Ms. Betty breaks out in even more tears as Saleem stops reading. Saleem starts smiling and hugs and kisses his mom.

She looked at him, saw the wide grin on his face, and said, "Why would you think this shit is funny? They are about to put us out. Boy, we're going to be on the street."

Saleem rises from his seat and walks out of the living room. He goes down into the basement and grabs some shopping money and the money to pay off the house. When he returns to the living room, his mother has her head down; she is covering her face.

Saleem said, "Mom stop crying here."

She looks up and sees Saleem holding stacks of money in his hand.

"Boy, where you get all this money? Oh My God, please don't have nobody run up in here. Did you kill somebody?" she exclaims.

"No Mom, go pay the mortgage off and relax. I told you one day I was going to take care of you, now the time," Saleem replied.

"Oh baby, I love you so much." She begins reigning kisses on him.

"Mom, Mom chill," said Saleem.

"Boy, you ain't too big for me to kiss you."

"I know Mom, I love you too," said Saleem, "mom, I'll be back later."

"Okay," replied Ms. Betty.

As Saleem walks to the bus stop to wait for Ayonna, he stops at the corner store known as Blacks. Saleem says hi to Mr. Kahn and buys two Phillies blunts which he says are for Mr. Carl across the street. Mr. Khan knows better but still passes him the blunts. He walks out of the store and continues to the bus stop the whole time, gutting the Philly so he can fill it with weed. As he sits on someone's steps waiting for the bus, he pulls the blunt and begins to choke violently.

"Oh Shit! This is a fire."

Once his lungs get used to it, he begins to take longer pulls. By the time Ayonna bus gets there, he's super high-looking Blackinese in the face; that's Black and Chinese. If you runnin' late, catch up as kids it the bus; some speak to Saleem, some nod, some shake their head, but that's it. Soon as Ayonna sees Saleem, her face lights up with a big smile.

"Oh My God, hey babe, what you doing here?"

"I told you I was going to get on my job, didn't I," said Saleem.

"Yes, you did baby," replied Ayonna.

Next off the bus is Ayonna's homegirl Tameka. Tameka is dark skin, down south phat and a cold-blooded freak. Scooby and I got the head last year before me in Ayonna started messin'. Scooby said the pussy is good as shit. I also heard she keeps an STD, so I ain't fuckin' with it. What Snoop Dog says, ain't no pussy good enough to get burnt while up in it, feel me. Anyway, her hatin' ass gets off the bus and rolls her eyes at me.

I said, "Girl go ahead."

She replied, "Boy bye."

I say, "I ain't sleep with you last night. I don't owe you nothin'.

She said, "Boy, please, nobody don't want you. I don't know what my girl sees in you anyway. You stay broke and always in somethin'."

"Broke? Girl, you must don't know," Saleem said, flashing a wad of money, then balls up a 20, throws it at Tameka and hits her in the face.

"Boy, why you do that and where you get all that money from?" asked Ayonna.

Tameka bends down and picks up to 20, tucks it in her bra and tells Ayonna to call her later. Then she turns to Saleem and tells him to suck her dick; then she takes off running down the street, laughing her ass off. Saleem and Ayonna burst out laughing themselves.

"Yo, you better get your crazy-ass friend," said Saleem.

"I will," Ayonna replied, "so whats up babe? Why do I have the pleasure of having my man pick me up from the bus stop?" asked Ayonna.

Baby, we goin' shoppin'; I wanna buy you a couple outfits, some sneaks, and some shoes.”

“Aww babe, that’s whats up,” Ayonna coos, “babe, you still didn’t answer my question. Where did you get all that money from?”

“Babe, I hit the lottery last night.”

“Boy stop playin’.”

“Listen babe, don’t ask questions and I won’t tell you no lies,” replied Saleem, “now go home, check in with your folks, do your chores, and meet me on 24th and Market Street.”

“Okay babe,” said Ayonna.

She then gives Saleem a hug and a kiss. Soon as Ayonna opens the door, she notices no one’s home. She hurries back outside and yells to Saleem, “Babe come here right quick!”

Saleem turns around and jogs back up the street to see what’s wrong. As he approaches Ayonna’s porch, he asks whats up. She said, “My parents ain’t here, come in right quick.”

“Girl, where are ya folks at?” asked Saleem.

“I don’t know. They are not here. What you scared?” asked Ayonna, “I know big bad Saleem ain’t scared,” Ayonna taunts.

“Nah, never that,” replied Saleem, “see the thing is, I don’t want your old man to pop up while we in the mix,” he said, stepping into the house, closing and locking the door behind him.

Then continues to speak, “as I was saying, I don’t want your old man to catch us fuckin’ and try to get at me for dickin’ down his little angel; then I have to put this hot shit up in ‘em,” he said showing his trusty .38 revolver.

“Boy why are you always got that thing with you all the time?” asked

Ayonna, "and you better not shoot my dad. Boy are you crazy? Well, never mind that last remark. I know you crazy." She laughs.

"Nah babe, not crazy, just a real nigga that don't take no shit," states Saleem.

"So, you just going to stand there and run your mouth or are you going to come get this pussy?" asked Ayonna in the most seductive voice she could muster.

"You ain't gotta tell me twice," said Saleem.

He grabs her hand and leads her to her room. He scans the room, finds her radio, and grabs her R. Kelly tape, then puts it on "It Seems Like You're Ready." Then he undresses Ayonna slowly, starting with her shirt and then her bra freeing her perfect perky titties, which are hard as missiles. He kisses her neck, making her moan, then kisses her shoulder bone, making her moan louder. He then makes his way to her nipples and begins licking and sucking them slowly and passionately.

"Saleem," she moans out, eyes closed, rubbing his head. He then unbuttons and unzips her pants. Then one by one takes off her sneakers; then pulls off her pants and panties all at the same time, exposing all of her sweetness. He kisses and licks her stomach, then tongues her navel as he continues down to her inner thighs, making her cry out with pleasure.

"Oh, baby, that feels SOOO good."

He eased his way to her clit as she screamed his name again.

"Saleem!!! Why are you doing this to me!"

He then slips his tongue into her witness, making her legs tremble as he licks and sucks her pussy ever so passionately. She grabs his head and begins to gyrate on his face. Saleem knows that she's about to cum, so he spreads up the motion with his tongue and just like that, her body convulses and she can't stop shaking.

"Oh my God! Oh my God!" she screams.

As soon as she stops, Saleem lifts her legs on his shoulders and eases his dick inside her tight wetness.

"Ahh," he moans.

She tenses a little from the thickness as he works his way inside her. As he fills her completely, he works up a rhythm, grinding his hips in and out, side to side, driving Ayonna crazy. As his rhythm quickens, he starts to slam into Ayonna's pussy with all he got making her scream with pleasure. He is about to cum; he can feel it deep in his balls then it comes, "Ahh!!! Shit babe, I'm cummin' Ahh!!! This pussy is so fuckin' good. Damn I love this pussy!" Saleem exclaims. They are both sweating profusely.

"Damn babe, that's the only thing you love?" asked Ayonna playfully.

"Girl, I love you more than anything in this world," he said, holding her in his arms and looking her dead in her eyes, letting her know that he was dead serious about the love he was confessing to her.

CHAPTER 9

Riverside Projects

Riverside Projects is considered one of the roughest areas in Wilmington, Delaware; this is the home base of the one and only Gangstar. A nigga that gorilla his way into position by putting fear in niggas hearts. At any given time, Gangstar might roll up on your block and smack the shit out of a nigga. Everybody on that block respect or fear and turn him into a coldhearted bitch in front of everybody. Well, on this day, he's looking like the bitch; he was just knocked out by Cousin Wayne from Northside in front of a crowd full of niggas and bitches. Some with a name, some without; one word has already spread like wildfire about what happened on 24th and Jessup Street at a local crap game.

He was sitting in his Chevy Suburban smoking a blunt with a knot on his head from the fall to the ground. It is hurting but even worse, his ego and his pride are crushed. Not really a shooter but will shoot. Gangstar sits in the SUV, contemplating his next move.

"Yo Gang' all you gotta do is give one the word big homie and that nigga Cousin Wayne is history," said one of his many flunkies.

"Nah, Lil' homey I've got to handle this one myself, ya dig. This shit here is about reputation; if I let this pussy get away with that lucky punch, everybody in the city'll think I'm sweet. So, this nigga gotta get laid out and dressed in his best shit," said Gangstar, "a Lil' homie, how that Biggie song go Warning?" asked Gangstar.

"Oh, you talkin' bout the part when he said, "It's goin' be a lotta flower bringin' and slow singin'.""

"Nah, asshole it's the other way around," said Gangstar.

"Oh yeah yup you right big homie my bad; I knew it was somethin' like that though," said the young crony, "so what you goin' to do Gang?"

"I'll think of somethin' trust me."

Just as Saleem and Ayonna get out of the shower, put their clothes on and step outside and make it halfway down the street, you hear a car system loud and clear.

"It's Biggie Smalls Cousin; you can tell by the voice; must be a song off the album."

When the car reaches them, it stops, and the window is so blacked out you can't see inside. Instantly I reach for my tray – 8; I put Ayonna behind me. Right before I raise my gun to shoot, the front window comes down; Scooby is laughing his ass off. He turned the music down and said, "I had ya ass, you know, was shook for a minute."

"Never that," Saleem retorts, "good thing you showed ya' self when you did 'cause you and that car was about to look like Swiss Cheese."

"Yeah, I seen you reachin' nigga," replied Scooby.

"Pull over nigga. Let me see the whip."

"Okay," responses Scooby.

"Yo, this shit fly," said Saleem.

"Yeah, you like it?" said Scooby, "well, wait til you see yours."

"Oh shit! You seen mines already?" asked Saleem.

"Yup and its all the to ma nigga," replied Scooby.

"But I didn't even give Cousin and them the money yet."

"I know, they paid for 'em and told us to drop it off."

"Oh, okay," said Saleem.

"So, what cha'll bout to do?"

"Shit, Imma bout to go get my car now, then Imma take my baby shoppin'."

"That's whats up," said Scooby, "come on, Imma take you to ya crib, grab that paper, then we goin' grab ya car and go to the mall," said Scooby. As the ride to Leem's crib Saleem sparks a blunt and passes it to Scooby.

"Yo ma nigga that shit kill kill," said Saleem.

"Oh, this shit from the…" then he stops when he realizes Ayonna is still in the car, but Saleem nods his head to reassure him that he's correct.

As soon as Scooby pulls on the patent weed, he goes into a coughin' fit.

"Oh, shit nigga pull over before you kill us all," Saleem said, laughing hysterically.

"Fuck you nigga this shit is crazy strong," replied Scooby.

"I told you nigga."

Ayonna is mad because she doesn't smoke and hates the smell of weed. They stop at Leem's crib, grab the doe then shoot straight to Que's house. As soon as they pulled up, they saw a brand-new money green Honda Accord, blacked out tints, five-star rims on it and a wing.

"That's you dog," said Scooby.

"Oh shit!" replied Saleem.

"Oh My God, Saleem, is this really your car?" asked Ayonna, all excited.

"Nah, babe, this our car."

She squills!!! She hugs Saleem and kisses him over and over again.

Cousin Wayne and Que come out front and toss Saleem the keys.

"Yo Lil' nigga, I see you like it. I knew you would," said Cousin Wayne, "you know I know ya flavor."

"Good lookin' out fam."

He gives Que and Cousin a hug after he passes off the money for the cars.

"Yo, y'all be safe. We'll holler at cha'll later; don't forget we goin' to the show tomorrow night, so be ready," said Cousin Wayne.

"A'ight," Saleem and Scooby both replied in unison.

"Yo let's go tear the mall up ma nigga," said Saleem.

"Nigga Imma beat you there."

"Bet a thou' you don't," said Saleem.

"Unh Ahn! Y'all ain't bout to do no racin' while I'm in the car. I'm too young and fly to die," said Ayonna. Everybody burst out laughin'.

Then Saleem said, "We goin' race another time homie."

"A'ight," replied Scooby," I'll take your money some other time he said with a smirk on his face. They both get into their new cars and head to the mall.

CHAPTER 10

The Jamaicans Are Found

Cash rules everything around me/C.R.E.A.M. get the money/Dollar Dollar bill y'all, C.R.E.A.M by Wu-Tang Clan.

"I grew up on the crime side, the New York Times side staying alive was no jive..." sang Cousins Wayne along with the song as he drove around town doing drop-offs and pick-ups.

He had been getting good feedback about the coke he got from Saleem and Scooby. He had made a mental note to see if he could buy a couple more bricks off them 'cause the coke he was getting from his Connect was baggage like a Mafucka. Right now, he was on his way to Vandever Ave. to drop off some work to a couple of niggas he fuck with down there, Lil' C. and the boy Mere-Mere two thorough Lil' niggas that get at a dollar and always come correct with that paper. He can see a lot of traffic in front of him. So, he makes a left on Pine St. by Walt's Chicken to keep straight up Pine, then makes a right off 23rd and Pine St. to circle all the way around to make a right by George Gray School so he can pop back up on Vandever Ave., but as he nears Vandever Ave., it's blocked off at the corner by the liquor store all the way down to the baseball diamond by Governor Printz Boulevard. So, he parks and gets out to see if he sees one of his young boys or anybody that may have an inkling about what's going on. Hopefully, none of his peoples got hit up. Automatically, he assumes it is shootin' 'cause it's the Northside of town, a.k.a. the north of death labeled after Philadelphia's Northside section of the city. The body count is already a staggering 28. It may seem like nothing to a major city, but it's a lot to a small one that only houses 65,000 residence and only

500,000 in the state period, so, you do the math. As Cousin Wayne reaches the corner, he sees an ambulance and coroner's vans in the middle of the street, which makes his assumption about a shooting correct. Now he hopes it's none of his peoples. Just as the thought enters his mind again, he hears his name being called.

"Cousin Wayne! Cousin Wayne!!" someone yells from across the street. He squints his eyes to see who's calling him. As the person across the street gets close, he notices it's Mere-Mere. As Mere-Mere approaches him, he extends his hand.

Cousin Wayne shakes it and asks, "Whats good Lil' homie."

"Man, it messy out here right now," replied Mere-Mere.

"I see," said Cousin Wayne, "what happened?"

"Man, they found the Jamaicans in they spot all dead and stinkin'. The lady that lives next door said she kept smelling a foul odor. At first, she thought a dead cat was in the alley, a possum or somethin', but when she went in the alleyway and backyard, she didn't notice anything. So, she went in the Jamaican's yard and the odor was stronger and smelt like it could be coming from the house. So, she called the police and sure nough when the cops kicked the door in, they saw Max and the other one besides Omega that be with them slumped on the floor decomposing."

"Damn, that's crazy," said Cousin Wayne, "so where Omega at?" asked Cousin Wayne.

"That's what I was about to tell you," said Mere-Mere.

"Oh, my bad, go ahead," said Cousin Wayne.

"Well, they went into the basement and found Omega with his head open and his neck slit from ear to ear. Everybody said it was a robbery.

The cops was bringing all types of machine guns and pistols out. Somebody had to catch them slippin' or it was an inside job because they had mad heat and didn't use none of them," said Mere-Mere.

"Yeah, somethin' ain't right, I don't see nobody getting the drop on Omega like that, but hey, everybody gets caught slippin' eventually. It happens to the best of us," said Cousin Wayne, "a-yo Imma get back at you and Lil' C. later when this heat dies down."

"A'ight," replied Mere-Mere.

"Peace," said Cousin Wayne, then headed back to his car.

"Damn, somebody slayed Omega shit real," he thinks to himself.

Also ponders on the thought of who could've done it. Then like a ton of bricks, it hits him hard, "Oh Shit!!!" he exclaims out loud as the realization of who had done it dawns on him Saleem and Scooby *Wow! Them Lil' niggas vicious; how the hell did they pull that off, he wonders. I should've put this together from the rip them niggas gave us two birds and 10 pounds of weed. I noticed the stamp on the bricks had marijuana symbols on them, but I never put it together. The marijuana symbol shoulda gave it away. That's Omega's trademark stamp, but hey, it is what it is. I definitely need to holler at the youngin', though and put them up on the game.*

He starts the car back up in the music flows out of the system smoothly. *"Cash rules everything around me/C.R.E.A.M. get the money/Dollar Dollar bill y'all…"*

"My thoughts exactly," Cousin Wayne said out loud as he drove in deep thought about everything he had just put together while continuing to do his pickups and drop-offs.

CHAPTER 11

Pulsations Night Club

"It's going down tonight; baby Pulsations Night Club is going to be bananas. The one and only notorious B.I.G. is going to be in the buildin' along with Keith Murray and Puff Daddy, be there or be square!" the DJ screams over the radio.

"Aww, I wanna go. It's going to be packed in there," whines Ayonna.

"Not this time babe, maybe next time; tonight, it's just the fellas," said Saleem.

"That's bullshit! You just bought me new clothes and shoes and I can't even floss in them!" said Ayonna angrily.

"Sure, you can and you will, just not tonight," said Saleem, "now cheer up, today been good; don't spoil it with all this unnecessary attitude," said Saleem.

Ayonna doesn't say anything; she just rolls her eyes and pouts.

"You better stop rollin' your eyes and making them faces.

"You know that Shit turn me on; gimme kisses," said Saleem.

"No boy, I'm mad at chu'," retorts Ayonna.

"Oh, it's like that, huh?" asked Saleem.

"Yup," responses Ayonna.

"Solid, Solid," replied Saleem.

Saleem looks over and sees Scooby flashing his lights trying to get his attention.

"Yo, I'm bout to go get dressed; meet me at Que crib after you drop her off and get dressed."

"A'ight," replied Saleem.

Saleem takes Ayonna home, makes her give him a kiss before he leaves then heads home to get dressed for the show. He can't believe he going to go see Biggie Smalls tonight. This is his first concert ever so it's a big deal for him; everything is fallin' into place.

It's time to celebrate tonight; then, it's all about business. As he pulls up in front of his house, he smiles, knowing that of the 'cause of that lick, he and his mom have a permanent roof over their head. As he walks through the door with all his bags, he smells a beautiful aroma coming from the kitchen. One thing for sure and two things for certain if my mom can't do nothin' else in this world, she damn sure can burn in the kitchen. As I enter the kitchen, she jumps, startled a little bit.

"Boy, you almost scared me half to death; announce ya' self when you come in this damn house. Where you been at? I been worried about you all day. They said somethin' happened to somebody on Vandever Ave. today."

"Oh, word!" They say who?" asked Saleem, not even thinkin' Omega and them 'cause she said it happened today, so he figured somebody got caught slippin' as usual.

"So, what chu' cookin' mom?" asked Saleem.

"Ya favorite."

"Swedish meatballs, macaroni and cheese and broccoli?" asked Saleem.

"Uhm hmm," replied Ms. Betty smiling from ear to ear, knowing how much he loves her Swedish meatballs and will kill somebody for a taste of her homemade mac & cheese.

"Boy, go wash up while I make you a plate," said Ms. Betty.

Saleem does as he's told, then comes downstairs and he and his mom eat and talk during their meal. At one point, Saleem tells her that he and Scooby are about to get their own apartment and from that day forth, she won't be payin' no more bills and if she wants, she can move and sell the house, or he can have this one remodeled. She decided to stay in the old house for now but would like to have it remodeled. He tells his mom thanks for the meal and that he's going out tonight. Hugs and kisses her, then heads upstairs to take a shower and get dressed so he can go meet everyone at Que's crib.

After his shower, he dresses, goes in the basement, grabs some paper for himself and Scooby and some weed for everybody to smoke. As he hits back upstairs, his mom tells him he looks handsome.

His arrogant ass replied, "I know," and looked in the mirror, "yeah, I'm fly, I'm definitely fly, but Imma stop at the shop and see if I can get a quick shape up though," said Saleem.

"Be safe tonight baby and stop being so conceited."

"A'ight, mom," replied Saleem.

He hops in his car and shoots straight to 24th and Market Street, parks and walks into Earnie's Barbershop, heads straight to the back and tells Mr. Earnie, "Hi, I got $25 for a shape up right quick and whoever next, I got $10 for you if you don't mind waitin'.

The next customer says immediately that Saleem could go before him. Reluctantly Mr. Earnie takes the money and allows Saleem to sit in the chair and shapes him up so sharp he can cut a niggas throat with his points. Saleem rises from the chair, thanks Mr. Earnie and heads straight to Que's house. Just as he's pullin' up, he sees Cousin Wayne, Que and

Scooby standing in front of Que's house; everybody lookin' their best. Cousin Wayne got on a pair of Tommy jeans, a Tommy button up and a fresh pair of white Reebok Classics. Que has on a sky-blue Polo tracksuit with a pair of fresh white Classics. Scooby is also fresh to death in a pair of Nautica swim trunks with a Nautica T-shirt and a pair of fresh white Classics with no socks and me, I'm Coogi down to the socks; like Big said in One More Chance, need I say more. As I approach the fellas', everybody says they whats up and compliments everyone's attire.

Cousin Wayne said, "Let me holler at you," with a serious face.

"Whats up Cousin Wayne, you okay?" asks Saleem.

"Yeah, I'm cool, me and Que just got done talkin' to Scooby right before you showed up."

"Oh yeah," asks Saleem, "what about?"

"Well, earlier when I was makin' my drop-offs and pick-ups, I went to go holler at a couple of my Lil' homies I fuck wit on Vandever Avenue. On my way down there, it was all blocked off, so I had to eventually park and walk down the street and see what was goin' on."

"Oh yeah," Saleem exclaims, cutting Wayne off, "my mom said somebody got hit up down that way today."

"Nah Lil' nigga listen, ain't nobody get hit today they found Omega and two other Jamaicans dead in the house nigga."

Saleem's eyes get wide, then he regains his composure and says, "What that got to do with me and Scooby?"

Cousin Wayne frowned his face, then replied, "Nigga I am ya ol' head you don't have to play dumb wit me nigga."

"What," Scooby said.

"Hunh," asks Saleem glarin' over at Scooby.

"Nah, Lil' nigga, after I heard what happened, I put two and two together and just like all day, every day it came out to four," said Cousin Wayne.

"Nigga what? Speak English," said Saleem."

"Look nigga, I know y'all robbed and killed them Jamaicans. How I know 'cause you gave me and Que two bricks of coke and 10 pounds of weed, all with Omega's trademark stamp, which is one of the reasons I wanted to holler at cha'll."

Saleem stands there listening to Cousin Wayne shocked and impressed that his ol' head is so on point.

Cousin Wayne continues with, "y'all need to change the wrapping on those birds and pounds or whatever y'all got with that stamp on it 'cause once y'all get moving and niggas see them stamps on the work, they going to automatically put two and two together like me and know y'all has something to do with what went down. I wouldn't be y'all ol' head if I didn't put y'all up on game. You dig me?"

"Wholeheartedly, big homie, that's why I fucks with you like I do," replied Saleem.

"Now, with that out the way, whats the numbers on them birds and that weed fire."

"To word it is, I bought some for us to smoke to," said Saleem.

"That's whats up," Cousin Wayne replied, "whats them numbers Lil' nigga," asked Cousin Wayne again.

Saleem laughs then said, "For you and Que 20 thous but everybody else 28 and for the pounds 1 thou' a piece."

"A'ight, Imma be hollerin' at chu', but right now, let's enjoy ourselves."

After their conversation, they head over to Scooby and Que. They walk around the corner, the block as usual is packed. Some of the bitches are on their way to see Biggie, so they got they Sunday Best on. Que tells everybody he's going across the street to the liquor store. Everybody passes off a couple of dollars for the drinks, blunts and Blackwood's. A couple of bitches call Cousin Wayne's name. He steps off to go holler at them. Hakeem and Khalif come over to holler at us. Hak and Leaf are Twins from the hood. These niggas are all dressed up to, but don't let the pretty boy attire fool you these niggas go in. We done been on plenty of missions together; they fuck with an ol' head that get at a dollar name Al.

"Whats good y'all?" asked the Twins in unison.

"All man you know, money, hoes and clothes are all a nigga knows," replied Saleem. Everybody burst out laughin'.

"Nigga you always keep somethin' fly to say said," Hak.

"I mean, what else is there to expect from a fly nigga," said Saleem.

"See what I mean," said Hak, "anyway y'all must be going to the concert."

"I see y'all all fly and shit," said Leaf.

"You know it," said Scooby.

"Yo, did you hear about Omega and them?"

"Nah," replied Saleem before Scooby could say anything.

"Well, they found them niggas dead and stinkin' today in they spot on Vandever Ave."

"Word, that's crazy," said Saleem.

"Niggas know who done that shit?" asks Scooby.

"Nah, I ain't heard no names yet, but you know this, Tellaware its goin' to come out eventually," said Leaf.

"I heard that," said Saleem.

"Yo, come on y'all, let's be out!" yells Que from across the street with a bag full of drinks.

"A'ight y'all, we'll see y'all at the club," said Saleem to the Twins.

"A'ight," replied the Twins in unison.

As we cross the street to meet up with Que, a car comes speedin' down the street with the lights off tryin' to hit Cousin Wayne, but he jumps out-of-the-way before the car can hit 'em. Nobody recognized the car but got an idea who it was or who had sent the driver. The car slows as it reaches the corner and then stops. Just as all the doors were opening, Hakeem and Khalif pulled out Twin Nine Double M Berettas and started squeezin' down the street at the car. "Boca Boca Boca," shattering the car's back window. The car pulls off and swerves into a parked car, backs up and speeds on down the street.

Excitedly Cousin Wayne yells out, "Good lookin'," to the Twins and says, "I owe y'all one!"

But they wave it off and say, "This the hood we pose' to ride like that."

Cousin Wayne nodded, then said, "Let's be out, it's about to be hot as shit…"

Before he could finish his statement, everybody could hear the sirens in the distance. Everybody clears the block, hops in their car and trucks and shoots up Concord Pike to get on the highway to head to PA to the

Pulsations Night Club to see Biggie Smalls, Keith Murray and Puff Daddy. Everybody in their respective vehicles is lost in their own thoughts. Everybody pretty much thinks that the attempted hit-and-run had somethin' to do with Gangstar from the projects. If it was, that was a bitch ass way to go about it, sucker ass nigga.

CHAPTER 12

Kurt Dies

Pulsations Night Club located in PA: the parking lot looks like a car and truck show. Bad bitches everywhere with they come fuck me hills and outfits on. Dress to impress and get sexed all crazy, hopefully by a baller with big cake and don't mind trickin' off a few dollars on some pussy. As Saleem looked for a parking spot, he observed everything takin' it all in. He sees hustlers he recognizes from the city; the most noticeable is this dude from Eastside, another section of Wilmington, Delaware. This dude goes by the name of B-boy, he gets crazy cake and he's been known to put that work in. This nigga is showing his money tonight. B-boy brought out his brand new pearly white 600 Benz. Nobody in Delaware has one of these at the time, not even the white people and nobody else in this entire parking lot has one out here. So, he's standing out, him and his crew.

Saleem finds a parking spot and meets up with Cousin Wayne, Que, Scooby, Al and the Twins. As soon as I walked up, Que passed me the blunt rolled up tight in the Blackwood's cigar rap he likes so much. I reach into my pocket and pass Que some more weed to roll up. As I pass the blunt to Cousin Wayne, he passes me a Heineken while we chill in the parking lot getting twisted. A lotta chicks were walking past, eyeing us all crazy. Scooby feeling the effects of the weed and beer, calls a light skin girl over to him and they start talking. Scooby sparks up another blunt and so does Que. The chick asked if she could hit the weed.

Saleem steps in and says, "You sure can but tell your girls stop being shy and come over here."

She smiles a beautiful pearly white tooth smile and turns and waves her friends over. The Twins come over and we all start hollering at all of them. Al, Cousin Wayne and Que are busy talking about whatever they're talkin' bout. Scooby grabs light skin girl's hand and walks her to his car and they get in.

"Yo Leem whats up with ya boy takin' off with the weed?" asked Hak.

"I see that ain't bout nothin' roll somethin' else and pass him some more weed."

"So you the weed man or something?" asked a pretty dark skin jawn with long, pretty black hair down her back.

I replied, "You can call me that."

"Oh, I can? What else can I call you?" she asked with a smile.

Saleem replied, "You can call me whatever you want but don't call me late for dinner or broke."

She laughs and says, "Boy, you are so silly.

"I say, my name is Saleem. I'm from Delaware. Whats ya name?"

She replied, "Simone and I'm from Chester."

"Oh, okay, what part?" I asked.

"I'm from Metcalf."

"Oh okay, the projects in the buildin'."

"Boy, what you know about the Calf."

"I know a Lil' somethin' somethin'. So, Simone, can I get cha' number so I can call you sometime? Maybe even come pick you up and take you to grab a bite to eat. I know you like Farillos on 9th Street."

"Oh My God! Boy, what do you know about Farillos."

"Girl, I just told you I know a Lil' somethin' somethin'. What you not use to niggas tellin' the truth?"

"Nah, it's not that. It's just I don't know; some guys say things just to sound good, but they not who they portray themselves to be."

"Yeah, I feel you on that, but I'm me. What you see is who I am. Where I'm from, all a man got is his word and niggas take it literally, so you live by ya word, feel me?"

"Yeah, I'm definitely feeling you. That was deep," Simone said, "do you mind if I ask you how old you are?"

"Nah, go head," replied Saleem.

"Well?" Simone said.

"I'm 15 yrs. old, why you ask?"

"Cause you seem so mature, so I figured you were older."

"Oh, thank you," Saleem replied.

"Well, don't you want to know how old I am?"

"Sure, but I was taught that I man should never ask a woman her age."

"True, see, that's what I'm talking about right there. Young guys my age are usually so petty."

"Well, I think that's how it is when you grow up sheltered; when you young and from the hood, you're forced to grow up fast and take on certain rolls. A kid our age ain't never been through those struggles of growing up without a dad, being hungry, wearing the same clothes, lights getting cut off, no heat, mayonnaise sandwiches, food stamps, that thick block of cheese that come in the cardboard box. They couldn't phantom drinking powder milk and when that runs out you gotta use sugar water for ya cereal or how about ya mom keep sending you to the neighbor's house to keep borrowing shit you know you ain't planning on giving back, changing diapers, I mean the list goes on I hope I didn't go too deep on you but for some reason, you feel so easy to talk to. I understand if you look at me differently now, but my life ain't always been sweet and I ain't ashamed of my past because it helps me become the strong person I am today," said Saleem.

"Nah, I can relate to a lot of what you were sayin'," replied Simone.

"That's whats up, so can I get your number or what?"

They exchanged info and promised to call each other when they got a chance and if they saw each other in the club, they'll have a dance or two.

"Go! Go! Go! nigga!" yells one of Gangstar's young boys, "get us to the hospital, Kurt back here bleeding real bad!"

Kurt is another one of Gangstar's young boys who was shot twice in the back when the Twins started shooting at their car on Jessup St. when they tried to run down Cousin Wayne in the middle of the street with their car.

"Yo Gangstar going to be pissed!" said one of the young boys.

"Word he is," said another.

"I told y'all not to do that shit in the first place; now Kurt all shot the fuck up. Hang in there dog. We on our way to the hospital."

"Hurry the fuck up dog he losing too much blood!" one of the young boys yells from the backseat.

"Man, I'm going as fast as I can," said the driver.

"Man, Gangstar said he was going to handle it now. We might've got them niggas on point now or they might try to send the wolves at us now," said the youngin' in the backseat.

"Yo Kurt, we almost there hold on dog. Kurt open ya eyes man don't go to sleep on me. Kurt dog wake up, yo Kurt, wake up oh shit! Man Kurt! Wake up! Wake up! NOOOOOO K-U-R-T! He dead y'all ma nigga dead y'all he ain't breathin' or nothing; this shit is fucked up! Them niggas gotta pay; they killed my baby word on Howie! Them niggas is dead even if I gotta kill 'em myself!" the young boy in the back cried and yelled out at the same time.

They take hurt Kurt to the hospital entrance and yell for help.

"Somebody call a doctor. My brother been shot! Somebody help!

Nurses come running and when they see Kurt, they all grab a part of his body and pick 'em up.

"Get a stretcher!" a nurse yells, but it's already too late Kurt is gone forever.

CHAPTER 13

˙ Crooks and Villains, Mafucka!

"Crooks and Villains, Mafucka!!! Crooks and Villains, Mafucka!!!" yells a rowdy group of dudes wearing Polo and Tommy Hilfiger shirts and jean shorts with Timberland boots; they gotta be like 30 deep. They're headed for the entrance of the club by passing everybody in line that's been waiting, including us.

Saleem is the first to speak, "Yo, who the fuck is those niggas?"

"I don't know," Al said, "but they deep as shit."

"Word they are," the Twins say in unison.

Cousin Wayne looks as if he wants to do something then his facial expression turns from a frown to a broad smile.

Saleem sees this and says, "Man, why you smiling at these niggas?"

"Cause they doin' what they want and don't give a fuck who don't like it and I'm willin' to bet they about to bum rush security and get up in the club free and they probably got they pistols on 'em," replied Cousin Wayne.

"You think so?" asks Saleem, "you want me to go to my car and grab ma shit?"

"Nah nigga, they ain't beefin' wit us they just on they rowdy shit tonight. This how these niggas have fun. They live for this drama shit," said Cousin Wayne.

"Well, Imma tell you right now if them niggas rush the door, I'm right behind them fuck that. I don't wanna pay and I'm tired of waiting in line."

As Saleem said that the group of dudes bum-rushed the security guard and mauled them over effortlessly, Saleem latches onto the group of dudes and pushed his way through just like he said he would. Cousin Wayne and the fellas laugh and shake their heads.

"That young boy crazy ass shit you gotta love that nigga heart," said Cousin Wayne.

As soon as Saleem and the dudes rush the dance floor chantin', "Crooks and Villains!!!! Crooks and Villains!!!"

As I stand off towards the side near a Picture Booth with a Biggie Smalls backdrop bitches everywhere just starin' at me. Probably wonderin' who I am 'cause I came in with a bunch of wild niggas. I probably look kinda young but with money or know somebody that gets money, whatever the case may be they eyein' a nigga and I'm definitely feeling myself.

As I look around the club, it's different levels, all around balconies everywhere and there all packed with people. There's a DJ on the stage playing songs from Biggie.

The atmosphere is intoxicating. Gotta know I'm feelin' good I've been blowin' omega all day and throwin' back Heinekens in the parking lot. My hair is diced, my Coogi outfit is shittin' on 'em all crazy.

Finally, everybody emerges through the entrance of the club. I say from the rip, let's go take pictures; everybody agrees. On the way to the booth, everybody's telling me how crazy I am for from bum rushin' the door with rowdy ass niggas I don't even know. As we approach the picture booth, mad bitches are eyein' us like a Mafucka, while we wait our turn. After we flick it up, we start to mingle through the club. We make our way up on the second balcony though landing where its sorta like a party of its own going on. I like this area because you can see the stage good, the dance floor and the other balconies across from you. All except for the ones above us, but I didn't give a fuck about what's going on up there. We grab a table; Que pulls out a bottle of Henny that he snuck in and we all pass it around like a cheap whore. I surprised everybody when I pulled out the weed I had on me and started rollin' blunts and even though it ain't a Blackwood Que is telling me, "Hurry up and spark that shit Lil' nigga," all thirsty and shit, everybody laughs. Once the weed hits the air niggas and bitches alike start askin' who got the weed for sale? Some even ask if they can hit it.

I'm like, "Fuck outta here this for the team; ain't no extras cornbread ass niggas," I say as two lame ass niggas walk away from our table.

As we all start feelin' the weed and liquor, we start dancin' randomly grabbin' bitches havin' a good time. When all of a sudden, the music stops and the DJ is yelling Chill! Chill! The Fuck out! Into the microphone. The crowd is departin' from up by the stage. As I look closely, I see the same crowd of niggas that bum-rushed the door throwin' blow after blow on two niggas that look helpless, but they still tryin' to fight all them crooks and villain niggas. After further observation, it's the nigga V. Meezy and the dude Feast, both from Delaware. I saw them niggas in the parking lot with B-boy and his squad. The nigga V. Meezy breaks free, but them niggas are still on his ass. I wonder where he's goin' 'cause the exit is the other way. When I look closer, the nigga B-boy and his squad are right beneath us. So, I guess he's tryin' to make his way over to them so they can see whats goin' on so they can help. V Meezy almost makes it there when a big fat dude catches him from the side, dropping him face first right at the feet of B-boy, who steps back out the way like he doesn't even know V. Meezy, which automatically pisses me off.

I shout from the balcony, "Help 'em y'all pussy ass niggas!"

Que grabs me and says, "Chill Leem that ain't our shit. Leave it alone."

I'm like, "Nah, them niggas 'pose to ride, they came together and they from Delaware," exclaims Saleem.

"You right Lil' nigga, but like I said it ain't our shit," said Que, "roll another blunt, fallback."

Reluctantly I follow his orders roll another blunt and spark it. Next thing I knew, a pair of hands covered my eyes and a sweet voice said, "Guess who?"

I smile because I know who it is.

"Simone," I say and turn around. She's all smiles.

"How you know it was me?"

"Cause how could I ever forget the voice of one of God's angels."

Instantly she blushes and a shy-looking smile appears on her face. I go in for the kill because Biggie said once she grins, I'm in game again. So, I pull her close, whisper in her ear, then suck on her earlobe and she moans a deep-throated moan. Then I look her in her eyes and she has a longing look in them. I lift her chin up, lean in, and kiss her with my tongue. She doesn't stop me or move away; she actually reciprocates my passion and for a second, it only feels like us in the entire club. When we finally break our kiss, she's still standing there with her eyes closed, then opens them slowly.

"Oh My God!" she exclaims, "I never had no one kiss me like that before. You got me feelin' all tingly inside and Oh My God, my stuff is soaking wet as if I peed on myself," she reveals.

I smile and say, "Here, take a couple pulls of this."

Meanwhile, everybody on my team are watchin' and so are her girls.

Cousin Wayne whispers to Que, "That Lil' nigga Smoove as shit he think he me or somethin'." They both shared a laugh.

Saleem and Simone start to dance. Saleem takes two more pulls then passes it to Scooby, who says, "Damn, I thought you was going personal," and they both start laughin'.

Next thing you know the crowd starts going crazy, bitches screaming. Everybody turns and looks to see what's going on. People point a hit the top balcony to the right of the stage.

"Oh Shit it's Big!" Saleem exclaims out loud, but like a ghost, he disappears from the balcony, but you can hear him through the speakers. Make his signature grunt, huh! What? The crowd goes bananas, then out of nowhere, in comes like 20 or so cops with shields, riot gear and helmets as if they're about to break the party up, but just as fast as they came in, they turned around and left.

Next thing I know, I hear, "Crooks and Villains Mafucka,! Crooks and Villains Mafucka,!"

Then a beat drops and them niggas is on the stage rappin' like an opening act or some shit. Then the music stops and Puff voice comes across the speakers.

"Yo, if y'all want my man Big to come out y'all gotta chill out, clear the stage. Big ain't comin' out until y'all clear the stage. Most of the Crooks and Villain niggas clear the stage, but it's still some up there. Then somebody comes running out the back of the stage and jump on top of a speaker and screams, "DJ, drop my shit!" The beat comes on and everybody goes crazy. It's Keith Murray singin' his hit "The Most Beautifullest Thing In This World," but his segment is cut short 'cause of the Crooks and Villains niggas that's on the stage grab 'em and try to jump 'em, but he breaks free and runs off the stage into the back.

They grab the mic and say, "Fuck that nigga we wanna see Biggie."

Puff comes across the airwaves and says, "That was foul what niggas did to Keith Murray, but if niggas wanna see Big, they have to clear the stage so he can perform."

Once again, only some of the Crooks and Villains niggas leave the stage.

"Tell the remainin' niggas on the stage to get off if they wanna see Big."

But them niggas said, "We ain't goin' nowhere."

Biggies voice comes across the sound system, "Fuck that Puff, I'm going out there."

Then all of a sudden, Biggie Smalls walks onto the stage in a tuxedo and a top hat and the biggest bottle of Dom Perignon I've ever seen in my life. He yells into the mic, "What the fuck is up Mr. C. drop my shit!" And just like that One More Chance comes through the speakers. As if none of the other shit happens, Biggie goes into his first voice of the song.

FIRST THINGS FIRST/I POPPA FREAKS/ALL THE HONIES DUMMIES/PLAYBOY BUNNIES/THOSE WANTIN' MONEY.

The crowd is gone while singing along with Big. I'm in awe, not believin' I'm even at the club seein' the Notorious B.I.G. in all of his greatness. Just as the second verse comes in the beat switches to the remix and niggas rush the stage. One nigga tried to grab Biggies signature Versace shades off his face, but Big blocked his hand and shoved him off the stage, sending him crashing to the floor. All hell breaks loose and Big is rushed off the stage and just like that, it's over. I wanna kill them niggas so bad, but it is what it is. Off the strength of those same niggas I saw Big for free the show comes to an end. I tell Simone I'm a call her when I get a chance. We kiss again and say our goodbyes. Me and the fellas head to the parking lot, which is flooded with cops and thousands of people.

"It's a cold-blooded zoo out here," Que said.

"Damn, it's so many bitches out here I didn't even see in the club," said Al.

"Word it is," said both of the Twins simultaneously.

Saleem pulls Scooby to the side, "Yo, I had a good time, I love this shit. Starting tomorrow, we on a money mission; you wit me nigga?" asked Saleem.

"You already know what it is ma nigga. What that nigga Tupac be sayin' M.O.B. money over bitches," they both say in unison.

Everybody hops in their cars and heads home with their own thoughts and plans and pondering over the events that took place throughout the day and this evening. Saleem his loss and thought about Simone and how they connected on a personal level so fast. He loves Ayonna but must admit there's something there with him and Simone.

CHAPTER 14

R.I.P. Kurt

The Riverside Projects is packed with family and friends. Gangstar is holding a visual for Kurt. Everybody got on R.I.P. Kurt shirts with his face on the front. Everybody's drinking, smoking weed and crying talking about how good he was and how much they miss 'em. They're talking about how they goin' out for they dog when the time comes. You know the same ol' talk everybody normally has when a soldier falls victim to these mean streets. Gangstar has called a meeting in the junkie crib named Ms. Ann. He is pissed off about last night's events that took place without his consent. Now, as a result, he has to bury one of his best soldiers.

"I told y'all stupid ass niggas not to make a move unless I said so!!!" he yells at everyone present at the meeting, "but no, you dumb ass niggas is hardheaded. Now I gotta bury my Lil' nigga Kurt!" he continues to yell at the top of his lungs. Then he lowers his voice to almost a whisper, "every one that was in the car, come stand up front next to me."

No one moves right away, so Gangstar yells, "What the Fuck I just say, you Mafuckas think it's a game! Get the Fuck up here now!"

Everybody that was in the car rushed to the front of the room, not knowing what Gangsta was about to say or do 'cause they knew when he gets mad, he can be very vicious and unpredictable. Everyone lines up side by side facing everyone else that either is sitting or standing up at the meeting.

Gangstar continues to speak, "I want everybody in here to take a look at the people who are responsible for killing Kurt."

"Whoa, Gangstar..." before the young boy could finish saying

Gangstar's name or whatever he had to say, Gangstar slapped the shit out of him in the mouth, causing both the youngins lips to bleed. You can hear some low giggles and a few daaammns!!!

But they are quickly silenced when Gangstar tells everyone to "Shut the fuck up! That's the problem with you niggas now y'all think everything is a fuckin' joke. You think it's funny Kurt dead, huh?!" he yells, "you dumb Mafuckas Ms. Nancy ain't got no more son 'cause assholes like these stupid ass niggas don't listen. Did I or did I not specifically say don't make no moves unless I say so?" asked Gangstar. Nobody said a word.

"Answer me!" he yells.

Everybody said yeah in unison.

Then he turns to the young boy standing up front, "Then why the fuck did you take it upon ya' selves to make a move? Don't everybody speak at once!"

"That's what I was tryin' to tell you Star; I told these niggas to fall back, but they insisted on going up Jessup Street to see if they saw Cousin Wayne so they could get at 'em for you," said the young boy Gangstar slapped earlier.

"Is this true?" Star asked the other young boys. They shook their heads hesitantly.

"Yo, sit down Lil' homie," Gangstar replied to the young boy he slapped, "now the rest of your stupid ass niggas are banded from the projects. I don't give a fuck if you live down here or not. You niggas can't follow orders properly. I don't need niggas on my team that are careless and gets they homies killed. Y'all niggas are poison, y'all lucky I don't put a bullet in y'all niggas. If I see anybody with these niggas y'all gone outta here and just so you know what I mean by outta here, take a look at the front of y'all shirts." Everybody's eyes are on the shirts. Sit in the Scripps the heart 'cause on the front of the shirt is the homey Kurt, who is no longer with them all because if you Homies ain't follow orders. The good definitely die young y'all careless ass niggas get the fuck outta my sight. If there's anybody that don't like my decision, y'all can roll too." Nobody moves.

"We family and we stick together, but if you niggas can't follow orders, then y'all don't need to be a part of this family. We live off of simple rules, loyalty and respect and what else, death before dishonor!" everyone said in unison.

Gangstar continues, "If you kill one of us, we kill 10 of them or die trying. Tonight, somebody got a pay for Kurt; I don't care who out there, they gettin' it."

CHAPTER 15

Biggie Gets Arrested

Saleem is up early in the morning. He just got done talking to Ayonna, telling her about the concert. He turns on the TV and sees Biggie in handcuffs, so he turns up the volume.

"A New York rapper known to fans is the Notorious B.I.G. was arrested last night after a performance here at the Pulsations Night Club. Delaware County Police report said that Christopher Wallace was arrested earlier this morning for Biggie pistol whipped a man he says owed him money. Mr. Wallace was released on bail but given a court date where he would have to appear in front of a judge. We'll have more for you later at 12 o'clock. I am Beverly Swanson reporting to you live from the Pulsations Night Club."

"Daaaamn, That's crazy Biggie a real nigga; he must've said fuck that rapper shit, where is my money nigga," Saleem said out loud, laughing to himself.

He reaches for the phone and it starts to ring.

"Hello," answers Saleem.

"May I speak to Saleem, please?" asked the female's voice.

"Yeah, this him. Whats up?" replied Saleem.

"Boy, you don't even know who this is," said the female's voice.

How many times I gotta tell you I could never forget the voice of one of God's angels," said Saleem knowing the voice on the other end was Simone from Chester. The girl from the club he met last night.

"Oh, I thought you was going to get me mixed up with one of your other girls," replied Simone.

"Girl, stop fishin'. You think you slick," said Saleem.

"Boy, what talkin' about?" asked Simone.

"Acting ignorant, you must be use to dealin' with slow niggas," said Saleem, "you and I both know that was your little way of tryin' to find out if there is another girl," states Saleem, "you ain't foolin' nobody." They both laugh.

"It ain't funny with ya slick self. I gotta stay on point with you, I see," said Saleem, then said, "you hear about Biggie getting locked up last night?" Changing the subject.

"Yeah, I just seen it on the news; that's crazy, right," replied Simone, not catching how Saleem just changed the subject.

He changed the subject so he wouldn't have to tell her about Ayonna because if she straight out asks, he ain't gonna lie to her. But, if he can avoid it, he plans on keeping it to himself 'cause he knows that if she finds out about Ayonna it's a possibility she might not wanna to deal with him like that no more. He doesn't want that 'cause he really wanna fuck Simone first.

"Well, whats good with you?" asked Saleem.

"Just wanted to hear your voice honestly." (Beep)

"Hold on, somebody on my other line…hello."

"Yo dog, wake up nigga," said Scooby.

"Nigga I been up," replied Saleem, "whats good though?"

"I was just calling you 'cause I figured you might wanna go check out our new apartment before we get our day officially started," said Scooby.

"Oh shit, are you serious ma nigga?" asked Saleem.

"As a heart attack ma nigga; I just got off the phone with Cousin

Wayne; he said to meet him on Miller Road at the Hot Spot Food Store," said Scooby.

"Say no more. I'll be there in a minute; let me finish this call," said Saleem.

"A'ight," replied Scooby.

(Clicks over)

"Hello."

"Yeah, I'm here," replied Simone.

"I apologize if I took too long, but I had to take that call. My peoples just told me that we just got our own apartment. I'm about to go meet him and check it out," Saleem said excitedly.

"Oh, that's whats up and I didn't mind you clickin' over. I'm not petty. I would've hung up on you," said Simone very sweetly.

"Well, I'm bout to throw something on so I can be out. Maybe one day I can show you what my apartment looks like," said Saleem.

"That would be nice," replied Simone.

"That's all it is then. When I get it situated, I'll let you know," said Saleem.

"Okay," replied Simone.

"Well, nice talkin' to you. It was nice to hear an angel's voice first thing in the morning," said Saleem.

"Boy, you a mess."

"Nah, not really, but I can be if that's how you like it," said Saleem.

"Bye Saleem, with your nasty self."

Saleem laughed and said, "A'ight," then hung up.

Saleem throws on a T-shirt and some Polo sweatpants and some Nike shower shoes, washes his face and brushes his teeth real quick. He grabs his keys, hits the stash, grabs some money and gets in his car and drives to Miller Road to meet up with Cousin Wayne and Scooby to check out the apartment. On his way to Miller Road, he sees Gangstar's truck ride past him, but it's not Gangstar drivin' it's a broad. He also notices white paint or something on the windows that say, R.I.P. Kurt.

"Damn, when Lil' Kurt got hit?" he thinks to himself, *"fuck it, better him than me."*

As he pulls up into the Hot Spot parking lot, he sees Cousin Wayne and Scooby's cars parked side-by-side, but they ain't in them. As he walks over towards their cars, he sees them in Hot Spot. They see him and walk out.

They all greet each other then Cousin Wayne says, "Yo, the apartment is official; it's right across the street in the Peeble Hill Apartments. I got it in my ol' mom's name; here go the keys right here. One for both of y'all it's $750 a month. I paid the security deposit, which was $1,200, so hit me Lil' niggas when y'all can."

"I got that for you right now," said Saleem and handed Cousin Wayne the money.

"Yo, on the way up here, I saw the nigga Gangstar truck ride past me, but he wasn't in it a broad was. I also noticed it had writing on all the windows that said, R.I.P. Kurt. I was thinkin' to myself when the fuck Kurt get hit," said Saleem.

"Yeah, yeah, I meant to tell y'all I was with the broad Sheema from Rive after the show and she was tellin' me that Kurt got killed last night. She said from what she heard, somebody on Jessup Street shot him in the back two times as he and these other young boys were ridin' through there. You know me, I put two and two together and realized he was one of the niggas that tried to run me down," said Cousin Wayne, "when the Twins got shootin' at the car, he must've been in there and caught some hot shit."

"Yeah, that definitely makes since ol' head," said Saleem and Scooby nodded his head in agreement.

"Well, y'all know shit probably bout to get hectic so stay focused and I ain't gotta tell y'all to stay strapped up 'cause I think y'all niggas been carryin' guns since y'all was in pampers," Cousin Wayne said with a laugh, "and I know y'all happy y'all got to own spot but everything ain't for everybody. Keep your spot low-key as possible. This where y'all rest at, you don't want people being able to know where y'all rest at and rule #1 don't keep no work at ya spot. Don't hustle out ya spot. Y'all about to start gettin' paper so y'all goin' have to move wiser. Just like how y'all preyed on Omega and them niggas goin' to eventually prey on y'all; especially once niggas realize y'all really touchin' paper. So roles are about to be reversed; the hunters are about to become the hunted.

"I heard that Cousin Wayne, that's some real shit, but I don't do the hunted thing," said Saleem, "to us these niggas still food; ain't no money goin' change us."

"Sure, ain't ol' head," added Scooby.

"If the opportunity presents itself again, a nigga goin' get it," said Saleem, "seriously, but we definitely feel what you put down. You know your word is always been good with us."

"That's whats up," replied Cousin Wayne, "yo, y'all be safe. I gotta make a run. I'll be at cha'll in a second for a couple more of them thangs."

"Okay," replied Saleem.

As Cousin Wayne gets in his car and pulls off, Saleem and Scooby grab a bite to eat out of Hot Spot, then go check out their new apartment. They also go pick up Ayonna and take her to IKEA to pick out some furniture for the apartment, so it can be delivered to the spot and told her to stay there till it comes. They gave her money to go shopping for toiletries and kitchen supplies and whatever else they may need. After that, Scooby and Saleem shoot to Saleem's mom's crib to break everything down and change all the packaging on the work. And split the rest of the money evenly and begin to assemble a squad that's goin' to shoot when it's time to shoot and get money when it's time to get money. After a few hours and some weed to help them ponder, they put a squad together, changed the wrappings on the work and are now ready to put the plan into motion. So they start gettin' money and begin what they both call operation takeover.

Saleem and Scooby have been passing out the work to the squad that they assembled on every side of town. On the Northside on Concord Ave., they gave Clark Bar and Buck a brick and 2 pounds just to see how things go. On the east side of town, they hit Cha' ball and Bell–Bell off with a brick and 5 pounds. On the west side of town, which is one of the biggest, if not the biggest side of town other than Northside, they gave Cheese and the boy Tiz a brick and 10 pounds of weed. Mostly weed 'cause that hood is known to move big weed over South Bridge Projects. They hit Animal and Shawn wit two bricks and ten pounds of weed. Animal can hold the extensions down and Shawn can hold the town side down. Now that everybody on every side of town is secure, the only thing to do is play their position on they block of 24th and Jessup Street.

CHAPTER 16

Cousin Wayne's Address

"Star! Star!"

"Ah! Ah! Yeah, Daddy Fuck me Fuck me Harder! Harder! Oh Shit this dick is so blazin'!" yells and screams Sheema.

"Oh Shit, bitch I'm bout to cum, I'm bout to cum," said Gangstar.

"In my mouth Dadddy, in my mouth!" yells Sheema.

"Ahh! Bitch open ya mouth. Ahh! Shit yeah, get it all bitch," Gangstar said while shovin' his dick down Sheema's throat, holdin' the back of her head makin' her gag and choke on his dick and his cum, "damn, you a nasty bitch, Gangstar said as he has to grab Sheema by her hair to get her off of his dick.

"Damn bitch, you goin' make a nigga kill somebody over that shot. If I was a week nigga I'll lock you down and try to marry you. They both laugh out loud.

"Here."

He gave her some money for the mission he sent her on, which was to get Cousin Wayne's address and try to find out if he keeps any type of work or money in the crib. She told Gangstar that she was just with 'em the night of the Biggie Smalls concert and Cousin Wayne took her to a house on 31St and Jefferson Street. And as far as she could tell, it was his main spot, but she wasn't for sure. She really didn't really get a chance to look around like that because they went to his room, did them and after they were done, he didn't really have too much rap for her; he made her get dressed and took her home. But she got the address like he had asked her to do.

"Thanks Daddy," she said after he passed her the money. Then she burps real loud, "excuse me," she said.

"Slurp, Slurp, I burp." Then her and Star bust out laughin'.

"Yo, you a crazy ass bitch, word get your ass outta my house," said Star.

"Are you sure you don't want no more of this head or this wet pussy?" asked Sheema seductively.

"Hell no, bitch you ain't bout to have me fucked up. That shot dangerous," exclaimed Gangstar with a big smile on his face.

"A'ight then," said Sheema but added, "don't be no stranger 'cause that dick blazin'. You ain't gotta pay me nothin' it ain't about that," she said with a half serious, half sincere voice 'cause she knows that if she can lock Star down, she won't have to do as much trickin' and schemin' on niggas like she does on the regular.

Sheema is a firm believer in you gotta use what you got to get whatever it is you want. Sheema gets dressed and leaves Gangstar sitting on his bed in deep thought. After a minute of pondering, Gangstar picks up the phone and calls his young boy B.G. and tells him Cousin Wayne's address and tells him to grab a couple more shooters and go lay on Cousin Wayne til dark and if they can get in his crib search for the money and drugs. Then hangs up. He then reaches over to his nightstand and grabs a pre-rolled blunt and sparks it up and begins to smoke while thinking bout the head and pussy Sheema just gave him.

"Damn, that's a good ass shot," he thinks to himself, *"why that bitch gotta be a whore, out there like that? Imma definitely see her bout somethin' again,"* he further ponders, *"this nigga Cousin Wayne must've*

thought I was going to let that lucky punch shit ride; he must be the fuck crazy. I've done shot and had people kill for less," thinks Gangstar to himself.

He then grabs the remote to the TV and turns on the news and sees the story about Biggie getting arrested and shakes his head sayin' to himself, *"these rapper niggas startin' to think they really like that until they come across a nigga that's really in the streets and get they shit pushed back. Let me get myself together so I can go check on this money. I know my Youngins better come straight today. I ain't with that short shit; no excuses. They know my motto, fuck you pay me bottom line or get cha' head cracked,"* as Gangstar further thinks, *"they goin' pay for Kurt's death too, all of them Lil' Jessup St., niggas; that's my word.*

CHAPTER 17

The Fight Ali Vs. Que

So, when you goin' stop playin' and give me some more of that pussy?" Que said to Carman.

"I don't know when you want some?" asked Carman in her sexy-ass Michelle voice.

"Shiit, I want some right now if it's like that," said Que.

"Nah, I'm bout to go to work, but we can definitely hook up later," replied Carmen.

Just as she said that a black or back Eddie Bauer pulls up bumpin' Tupac's song "Shed So Many Tears."

"Oh Shit!" Carmen said with her eyes wide is if she seen a ghost, "Que that's Ali. I know he bout to trip," said Carman in a scared and shaky voice.

"What, that nigga own you or something?" asked Que.

"No, but we are kinda together," replied Carmen.

"Well, check it if he comes over here and asks whats up just say nothin'. I was trying to holler at chu', but you was just tellin' me you gotta man and was about to walk away when he pulled up" said Que.

"Damn, you think fast," said Carmen.

"I mean, when you in the streets, thinkin' fast and ahead is a must."

Ali jumps out of his truck and leaves it in the middle of the street, the door open with Tupac blaring from the speakers.

"Yo, what the fuck is this!" yells Ali.

"Babe, it ain't nothin'," said Carman, then goes right into the story Que told her to run in one breath. Ali softens a bit but a crowd has started to form, so he wants to draw a little just to heart test and see where Que's heart at 'cause he recognizes the nigga from Northside. He thinks Que it's just a pretty boy and the nigga Cousin Wayne is the one that's really built like anything. So, he thinks he figures he can chump Que and make him look like a bitch in front of everybody, especially Carman. Knowin' he don't really wanna get nothin' started, but if it pops off, then it will pop off, Fuck it!

So, he said, "If what you say is true, why this bitch ass nigga still standin' here lookin' dumb?"

A couple of people in the crowd snicker and some laugh out loud. Que replied smoothly, "Listen my man, watch cha' mouth. Imma let that slide 'cause I can see you emotional right now. Ya lady told me the look and I respect it but don't even in ya life disrespect me like you just did."

"Nigga don't try to play tough and get cha' self-hurt out here trying to show off, fake ass pretty boy. You take all that rap back over Northside," said Ali.

"Yeah, a'ight whatever nigga," replied Que.

As he begins to walk to his car and stops and said to Carman, "When you get tired of being smothered by this goofball ass nigga let me know," he then gives a smile and a wink which automatically pisses Ali off.

"Nigga is you retarded? You think you can come on my side of town by ya' self, disrespect me and get away with it?" asked Ali while approaching Que.

Que meets him halfway, looks him dead in the eyes and says, "What nigga!"

Ali hesitates and tries to swing on Que. Que blocks it and Ali grabs him and tries to wrestle, but Que breaks away.

"Nah Nigga, ain't no wrestling pussy whats up."

People in the crowd yells, "Fuck 'em up Ali!"

They square up and Carman gets between them, "Come on y'all, this ain't even worth it!"

Ali mushes her in the face, "Bitch move, I'm bout to fuck this nigga up," said Ali.

Ali rushes Que with a wild swing. Que side steps Ali and catches him on the side of the head.

Ali grabbed the side of his head then said, "That's it pussy, that's all you got?"

Que said, "Come and see nigga!" Ali rushes Que again and tries to fake a swing with his left tryin' to throw Que off so he can really throw the right. Que was about to duck but sees Ali ain't throwin' the punch and sees the right comin', so he dips under the punch and catches Ali with a left hook to the ribs, then follows up with a right hook to the jaw, stumbling and dizzying Ali. Ques sees this and then goes in for the kill when a nigga sneaks Que from the side.

"Nah nigga, you ain't about to get no win over west side nigga. Que shakes the punch off and turns to fight the dude that stole on 'em. This niggas guard is weak, notices Que. He goes old school on 'em, throws the fake kick makin' the dude try to block it with both hands leavin' his face wide open. Que takes advantage of the opportunity and catches him on the chin putting him down, half sleep, moanin' on the ground. Hearin' people in the crowd getting unruly, he turns and runs to his car. Ali takes off after him, but Que reaches his car, gets in and closes the door, but the mob surrounds the car, so he can't leave. Not being able to see through the tints, they can't see Que going under his seat, grabbing, and cocking his 45 automatic.

Que rolls down his window, points the gun out the window and yells, "Back the fuck up!"

The crowd on his side of the car scattered, but the people on the other side were still kicking his car. So, he jumps out of the car and yells, "Back the fuck up!"

Everybody scatters. He then turns and sees Ali and aims his pistol at him. Ali eyes widen.

"Yo! Yo! Chill! Fam!" exclaims Ali scared to death.

"No Que, please don't!" screamed Carmen.

"Tell everybody to stay back while I pull off nigga!"

Immediately Ali yells, "Everybody Fall back! Fall back!"

Everybody does as they're told. Que goes back to his car. Before he gets in he says, "Let's leave this shit here; we fought, that's it. Don't let your pride get the best of you," then hops in the car and pulls off, thinking to himself, *"damn, I was glad I didn't have to shoot nobody out there. It was too many people for that."*

Meanwhile, on 24th and Jessup Street, things are flowin' smoothly. Money comin' everybody loves the new work. Saleem and Scooby are about to walk up 24th and Market Street to a Chinese store called Golden City To grab a couple of fish sandwiches. What's crazy is Saleem just came home from a bid not too long ago last year for robbin' the same Chinese store three times back-to-back with no mask but ended up getting the charges dropped 'cause niggas from the hood made the Chinese people not show up for their court dates. But since he been home, he still eats there like nothin' never happened. Crazy, right? As they walk into the store, it smells like weed heavy.

Saleem said, "Who is smokin' that dirt? That shit stinks."

The boy Buck-Jones said, "Shiid, all I smoke is fire."

Saleem said, "I heard that; roll this up," then walked over to the counter with Scooby in order of his food.

"Yo dog, you don't be scared them Chinese Mafuckas ain't goin' do nothin' to ya food?" asked Scooby.

"Nah man, they know if I find out, I'll burn this whole shit down with them in it; If not me, the hood."

"True, true," reply Scooby and they share a laugh knowing that every word Saleem said was true.

"Yo *"coughin'"* this *"coughin'"* shit is kill dog," said Buck-Jones tryin' to get himself together.

"I told you nigga you."

"Yo, sale me some of this shit dog."

"Nah, let me talk to you outside for a minute, baby boy, up top of two-four is called Turf; it's also known for makin' crazy money off of weed."

"Yo, I fucks with you, Lil' Bush and Cum-Cum Lil' crazy ass, plus I know when y'all focused y'all get at a dollar. I got some of the same weed for y'all if y'all tryin' to get this money."

"Man, it's whatever 'Leem."

"That's all I needed to hear. Imma send one of my peoples up here with the work. Can handle 10 pounds?"

"Damn right, that shit goin' sell itself said," Buck-Jones.

"OK, be ready," said Saleem, then walked back into the store.

Saleem grabs his food, then he and Scooby start walkin' back down the way. He begins tellin' Scooby the plan for Buck-Jones and his crew. Scooby agrees it's a good move for the both of them.

"Yo dog, we gotta find an A-1 Connect so we can keep things goin' and keep getting this money," said Saleem.

"I know, we should've been pulled somethin' like this off," said Scooby, "we young bosses."

CHAPTER 18

Saleem's New Place

"Yoou you remind me/of a love that I once knew is it a dream/or is it déjà vu I just had to let you know so/I had to sing it." (Mary J Blige Remind Me)

Ayonna is doin' her best Mary J. Blige rendition of the song while she prepares fried chicken, yellow rice and string beans for her, Saleem and Scooby. If he would like some, she has already decorated the apartment and had the movers place everything in place how she wanted it and the place looks very nice and comfy. She even took the time out to fill the refrigerator and cabinets and went as far as makin' up the bedrooms. She can't wait till Saleem and Scooby come home and see what she's done. I saw you before baby/is it déjà vu she continues to sing while cooking for her man and friend.

"A Scoob, I need you to hold the block down. Imma bout to go check on Ayonna and the spot and make sure everything's alright," said Saleem.

"OK, I got it dog," replied Scooby.

Saleem walks down the corner where his car is. He notices a couple of bitches from the hood standing by his car smokin' a blunt. As he gets closer, he sees it's Shontay, Gutlynn and Dina.

"Saleem! they all say in unison.

"Hey, whats up y'all," replied Saleem as he walked to his car to open up the door.

"Damn, that's all we get is a whats up y'all?" asked Gutlynn.

"When niggas get a couple dollars, they change up," said Dina.

"Stop y'all, leave him alone before he kills all of us; you know he's crazy," said Shontay jokingly.

"Nah, never will I change and the only thing I'll kill on y'all is them pussies," replied Saleem with a smirk on his face, showing his deep dimples on his sexy caramel face.

"Boy, you ain't killin' nothin' with that little ass dick," said Gutlynn.

"Yeah, that's what they all say til dick in they stomach then it's Saleem, Saleem you in my stomach, you in my stomach and um like."

"Nah, little dick remember girl, yeah right," said Dina.

"Girl, I ain't goin' lie Ebony said he can fuck his ass off," said Shontay tellin' Gutlynn and Dina.

"What they other friend told her who Saleem fucked, not Summer?"

"Well, let me feel it then," says Gutlynn.

"Girl, I'm outta here," said Saleem.

"Ah! Ha! He scared y'all!" yelled Gutlynn. Dina and Shontay both laugh.

Saleem walks back around the car over to them and they stop laughin'.

"Boy, we was just playin'."

Thinkin' Saleem was about to be on some bullshit. Saleem then pulls his dick out and they yell, "Oh My God! Boy you crazy."

Gutlynn freak ass grabbed it and said, "Damn, it is a nice size and it ain't even all the way hard."

"Let me feel it; yeah, me too," Shontay and Dina said with lust in they eyes.

Saleem lets them get their feel on, then he puts his dick away and walks back around to the driver's side so he can leave. Before he got in Gutlynn said, "I'm with you tonight."

Saleem laughed and said, "Nah, ma dick too little, remember," and got in his car.

"Boy, we was playin'," the said before he pulled off heading home.

Saleem turns the key in the lock to open the door; he can smell the aroma of fried chicken. As he walks through the door, he sees the place for the first time.

"Damn, this shit fly; I could get use to this."

He also heard Ayonna singing, but he doesn't see her; it sounded like she's in the bathroom or the bedroom. He locks the door behind him and decides to creep up on Ayonna and scare her. As he gets closer, he notices that she's singin' in the mirror, butt naked dryin' off. He hides outside, waiting for her to come out. She wraps the towel around herself, then walks out towards the bedroom, not noticing Saleem and without warning, he grabs Ayonna from the back and tackles her on the bed.

She screams at the top of her lungs and yells, "Help!!!"

Saleem flips her over so she can see it's him. She starts windmill punching and kicking him with her feet.

"Boy, why you do that!" she screamed.

Saleem grabs her legs and spreads them apart, "I apologize baby, let me make it up to you."

Then he goes in for the kill, licking and sucking her clit. She moans out in pleasure diggin' her nails in his head.

Oh My Fuckin' God! Boy, why are you doing this to me!" Ayonna whines, "I hate chu' Imma bout to cum already. Shit boy!" Ayonna exclaim. Then gushes a river of cum out of her pussy into Saleem's mouth.

"Argh!!!" she growls and begins shaking all crazy, locking her legs around Saleem's neck, suffocating him momentarily.

When she finally relaxes, Saleem takes off his clothes, dick hard as a missile, climbs on top of her and puts her in the back and deep dick that sweet tight pussy like it's the last one he'll ever get to enjoy. Instantly Ayonna's cumming again, clawing Saleem's back screaming his name, cussing out God and everybody else. She's out of it; she's in pure bliss. What she won't do for this man. Within minutes Saleem finds his release.

"Argh!!!" exclaims Saleem, "girl, I will kill you if I ever find out you given my pussy way."

"Boy, stop playin', ain't nobody gettin' this pussy; ya name is tattooed all in this pussy."

"It better be," said Saleem.

"Babe, do you like what I did with the place?"

"Yeah babe, it's fly as shit. Mwaah!"

He kisses her on the lips.

"Babe, you hungry? I cooked," asked Ayonna.

"Yeah babe, I'm starvin' now; I done worked that fish sandwich from Golden City off fuckin' with you."

They both burst out laughin'.

"Boy, get up so I can make you a plate."

As she gets up, her ass wiggles and Saleem smacks it playfully.

"Boy stop," Ayonna said with a giggle.

Saleem lays back and contemplates with his hands clasped behind his head and his feet crossed at the ankles thinkin' how his life has changed in a day or so and how it's about to change for the good and not for the worst.

Cousin Wayne just came from G-N-P's, a popular sub shop on the Northside located on 28th and Market Street, across the street from the Rite-Aid. As he cruises down Market Street, he sees the young girl Tameka that be with Saleem's girl Ayonna.

"This young girl is built like a buffalo, but she's too young," thinks Cousin Wayne to himself, *"she stay tryin' to flirt though. Que nasty ass and Lil' Scooby both said the head and pussy good. Imma see where she's going."*

"Burmp! Burmp!" Cousin Wayne blows the horn at her. She tries to ignore the horn as if she ain't payin' it no mind. She begins to switch harder as she walks, hoping that whoever it is its worth turnin' around for, but she doesn't want to seem desperate, so she keeps walking.

"Burmp! Burmp! Tameka!" Cousin Wayne blows the horn and yells out her name with the window down halfway. She stops dead in her tracks, and spins on her hills wondering who's calling her name from a car. When she sees the car, she automatically knows it's Cousin Wayne, Saleem and Scooby's ol' head.

"Come here girl," said Cousin Wayne.

She smiles from ear to ear and sashays over to the car.

Cousin Wayne pulls over closer to the curve, "Damn what chu' ignorin' me now?" asked Cousin Wayne.

"Never that," replied Tameka, "I didn't know it was you."

"Oh," said Cousin Wayne, "I was tryin' to see where you was goin' and if you needed a ride."

"Oh, nowhere really. I was just walkin' tryin' to find somethin' to get into," said Tameka with a flirtatious voice.

"Oh, is that right," said Cousin Wayne, "well, if you tryin' to get into somethin' you can start by gettin' in here," Cousin Wayne said, unlocking the passenger door. Without hesitation, Tameka gets in.

"So, whats with you? What chu' tryin' to do?" asked Tameka.

"I know what I'm tryin' to do, but I know you kinda young," said Cousin Wayne.

"Boy, age ain't nothin' but a number," Tameka replied, quoting Aliyah's song.

"Yeah, I heard that," said Cousin Wayne pullin' away from the curb, then drivin' up a couple of blocks and makes a left, then drives down 26th Street down Prices Park and pulls over. Then put in Jodeci and Forever My Lady comes through the speakers.

"Oh My God, this is my song," said Tameka, "why we stop here?"

"Cause I'm tryin' to see what you can do with this," Cousin Wayne said pullin' out his dick.

"Damn, I ain't know you was holdin' like that. It's all long and thick," said Tameka.

"Whats up, can you do something with it?" asked Cousin Wayne.

"Yup, hold up, let me spit out my gum," said Tameka, "lean ya seat back some." She reaches over, grabs Cousin Wayne's dick with both hands, and gently puts him in her mouth.

"SSST!" Cousin Wayne hisses like a snake 'cause of the warmth of her mouth. Like a bobblehead doll Tameka bobbles her head up and down each time takin' Cousin Wayne deeper in her throat, causing him to moan and shift his seat.

"Damn young girl, you the shit," said Cousin Wayne.

"Umm hmm, you like that, huh?" Tameka asked, taking Cousin Wayne out of her mouth and starts smacking her mouth and her face with his dick. Then she spits on it a couple of times then, jerks him off a little bit, then places him back and her mouth then begins to suck hard and slow.

"Oh Shit!" exclaims Cousin Wayne.

Tameka feels Cousin Wayne starting to swell in her mouth, so she knows he's about to cum. So, she speeds up, still sucking hard and taking as much of him as possible in her mouth and throat.

Cousin Wayne grabs the back of Tameka's head so she can't move and rotates his hips, forcing most of his dick down her throat. Like a champ, she holds her head steady and waits for him to cum. A couple more thrusts later, Cousin Wayne shoots his load down Tameka's throat.

"Argh!!! Shit!" yells Cousin Wayne.

"Uhmm," Tameka said, then giggled, "how did I do?" asked Tameka teasingly, knowing damn well she handled her business.

"Girl, stop playin' you are Fuckin' beast," said Cousin Wayne, still layin' back tryin' to get himself together, "Tameka whats up?"

"My pussy is so wet right now could you please fuck me now."

Cousin Wayne looks over at Tameka; he can tell she is horny 'cause she keeps licking her lips and grinding in her seat.

Cousin Wayne said, "Right, we goin' to shoot to my crib; you better not run ya mouth about this and you better not tell nobody where I'm bout to take you.”

“Boy, I don’t get down like that and even if I did it most definitely wouldn’t be you. I got mad love; you already know I’ve been tryin’ to get you to fuck me for the longest,” said Tameka.

While Cousin Wayne is talkin’ to Tameka he doesn’t see the young boy from River slow down tryin’ to see if anybody is in the car. They were on their way to lay on him at the address Gangstar gave them, but on the way, they noticed his car part down Prices Park. So, they decided to see if Cousin Wayne was in the car or if he came out from somewhere so they could ambush ‘em instead of having to go to his house and wait.

“B.G. ain’t that the nigga Cousin Wayne’s car right there?” asked a young goon from the backseat.

“Yeah, yeah, it sure is,” said B.G. as he slowed down, trying to peek into the car to see if anybody was in it but couldn’t really tell ‘cause of the dark tints on the windows.

“Yo let’s air that nigga out right here, fuck goin’ to wait at his crib,” said another young goon from the front seat.

“Nah, we not going to do it right here. It’s almost dark out but still kinda too light. But we are going to park and wait to see if he’s in the car or where he comes from, then follow him. Gangstar told me to go to his crib and try to get in and see if we can find some money and work up in there, said B.G., “so you know I ain’t tryin’ to fuck this up; you see what happened to Pookie and them. They got burned from the hood. I ain’t tryin’ to have that happen to me.

“Yeah, I feel you dog,” the other two goons both agree.

Well, we might as well smoke something; smarts this up and turn the music up a little bit. While we wait, Tupac comes through the speakers.

I see death around the corner gotta stay high while I survive/In the city where the skinny niggas die/If they bury me, bury me as a G. nigga/No need to worry/I expect retaliation in a hurry," they all sang Tupac's verse.

CHAPTER 19

Back on the Block

Back on the block, Que is tellin' Scooby and the Twins what happen over Westside. Everybody is ready to shut the block down, suit up and ride out

But Que is tellin' everybody to chill.

"We going to play the tapes through. I handled my business for right now," said Que.

"Well, whenever you ready to put that work in you already know we ridin' like a bus down a hill with no brakes," replied one of the Twins. Scooby and the other Twin both nod in agreement and support of what the other Twin just said.

"Yo, somebody roll somethin' up," said Que, "Imma bout to go to the liquor store right quick."

After Saleem and Ayonna finished eating, they took a shower, got dressed, then headed for Saleem's car so he could take Ayonna home. After Saleem drops Ayonna off, he shoots to the block so he can see what's going on. On his way, he sees Cousin Wayne comin' from the Prices Park Way, so he speeds up so he can catch 'em to try and scare 'em. He catches up to Cousin Wayne and starts tailgating him, shining his high beams on him.

"Who the fuck is that ridin' me like they crazy," Cousin Wayne said out loud, "yo Meka pass that gun outta the glove box right quick; somebody must be tired of livin'."

Tameka does as she's told; she doesn't at all seems scared. Cousin Wayne said, "When I get to this stop sign Imma jump out and see whats up with whoever is following me all close."

"Man, you peepin' this shit?" asked B.G.

"Yeah," said the other goons.

"But who the fuck is that?" asked one of the goons.

"I don't know, but whoever it is, it looks like they bout to do us a favor," replied B.G.

Suddenly, Cousin Wayne's car stops and his door flings open with his gun tucked behind his back.

"Whats up pussy!" he yells at the car with both his hands in the air.

Saleem rolled the windows down, tryin' to hold back his laughter and said, "The sky Mafucka,," then burst out laughin'.

Cousin Wayne looks closer and realizes it's Saleem's retarded ass.

"Yo, what the fuck is ya problem, you dumb bastard. You playin' bout to get ya head blown off," said Cousin Wayne.

At this point, Saleem is in tears; as he pulls himself together, he gets out of the car and walks over to Cousin Wayne and they begin to slap box a little bit, then hug. Saleem peeks into Cousin Wayne's car and notices a female but can't really tell who it is, so he says, "Oh my bad player, I ain't mean to bust ya groove big homie."

"Nah, nah, you good baby boy," said Cousin Wayne.

"Well, who that, she workin'?"

Cousin Wayne laughs and says, "Yes, she workin' the head crazy um bout to see what that pussy bout right now but if you want some head right quick, hurry up," said Cousin Wayne bout to set Saleem up for failure so he can get his left off now.

"You serious?" asked Saleem.

"Yeah, go ahead right quick."

Saleem rushed over to the car, hopped in and said, "Whats good sweetheart?"

"Boy ain't nothing good!" yelled Tameka.

"Oh shit! Girl, what the fuck you doin' in here?" asked Saleem surprised.

"None of your business and where Cousin Wayne at? What chu' thought I was somebody else with ya trifling ass. Imma tell Yonne too," said Tameka.

"Girl, chill, damn," said Saleem.

"Well, I need huge money then."

"Girl, you scandalous, here," Saleem said, passing her a twenty.

"Nice doing business with you."

"Now get out right now, but you better not say nothin'.'"

"Boy, I'm not. I been told my girl you ain't shit. She's just dick-whipped right now."

Saleem sucks his teeth and gets out to a laughin'.

"Cousin Wayne you a sucker, Cousin, you got that though," said Saleem, "Cousin Wayne, you ain't shit, you better strap up, they say she keep something but the pussy good."

Good looking Lil' homie; look Imma need you to bring me two of these things to the crib but give me some time to hit Sheray off, a'ight," said Cousin Wayne.

"A'ight," replied Saleem.

Look at the sucker ass niggas. We should kill both of these pussies right now," said B.G. And when did that niggas get a car? Them Jessup Street niggas must be eatin' like a Mafucka, them niggas gotta get got."

"I'm wit you dog," said both of the goons.

"That's whats up, but we're going to handle that another time right now. Let's keep followin' this nigga Cousin Wayne," said B.G. with hate and envy in his eyes.

Meanwhile, back on the block, the Twins, Scooby and Que, are smokin', out drinkin' Hennessey, talking shit to each other, and the bitches as well.

"A Scooby, where that nigga Saleem at?" asked Que.

"He went to go check on his broad, the new spot we just copped," said Saleem.

"Oh word, y'all got the spot."

"Yeah."

"Damn, y'all Lil' niggas comin' up in the world. I'm proud of y'all niggas."

"Speak of the devil," said one of the Twins seekin' Saleem comin' up the street bumpin' Pac. *"It's just me against the world baby/me against the world/I got nothing lose/it's just me against the world baby/"* sings Tupac as Saleem pulls up and parks but leaves the car and the music on.

Bitches start dancin' and singin' along with the song and so are the Twins. They swear they are Tupac.

"Whats up?" said Saleem as he approached Scooby and Que.

"You tell me big money with the new apartment," said Que.

"Nah man, I ain't doin' nothin' you ain't done and still doin' big homie."

"What happened to ya neck and shit?" Referring to the scratches on 'em from the scuffle over Westside.

"All man, had a little situation with them, Westside niggas, but I'm good though," said Que.

"Nah Fuck that. Let's go handle that right now," said Saleem.

"I said the same thing," said Scooby.

And the Twins added their two cents, "Us too," they say.

"Nah, it's a time and place for everything and now ain't that time."

"Man, you better than me," said Saleem.

"Imma bout to bust a move for Cousin Wayne right quick."

"Oh word," said Que.

"Where is that nigga at trickin'?"

"Oh, yeah,"

"With who, hot ass Tameka?" asked Scooby.

"Yeah."

"Oh Shit," said Scooby, "that nigga better be careful. That shot crazy."

"Word it is, for a young girl," said Que.

"Well, tell that nigga I asked for 'em."

"A'ight," said Saleem as he shot to his mom's crib to grab that work for Cousin Wayne and Buck-Jones to kill two birds with one stone, he figured as he pulled up in front of his mom's crib. He notices her sittin' on the porch with her friend, Miss Carletta.

As he approaches, Miss Carletta yells, "Hey tinky butt!" in her baby voice.

"Hey Miss Carletta, hey mom."

"Damn Betty, tinky butt gettin' big with his handsome self."

Saleem started smilin', saying, "A lotta stuff got big on me."

"Oh My God, listen at tinky butt talkin' shit." She burst out laughing.

"Boy, watch chu' mouth," said Miss Betty, laughin' herself.

"You better get her then mom," Saleem said as he went into the house.

The phone starts ringing, so he rushes to answer it.

"Hello."

"Hi, may I speak to Saleem, please?"

"Yeah, this him," said Saleem, "whats up with you sexy?"

"Boy, you swear you know my voice."

"I told you whats up with that," said Saleem.

"Yeah, I know, and you never forget one of God's angel's voices," Simone said, mocking in her best Saleem voice. They both began laughin' at her mockery of him.

"So, how's everything?" asked Saleem.

"Everything's OK right now, but next week it won't," said Simone.

"Oh yeah, why you say that?" asked Saleem, concerned.

"Well, my mom just got a job," said Simone.

"That sounds good to me. Why you sound so down?" asked Saleem.

"Because it's… in …Atlanta," cries Simone, not able to hold back her tears any further.

"Aww baby, it can't be that bad. Stop cryin' everything will work itself out," said Saleem.

"I sure hope so," said Simone, sniffin' holdin' back her tears as best she could.

"Why don't you wanna leave?" asked Saleem.

"Cause all my friends are here; all I know is the Calf referring to her projects, "and I was just getting to know you and you never got a chance to take me to Farillos or nothin'," said Simone.

"Girl, are you serious? That ain't bout nothin'; first chance I get Imma come up there and see you and take you to Farillos," said Saleem, laughin'.

"Why are you laughin' at me punk?" asked Simone, "Saleem."

"Yeah, whats up?" asked Saleem.

"Are you really goin' to come and see me before I leave?" asked Simone.

"Yeah, no doubt," replied Saleem, "now cheer up."

"Okay," replied Simone.

"Well, I gotta make a run right quick but'll holler at chu' though. Stay sexy," said Saleem.

"Okay, I will," replied Simone.

After Saleem hangs up, he shoots down to the basement and grabs the work for Buck-Jones and his crew and the work Cousin Wayne asked for.

CHAPTER 20

187 on Cousin Wayne

"Stay a couple cars back," said a goon in the backseat to B.G.

"Nigga I got this, you just be ready," replied B.G.

"Nigga I was born ready," said goon.

"Yeah, we'll see," said B.G.

"Yo, look this nigga goin' to turn into the gas station," said B.G. to the goons.

"Man let's just do this nigga and get it over with," said the goon in the front seat.

"Nah nigga Imma just go to his spot and park like we was told, but if you wanna be a wild cowboy, get out and go against Gangstar wishes be my guest," said B.G.

"Nah, I'm good," said the goon.

"Like I thought," said B.G.

Cousin Wayne pulls into the gas station.

"Yo, you want something outta here?" asked Cousin Wayne to Tameka.

"Yeah, can you get me a Pineapple soda and some BBQ sunflower seeds?" asks Tameka

"Sunflower seeds?" asks Cousin Wayne with a laugh.

"Yeah Boy, they the look," replied Tameka.

"A'ight," said Cousin Wayne, then went into the store.

As he enters, he's greeted by several people that know 'em or know of 'em. Cousin Wayne grabbed a pack of condoms and the pineapple soda, but he didn't see any BBQ Sunflower Seeds, only plain. So, he goes to the door and yells out to Tameka, who sees him and rolls down the window.

"They don't got BBQ, only plain," said Cousin Wayne.

"Okay, get the plain ones please," said Tameka.

"A'ight," said Cousin Wayne and walked back into the store but was stopped briefly by two females coming out that said, "I see you babysitting tonight; when you ready for a woman holler at me," one of them said and they both start laughin'.

Not waiting for a response, Cousin Wayne just smirks and goes up to the counter and pays for his merchandise, then exits the store, hops in his car and heads home so he can see what this pussy is hittin' for. If it's anything like that head, she might be one of his new young whores. He usually just let 'em suck 'em off every now and then 'cause they're too young to be dickin' down and he ain't wit no rape charges.

Saleem goes up top of Two-four first to drop off the ten pounds of weed to Buck-Jones and them.

"Yo good lookin' homie," said Buck-Jones, thankful for Saleem hittin' him and his crew with the weed.

"You already know I fuck with y'all niggas like that, so why wouldn't I wanna see y'all get money," said Saleem, "real niggas do real things, right?" asked Saleem.

"No doubt," said Buck-Jones, "man, as soon as we done, we goin' get at chu'; word just keep hittin' us."

"Don't sweat it, I got chu'," said Saleem.

"That's all it is," replied Buck-Jones.

"Buck! grab that nigga!" yells Cum-Cum.

Buck-Jones turns and sees a man running in his direction. As the man tries to run by, Buck-Jones catches him with a hook stumbling the man off balance. Niggas in the Chinese store see what's going on and swarm the guy and start beating the shit out of the dude to the point where it looks like they bout to kill 'em.

I grabbed Buck-Jones and said, "Yo, be out Lil' homie, so put that work up. It's bout to be hot out here. Just as Saleem said that shots ring out Pop! Pop!

"Snatch another pack Mafucka,!" yells Cum-Cum, who shoots the half-dead guy in his hand and foot. Everybody backs away and walks off, leaving the dude for dead.

"Yo y'all Lil' niggas crazy up here. Imma holler at cha'll," said Saleem.

"A'ight," replied Buck-Jones Saleem got in his car and headed to Cousin Wayne's crib to hit 'em off.

As Cousin Wayne and Tameka pulled up to his crib, Tameka said, "This a nice neighborhood. I wish I lived in a house like this."

"Girl, this ain't shit. I want something way live than this," said Cousin Wayne, "you ready young girl, don't get scared now."

"Boy, I ain't never scared of no dick; it's big, but I can handle it. You seen my head game some, so you can only imagine what this tight net pussy hittin' for," replied Tameka.

"Okay, I like that slick ass mouth, talk that same shit when this python up in you," Cousin Wayne said with a smirk on his face knowin' he bout to kill this young girl for talkin' all that shit. Tameka reached over and grabs Cousin Wayne's dick and said, "A gardener snake maybe but not no python," she said with a giggle.

"I can show you better than I can tell you. What you forgot how big it was that fast? You could barely get the head in ya mouth. Argh! Argh!" Cousin Wayne imitates that sounds Tameka was makin' when she was chokin' on his dick.

"Fuck you, Cousin Wayne," said Tameka.

"Fuck all this talkin'. Come on so I can shut chu' up."

There that nigga go right there pullin' up," said B.G., "y'all niggas ready to put this work in?"

"Yeah," one goon said.

"You already know," said the other.

"Well, mask up then so we can handle this nigga Riverside style. Y'all know what that is niggas?" asked B.G.

"Of course," said the young goons.

"Then let me hear it."

"187 nigga," replied the young goons.

"Exactly, now let's do this shit for Kurt."

Cousin Wayne and Tameka both get out of the car laughin' and gigglin' and start towards the house.

Cousin Wayne stops, "Damn, wait right here," he said to Tameka, "I forgot my pistol."

"Boy, hurry up; my pussy bout to bust out my panties fuckin' with chu'," said Tameka.

"Girl, you crazy," Cousin Wayne said, opening the car door and grabbing his gun outta the glove compartment and discreetly tucking it under his shirt. *"Newsy ass neighbors stay lurking',"* he thinks to himself, closes the car door, then heads back towards the house, not noticing the masked-up niggas creeping in between cars headed in his direction. As Cousin Wayne puts the key in the door and turns the knob, he hears the cock of a gun, and somebody says, "Got cha' ass right where we want chu' now nigga."

'They'll never take me alive/I'm gettin' high wit ma fo-five cocked/on these suckers time to die," raps Tupac from the speakers of Saleem's car on his way to drop off the work that Cousin Wayne asked him for. He figures Cousin Wayne should be done freakin' off with Tameka by now.

"That Lil' Bitch a whore; she lettin' the whole crew run through her," Saleem thinks to himself.

"Bust on Mafuckas with a Passion/better duck 'cause I ain't/lookin. when I'm Baum base blastin'," Tupac continues to share his pain throughout the song. Pain from the Above the Rim soundtrack.

"Let me turn this shit down before these nut ass neighbors call the cops," Saleem thinks to himself, *"and plus, I got this work on me too. I gotta stop listening to Pac got me all amped up and shit."* Saleem thinks as he turns down Cousin Wayne's block.

"What the fuck!" Saleem exclaims out loud as he stares in disbelief, not believing his eyes. It looks like he saw niggas with masks pushing Cousin Wayne into the house.

"Damn, what the fuck!" thinks Saleem said to himself.

He pulls over, turns off the car, pops his trunk and grabs his hoodie and puts it on and pulls the hood over his head and tightens it over his face and creeps through the alley and peers through the window, trying to get an angle on where everybody is at so he can try to figure out his next move.

"What the fuck!" exclaims Cousin Wayne.

"Oh My God! shrieks Tameka both caught off guard by the masked gunmen.

"Don't say shit. Just tell us where everything is," said the masked gunmen.

"I don't know what you'll talkin' bout I don't got nothing in here," said Cousin Wayne.

"Whack!!!"

"Ahh shit! nigga," said Cousin Wayne in pain from the blow to the head, which made Cousin Wayne's head start to bleed and swell.

"Now stop Playin' games nigga before I start lettin' this gun bark," said the masked gunman.

"I told y'all niggas ain't nothin' in here, or else I would give it to y'all," said Cousin Wayne, tryin' to sound convincing.

"Well, where it's at nigga!" yells the gunman.

"At my other spot," said Cousin Wayne, quickly hoping that the gunman was stupid enough to believe him.

Cousin Wayne can tell they are young and they're amateurs cause they never even checked him for weapons. So, the first chance he gets, he plans on cookin' every last one of them.

"Man, we gonna check here first. It better not be nothin' here," said what seems to be the main spokesperson for all the gunmen.

"I told you ain't nothin' here y'all bout to waste y'all time when we could be goin' to the other spot and making' this easier for all of us," said Cousin Wayne.

"Man shut the fuck up; we got this. You just better hope we don't find nothin' in here, or you goin' get more than a lump on ya head nigga. Matter fact, you talkin' too much. Yo gag this bitch ass nigga and tie his hands behind his back, then check his pockets!" barks the spokesperson for the gunmen.

Cousin Wayne is losin' hope now that he's being tied up.

"Yo, this nigga gotta gun on 'em dog," said the goon as he continued searching Cousin Wayne.

"Oh, you think you slick nigga you couldn't wait to catch us slippin'," said the spokesman, "I should pop ya dumb ass right now."

Then walks over and smacks Cousin Wayne in the face with an open hand causing Cousin Wayne to grimace and mumble something unrecognizable from his gaged-up mouth.

"Yo dog what we goin' do with this bitch," said the other gunmen.

"Man fuck that bitch. I ain't never like her anyway," said the main gunmen.

"Fuck you too B.G., Rome, and Scotty, I know who the fuck y'all are. Y'all can't hide behind these masks; I went to school with all you dumb ass niggas," said Tameka.

"Oh shit! Dog she recognizes us," said Rome, "you dumb ass bitch I was goin' let you live too," said B.G., "tie that Bitch up. Got something for her," said B.G. unbuckling his pants.

Tameka's eyes got wide.

"Hold that bitch down."

B.G. rips her shirt open and her bra freeing her wholesome titties and begins licking and sucking them ravishingly. Then he pulls her jeans and panties down at the same time, exposing her pleasure box. Then he climbs between her legs through her jeans 'cause there still on, then forces himself in her causin' her to cry out a muffled scream.

"Yeah Bitch take this dick you use to act like you was too good for me anyway," said B.G. "and this pussy good too. Damn I'm about to cum already, Argh!" B.G. pulls out and nuts all over Tameka's stomach.

"Let me at her dog!" yelled Rome.

"Here do ya thang."

Back and forth, they all continue to rape Tameka while Cousin Wayne watches heatedly, swearing to himself that all three of them niggas are dead if he makes it out of this alive.

Saleem has seen enough. He sees that all the gunmen are preoccupied with raping poor Tameka, so he decides to just kick the front door in and come in shootin' 1, 2, 3, counts Saleem, then Boom!! The front door come's crashing in, catching everyone by surprise. Without a second thought, he shoots the first gunmen in the back which is B.G., then he shoots the second gunman in the shoulder which is Rome, and the third gunmen which is Scotty, twice in the back of the head while he's still on top of Tameka who is layin' there in a daze unaware of what's going on at that point due to the brutal rape she just had to endure.

"Cousin Wayne, you good?" asked Saleem as he untied and ungagged him without a word Cousin grabbed his nine off the floor and shot Rome in the face making sure that he'll have to have a closed casket funeral. Then he walks over to the leader of the gunmen and pulls off his mask and flips him over on his back.

"OHH!" gasps B.G.

"Oh, shit, that's B.G.," said Saleem.

"You know this nigga?" asked Cousin Wayne.

"Yeah, that's one of Gangstar's young boys," replied Saleem.

"Oh, that's who sent them, that's all I wanted to know." Then Cousin Wayne empties the rest of his clip in him unmercifully.

"Damn man, look at what they did to Meka. She looks out of it dog," said Cousin Wayne.

"Man, it's all my fault, I shoulda been on point."

"Nah Cousin, you can't put that on ya' self; shit happens. How it happened, we in the game, shit like this happen all over the world when you live this kind of lifestyle. Shit, somewhere in the world, this same shit is happening right now," said Saleem trying to stop Cousin Wayne from stressing himself over the situation at hand.

"Man, we gotta bounce before the law come my nigga," said Saleem.

"Nah, you go, I can't leave Lil' momma here like this. This my crib I got a permit for my gun. Imma say they rushed me and Tameka and tied us up; I got loose while they was raping her, grabbed my gun and started shootin'.

"What about the bullets I let off?"

"I'll cross that bridge when I get there."

"A'ight, I'm out Cousin."

"A'ight," said Cousin Wayne.

Saleem runs down the street with his hoodie on, jumps in his car and backs down the one-way so the neighbors can't get his license plate number if they're looking out of the window. He then heads to the block to inform Que and Scooby about what took place at Cousin Wayne's crib.

Cousin Wayne scrambles around the house, grabs anything illegal, puts it in a duffel bag, and then takes it to his truck instead of the car he and Tameka were in. Then he takes the key to his truck off his key chain and hides it. So, if the cops get to checking his key chain, they won't find another vehicle key beside his car key.

CHAPTER 21

Saleem Informs Them of the Events

Saleem pulls up on the block and approaches Scooby.

"Yo, where Que at?"

"He just went to the crib. Why whats up?" asked Scooby. "Come on dog, let's drive around there. I wanna park my car in Que's back lot."

"A'ight," replied Scooby.

As they parked Saleem's car in the back lot, Scooby asked again, "Whats up dog and don't say nothing 'cause I can see it all over ya face."

"Imma spit it out when we get in Que's crib," said Saleem.

"A'ight dog."

Saleem knocks on Que's door; within a minute, Que looks through the peephole, sees who it is and then answers the door.

"Whats up y'all? Come in," said Que.

"Yo, you got company in here?"

"Nah, it's just me; why, whats up?" Que asked cautiously, sensing that's something wrong.

"Man, remember I came to the block and told y'all I was bout to bust a move for Cousin Wayne and he was with Tameka?"

"Yeah," Que replied.

"Well, I shoot to his crib to drop off the situation he asked me for and as I'm coming down his block, I swear I see some niggas in masks pushing him and Tameka in the house. So, I pulled over, parked, jumped out, went through the alley and peeked in through the window tryin' to see if I can get a visual of whats going on. I peek through the window and see three niggas in mask with guns out. To make a long story short, shit got ugly quick. Cousin Wayne ended up getting hit in the head with a gun and all three of the masked-up niggas took turns raping Tameka. I couldn't watch no more, so I just kicked the front door in and came in gun blazing."

"So, where Cousin Wayne and Tameka at right now?" asked Que.

"Man, that nigga stayed at the scene and said he couldn't leave Meka there like that. She was laying on the floor with her eyes wide open, no blinking, just staring off into space.

"Damn, that's deep," said Scooby with a look of bewilderment.

"Y'all don't know who the niggas was?" asked Que.

"Yeah, it was B.G., Rome and Scotty from the projects. Gangstar must've sent them," said Saleem.

"Yeah, I was thinking the same thing," said Que.

"So, whats next Que?" asked Saleem.

"Man, we gotta make sure Cousin Wayne good, then we goin' to have to put an end to this shit with Gangstar 'cause shit is starting to go too far. Too many niggas dying already we 'pose to be tryin' get this money we can't do that if we beefin' every second. Imma bout to go check on Cousin Wayne; y'all hold the block down or put somebody in charge. Stay on point wherever y'all are," said Que. Everybody leaves Que's house. Que jumps in his car and pulls off while Saleem and Scooby head back to the block.

"Yo, hold up, Scooby let me do something right quick."

Saleem runs into a nearby alleyway for a minute, then comes back out.

"What, you went back there and took a shit?" asked Scooby jokingly.

"Nah nigga I had to put that pistol up that shit hot. I gotta grab my other joint when I get a chance."

"Yeah, 'cause you know it's bout to be on once shit hits the fan," said Scooby.

"Word it is," replied Saleem.

"So, Tameka fucked up, huh?" asks Scooby.

"Yeah, she looked like a Zombie. She get on my nerves and shit but she didn't deserve that."

"I know my baby Ayonna gonna be hurt about this; you know that's her road dog."

"Yeah, I know," said Scooby.

"Yo, let me see ya car real quick so I can go grab my other pistol and put that work up that I was about bring Cousin Wayne."

"A'ight," replied Scooby tossing Saleem his keys to his car.

It's a war going on outside/no man is safe from you can run but chu'/can't hide forever from the streets that/we done took you walkin' wit cha' head down/scared to look, you shook 'cause ain't no such/thing as halfway crooks.

"Let me find out this nigga a mob deep fan on the low," thinks Saleem to himself as the music comes through the speakers in Scooby's car.

"Only the Strong Survive is my shit. I definitely feel like this right now," thinks Saleem as he picks up the work from out of his car then heads to his mom's house. As he pulls up, he cuts the car off, observes his territory, then goes in the house, puts the work up, grabs his chrome .38 snob nose revolver and tucks it in the small of his back. As he opens the refrigerator in search of a snack, he sees some leftovers, but he's too lazy to heat it up. So, he just grabs his mom's pitcher of Kool-Aid and drinks straight from the pitcher, leaving a swallow in it knowing his mom is going to kill 'em for that 'cause he knows she hates for anybody to touch her Kool-Aid period, then has a nerve to only leave swallow. Yeah, he goin' have hell to pay when she sees that. Saleem shoots upstairs to his room, grabs the phone and calls Ayonna to inform her briefly of the events that took place and to let Tameka's mom know that Tameka is in the hospital.

"Hello."

"May I speak to Ayonna, please?"

"This her."

"Hey gorgeous."

"Hey babe, whats up?"

"All you know same ol' same ol' tryin' stay away from the lame-o."

"Boy, you crazy always got a sayin' for somethin'," said Ayonna with a giggle.

"Yeah! I just want to tell you I love you."

"Aww, I love you to baby," squeals Ayonna.

"Look, I want you to be strong; for one, right now, brace yourself for what I'm about to tell you."

"Boy, what you talkin' bout?"

"Just listen, Tameka is in the hospital."

"What boy! Stop playing. In the hospital for what?"

"Just listen, she got raped tonight by like three niggas, I need you to tell her mom she in the hospital."

"Oh My God!" screams Ayonna, "are you serious? How did this

happen?"

"Look, I can't go into details just call her family and let them know she's in the hospital, Okay?" asked Saleem.

"Okay," Ayonna replied cryin' with a shaky voice.

Then he hangs up and calls Simone.

"Hello."

"Yes, can I speak with Simone?"

"Saleem is that you?" asked Simone recognizing the voice on the other end.

"Immediately, the one and only," replied Saleem.

"Boy, whatever, whats going on?" asked Simone.

"I'm good sweetheart, I was thinking about coming to see you tomorrow."

"Oh My God, are you serious," squeals Simone.

"Yeah, of course, I am, so be ready when I come through. Meet me on 9th St. at the A-Plus gas station. Imma Park by city grill 'cause I know some good dudes over by that bar that I need to holler at," said Saleem.

"Okay, what time?" asked Simone.

"Bout 12:00."

"Okay, bye."

"Bye."

Saleem sits on his old bed and thinks about the events that took place at Cousin Wayne's crib. He then pulls himself together out of his reverie and decides to take a shower and dispose of his clothes because his pretty sure they have gun powder residue on them. After his shower, he bags up the clothes, gets dressed and heads back to the block.

"Thanks for coming to get me from down this nut ass police station," said Cousin Wayne.

"Man, you know I was comin' to see what was what once I caught wind about what happened," said Que.

"That's whats up family; that's why you my nigga."

"So, what was the Jakes talkin' about?"

"Man, they was on me hard, but I'm registered and them niggas was in my house, so I had a right to bear arms," said Cousin Wayne, "I'm straight said I was giving Tameka a ride home when I told her I needed to stop at my house first and when I opened the door some masked man rushed us, tied us up, and started askin' for money. I told 'em I got some in another spot. They didn't believe me at first, so I guess in an attempt to make me tell what they thought was the truth, they started raping Tameka mercilessly. It was sad dog; I couldn't watch that shit. Next thing I know, Saleem bust through the door and start cuttin', but I told the cops I got them to let me go. After they raped Tameka, I got a hold of my gun and started layin' niggas down. I don't think they believe everything, but right now, it was enough. Detective Cropper said he would be in contact with me if he needed more info."

"Man, that's some deep shit," said Que, "I'm sure glad Saleem came when he did or the story might've played out differently."

"Yeah, I know," said Cousin Wayne, "I love that Lil' nigga; he reminds me of myself at his age. Imma make sure I let him know that personally tomorrow, but tonight Imma go grab a room at the Marriott and get my head together."

"Well, a'ight get at me tomorrow."

Then they both parted ways, lost in their own thoughts, knowing things were getting crazier every day and they needed to clear all of this shit up with Gangstar, but they knew tryin' to talk to him would be useless at this point because too much blood has been shed already and war has already been declared. So, they would have to stay on point and be prepared at all times 'cause in Delaware, if you get caught slippin', you end up missing its niggas that's been missing in Delaware longer than Jiminy Hoffa.

CHAPTER 22

Detective Cropper

Wilmington Police Department located on 3rd and Walnut Street across from Compton Towers Apartments and right in the back of the police station is Chadwick Apartments on the city's Eastside. Detective Cropper is sitting in his cubical going over the different homicides that have recently plaques the city. For some reason, he feels they're somehow related, but he can't really say for sure. He only has a couple of clues, like the area they've been occurring on the Northside of town and it seems that someone has been using a .38 revolver in a lot of these homicides. As of yet, the ballistics hasn't come back to determine if the bullets came from the same gun. While Det. Cropper is pondering. Chief Douglas approaches him and breaks him out of his reverie.

"Hey, Cropper, what the Hell are you doing sitting here with your dick up your ass!" screams the chef, "fucking kids and adults are getting murdered in cold blood right under our noses and you're sitting here jackin' your dick off. Do you have any idea the heat the mayor is runnin' on me and this fucking department?"

"Well, I uh."

"Shut the fuck up! You don't know 'cause you're in here staring off into space. You know, when the mayor comes down hard on me, I come down even harder on this department. I don't wanna hear no fucking excuses just start solving these fucking cases, or you can put your shit in a box or up your ass right now and get the hell outta here!"

Without waiting for a response Chief Douglas Storms off and leaves Det. Cropper sitting in his cubical, slightly pissed but not so much so 'cause he knows that it's all a show for the mayor.

Chief Douglas always puts on a show whenever the heat gets put on him; in all actuality, he's a big softy.

"Cropper, I see the chief is on you pretty heavy," said Det. Smalls.

"Yeah, you know how it goes when he gets put under the gun when a certain department gets a pile of cases back-to-back before anyone has a chance to solve any of them."

"Well, you know if you need me, I'm here for you," said Detective Smalls.

"Thanks pal, that's nice to know."

"A'ight, Cropper see you around."

"I just need to ruffle some feathers out on the street. I'm pretty sure I can get one of these rat bastards in this city to tell me something," thinking Detective Cropper to himself, then takes a sip of coffee, wondering where he should start at with his rival up of petty thieves and hustlers that don't mind snitching. Truth be told, he hates a snitch, but the bastards come in handy when you can't seem to put a case together on your own; you can depend on a rat bastard in this city to come through for you like Michael Jordan in the clutch. So, he takes another sip of coffee, a bite of a jelly doughnut, grabs his keys and hits for his Cruiser to see if he can find someone who knows anything about the murders that's on his case load that's been plaguing the city faster than the HIV virus, which is heavy in the city of Wilmington.

CHAPTER 23

Gangstar Discovers the 187

"Man, this is a brand-new Sega Genesis. All I want is a Ballgame for it which is 3.5 grams of crack cocaine. Come on man, I know you got it is time," said Buggy, the crackhead to one of Gangstar's young boys.

"Buggy man, go head with that bullshit ass game system that don't even probably work."

"It works, young blood. We can go hook it up right now," Buggy persisted.

"Buggy, I need money fuck a game."

"Hey, what the fucks goin' on over there? What y'all think this shit legal!" yells Gangstar from the green box he's sitting on, "how many times I gotta tell y'all niggas keep all transactions short!"

"I know Star, I told this Mafucka, keep it movin' he tryin' to sell this nut ass, Sega Genesis, for a Ballgame. I told 'em I need money fuck a game system," said the young boy.

"A Buggy come here," said Gangstar.

"Nah, I'm good Gang. Imma leave right now," Buggy said, knowing how Gangstar can be on some bullshit, especially in striking distance.

"Yo, what the fuck I say!" yells Star, "get the fuck over here. I just wanna take a look at the game system asshole, I might wanna put it in my truck!"

"Oh a'ight, my bad."

Star said, "Buggy."

As soon Buggy gets within reach of Gang, Gangstar hops off the green box lightening quick and grabs Buggy by the throat then snatches the bag with the game station in it.

"The next time I say come here Mafucka, don't hesitate just come. Pussy, if I say jump, you say how high you hear me nigga?"

"Ye..ah I...I he..ar you," said Buggy through the tight grip of Gangstar's hand around his throat.

Buggy's eyes begin to roll up in his head, showing he's either about to pass out or die.

"Star! Star!" yells a young goon running full speed towards Gangstar.

Instantly Gangstar let's Buggy throat go and he hits the ground like a sack of potatoes gasping for air. The young goon approaches, almost out of breath.

"Whats up Lil' nigga? It better be good screaming my name out loud like you crazy."

"Star man shit went down," said the young goon.

"Lil' nigga, what the fuck you talkin' about?"

"I just came from my girl crib on 32nd St. they got everything blocked off police, ambulances and fire trucks everywhere."

"Yeah, so what the fuck that got to do with me?" asked Gangstar.

"O.G. I went to go see what was going on and they was bringin' bodies out of the house on 31st Street."

"And, nigga get to the point," said an irritated Gangstar.

"Well, as I was watchin' one of the cops started walkin' down the street lookin' at cars, then he came to a stop at a brown Oldsmobile, opened the door and begin searching it as I try to think where I know this car from when it hit me."

"Oh shit!" exclaims Gangstar, finally putting it together, "B.G. and them I sent them niggas on a mission tonight in that same squatter."

"Yo, you think the bodies I saw was them?" asked the young goon.

"I don't know Lil' homie; I hope not Fuck! Fuck!" exclaims Gangstar, "yo good lookin' Lil' nigga Imma see whats what then I'll let everybody know what it is and what it's going to be. If it's my Lil' niggas, then Jessup St. niggas might as well start picking out they Sunday's best 'cause it's goin' be a lot of funerals."

"That's whats up, big homie. You already know how Riverside ride 187 style."

"Lil' homie 187 style," said Gangstar, "come on, take a ride with me; you strapped up, Lil' nigga?"

"You know I can't go no where without mines, big homie."

"Say no more then."

"It's so much money out here tonight," said Hakeem.

One of the Twins, "Yeah."

"Word it is," replied Khalif.

The other Twin, "Yo, go grab some more blunts out of the L.Q. before it closes and some cigarettes to dog," said Hakeem to his brother.

Who replies, "A'ight," and goes across the street to the liquor store to make the purchases before the store closes.

"Hey Unc over here, what chu' lookin' for? I got dimes," said Twin to the junkie walkin' across the street.

In the hood, male junkies were sometimes called Unc and the female ones were called Auntie basically to make them feel like family and sometimes 'cause you just didn't know their names.

The junkie crosses the street, "A man you got nicks or dimes?"

"Dimes," said Twin, "how many you want?"

"Let me get two for 15."

"A'ight, hold on." Twin turns his back and bends down to dig his pack out of the dirt hole he made to hide his package, never seeing the junkie walk up the street to someone outta sight.

Que pulls into the Gulf gas station located on Governor Prince Blvd. so he can grab some Backwoods so he can take it in for tonight; too much shit has been going on. It's been a long day, so he just wants to take a shower, eat, smoke out and hopefully find something on TV. He approaches the window and makes his order for the Backwoods. Coming across the bridge Det. Cropper is still in search of a snitch so he can begin putting some of his many cases together. As he hits Governor Printz Blvd., he sees a familiar face.

"Well, I'll be damned if it ain't Quincy Smith, one of Northside's finest. I bet he knows what the hell's going on over this side of town. The question is, can I get this asshole to run his mouth."

Det. Cropper pulls into the gas station and gets out of his Cruiser and yells, "Hey asshole, don't move!"

Que recognized the voice Immediately and exhaled, "All man, what the fuck you want with me? I'm twenty-nine negative," said Que using the Police lingo, which means he's clean.

"You're a piece of shit; do you know the code for that dick head?" replied Det. Cropper.

"Come on man, with the bullshit; just tell me what you want so I can be out. I had a long day."

"I don't give a fuck what type of day you've had asshole, I seen you down the station not too long ago with your partner in crime Wayne Reeves. You need to let him know I don't buy that bullshit story he ran down one bit and if I find out that it didn't happen, how be said it did I'm going to have his ass in a sling. You can bet your sweet little drug dealin' ass on it."

"Man, if you not about to arrest me, I'm about to be on my way," said Que.

"You're not going anywhere until I say so asshole. Put your fucking hands on the car."

"Man, this some bullshit, for what?" asked Que.

"Boy, 'cause I Fuckin' said so. That's why you fuckin' idiots think you run this city, well, you're a fucking fool if you think that. You see, dick head this is my city I run this shit. Now tell me what you know about all these shootings?"

"Man, I don't know shit about shit."

"Stop fucking trying to insult me, you piece of shit. I know anything that happens on this side of town. You catch wind of it one way or another. Hell, you probably got something to do with it."

"Come on Cropper, you know I don't get down like that."

"Yeah, I know, but I bet you know who does, so why don't you scratch my back and I'll scratch yours when you need it. Tell me first, what happened at your buddy Reeve's house where these fucking teenagers were gunned down and a teenage girl was repeatedly raped. Then tell me about them fucking Jamaicans and anything else you know."

"Man, I wish I could fill in all those blanks for you," said Que, "but I can't tell you what I don't know."

"You Fuckin' little cocksucker, you wanna play games, huh," said Det. Cropper heatedly, "spread your fucking legs."

"A'ight man, damn, take it easy!"

"Shut the fuck up and spread 'em wide. Do you have anything on you that can stick me any drugs or weapons on you?"

"Nah man, I ain't got shit!"

"Oh yeah, well, why do you have these?" said Det. Cropper, pulling out the Backwoods cigars box."

"Since when has it become a crime to have cigars?" asked Que.

"When you assholes decided to start putting Marijuana in them.

"You do know Marijuana is illegal, don't you asshole?" retorted Det. Cropper.

"Well, I don't have that problem, I don't smoke weed and I don't have anything on me. So, if you can just let me go on about my business, I'd really appreciate it," replied Que snidely.

"Yeah, not now, but just know when you slip, I'll be there to make sure you stay down for a very long time," replied Detective Cropper.

"Am I free to go?" asked Que. "Yeah, for now, you low-life piece of shit," retorted Detective Cropper. They both make eye contact as Que hops back in the vehicle pulled off heatedly.

Pace both equipped with semi-automatic handguns, the young goon with a nine caucus and Gangstar Glock .45.

"Yo, I hope they fat, man I don't want no skimpy shit," said the Junkie to Twin.

"Man, all my bag fat Unc here," Twin said, handing the junkie two rocks of crack for his 15 dollars, never noticing that the junkie was acting shifty and antsy.

Had he been paying attention, he would have probably been on point enough to notice the two guys walking extra fast with one hand slightly behind their back to conceal their weapons until they were ready to use them. By him not payin' attention may cost him dearly. After he hands the junkie the rocks, the junkie backs up slowly, turns on his heel and breaks into a run that turns into a sprint which baffles Twin.

Then he examines the money, "What I know this money ain't..." before he could finish the words he was thinking out loud, gunfire erupts

"Boom! Boom! Doom! Doom!"

The young goon and Gangstar let off shots at Twin simultaneously, catching him by surprise. Twin turns towards the shots only to be met by three of the first four shots, two in the stomach, one in the shoulder and one in his chest. Twin tries to scream out in pain, but the slugs knock the wind out of him on contact and he hits the ground hard. The other Twin hears the shots and automatically grabs his gun off his waist and rushes out of the liquor store, leaving everything he just purchased on the counter and rushed out of the door seeing two people running down the street. Then sees his brother layin' by the curb across the street, so he aims at the two figures and begins shooting in their direction.

"Boc! Boc! Boc!"

"Ahh!!!" one of them yells and falls to the ground but gets back up and tries to run again, but wherever he's hit slows him down. The other guy bends the corner leaving his boy behind. Twin squeezes his gun off again, missing the limping gunmen. Twin thought of chasing the gunmen, but he wanted to see how badly his brother had been hit.

As he approaches his brother, he yells, "Somebody call an ambulance! Oh no Hak!!! Hang in there, you goin' be a'ight!"

"It's burnin' man, its burnin' it startin' to get cold dog."

"Coughin' Coughin' Urgh!!" Blood spews out of Twin's mouth.

"Stop talkin' dog."

"Watch out, watch out," said Scooby bogarting his way through the crowd that has formed around the Twins, "get the fuck out the way before I pop one, you Mafuckas!" exclaims Scooby.

Once he sees Twin laying their all hit up he says, "Nah man, not my nigga! Who did this shit?"

"I don't know man. I was in the liquor store when the shots went off. When I came out, I seen two niggas runnin' down the street, so I started shooting at them. I hit one of them. He fell but got back up and kept runnin' but with a limp."

"Damn; Damn, Damn it! I knew I shouldn't of went in Mrs. Debbie crib."

"Why was you in there man?"

"You know that head like that," said Scooby.

"All man, you better stop trickin' for your dick fall off," said Twin.

"Cough, cough, ugh!!" the other Twin that's shot goes back into a coughing fit and throwin' up blood again. Sirens are getting closer.

"Yo, give your gun so I can put it up before the law get here."

Twin passes both his and his brother's gun before Scooby dips off to put the guns up.

The wounded Twin speaks, "I...love... y'all... man...they caught... slippin'."

"We love you too. You goin' be a'ight hang in there."

An ambulance pulls up and both paramedics jump out with equipment.

"Coming through comin' through!"

The crowd parts to allow them through and they immediately start working on Twin.

"Get a stretcher!" yells one to the other.

Scooby slides off 'cause he knows that the police will be there any minute and he doesn't wanna get caught wit the guns.

"Yo, Imma put these up. I'll be back."

"A'ight," said Twin.

The Paramedic arrives with the stretcher at the same time Det. Cropper and some black and whites pull up on the scene Det. Cropper had to let Que go so he could make it to the shots fired call that came over the radio. No sooner than Det. Cropper and the black and whites pull up; Que pulls up and hops out of his car and approaches the crowd to see what's going on as the paramedics hoist Twin onto the ambulance Det. Cropper comes over and sees Twin shot up pretty bad and from the looks of him, he doesn't think Twin will make it. The other Twin tries to climb into the ambulance with his brother.

Det. Cropper grabbed his shoulder and said, "I need to talk to you."

Twin snatched away from him and said, "You talk to me at the hospital. I'm going with my brother.

Det. Cropper stared at him, then said, "I'll be there," then turned around and told everyone to "backup this is a crime scene; unless you want to be a part of this case, I suggest you back up!"

Nobody wants any parts of the case 'cause they know if anybody gets caught snitchin' that'll be consequences and repercussions for their actions.

"Officers secure this area; tape everything off and keep these people back. If anyone can't seem to follow directions, arrest them for interfering with a police investigation and whatever else you can think of."

Saleem turns the corner in Scooby's car and sees what looks like a million people on the block. Ambulances, fire trucks, and police cars were everywhere.

"What the fuck is going on up here?"

Saleem wonders to himself as he pulls over and decides to walk up the block to find out what's going on. As he gets closer to the scene, he sees Scooby coming out of the side alley way, so he heads in his direction.

"Yo Scoob!" calls Saleem. Scooby stops and looks to see who called him; as he looks, he sees Saleem waving his hand to get his attention.

Scooby strolls over to him and gives him a dap, and says, "Yo, dog shit got messy."

Que sees Scooby and Saleem across the street ad says, "Yo!"

So he can get their attention; they both see him and walk up to him.

"Whats up y'all what the Fuck happen out here?" asked Que.

"I was just about to tell Saleem right before you called us."

"Oh, before you do, let's walk to my crib so we can get off this hot ass block," said Que.

As they walk to his crib, he updates them on Cousin Wayne's situation and how right before whatever just happened around here, he was being harassed by Det. Cropper about shootings in the city.

"Damn, that's crazy," said Saleem.

As they go inside Que's crib, they find seats. Que cracks the Backwoods he bought from the gas station and begins rolling up a blunt so they can smoke while they converse. Que sparks it and takes a couple of deep tokes and passes it to Scooby, who's the closest to him. Scooby takes a few tokes and then passes it to Saleem, then he begins to tell his story about what happened.

After the story, Que said, "Did Twin say who it was that shot him."

"Nah," said Scooby.

"Did the other Twin say he knows who was shootin' at?"

"Nah, he said he hit one of them and they ran this way like down here towards ya house, so they must've been parked around here somewhere," said Scooby.

"Well, if one of them got hit, it should be blood across the street or somewhere out front. Come on, let's go out front and check right quick," said Que.

Everybody exits the house and begins looking at the ground. As they crossed the street, you could see blood spots trailing down the street, so they followed the spots that ended at what could've been a parked car.

Ms. Edna across the street startled everybody when she said, "They been left."

Everybody looks up at the same time to see Ms. Edna in her window smoking a cigarette. Ms. Edna is Que's neighbor who always be in everybody's business. Word is she likes younger men; a couple of dudes from the hood have been known to creep over her crib late at night. You can tell back in the day, Ms. Edna used to be something to watch 'cause she still got a nice body and her face is still decent looking for her age.

"Hey Ms. Edna, did you see who it was or what type of car they was in?" asked Que.

"Yup, I sure did."

"So, can you tell us what you saw?" asked Saleem.

"I can, but whats in it for me?"

"All come on Ms. Edna, I been your neighbor forever and besides, one of the Twins got shot pretty bad," said Que.

"Oh My God, not Kim son?" Gasps!

"Ms. Edna yeah, Ms. Kim son."

"That a shame. I just seen him the other day when I went to the liquor store to get me some cigarettes. Well, I heard all them shots. I automatically hit the floor 'cause you know bullets ain't got no name on them when they get to flying and y'all young people don't know how to shoot no damn gun. Hitting people that don't even got nothing to do with nothing. Anyways after I realized I wasn't dead and ain't no bullets come through my window, I rushed to the window to see if I could see anything."

"I bet you did with ya nosey ass," mumbles Saleem.

"Excuse me honey, what was that?"

"I said, could you please tell us if you knew any of them," said Saleem.

"Oh," said Ms. Edna, "I thought you said something smart with your handsome self. You know you ain't too big for a good spanking," said Ms. Edna with a wink making Saleem shake his head and think to himself,

"Man, this old lady really a freak."

Que cuts in Ms. Edna and says, "Then what chu' see?"

"Oh, I'm sorry baby, well as soon as I get to the window, more shots go off, I duck again, but I hear somebody scream out in pain, so I peak back out the window and see a big dark skin guy running full speed with a gun in his hand towards a black truck that was parked where y'all standing at right now, but he doesn't appear to be hit. Then a few seconds later, a little boy about Saleem's and Scooby's age come limping around the corner. By then, the big dark skin guy was getting in the truck, ready to pull off, until the other guy started yelling stop Star wait for me! The big guy jumps out of the truck, gun in hand, and helps the younger boy in the truck, then pulls off."

At the mention of Star's name, everybody knows that it was Gangstar and one of his young boys behind the shooting.

"Thank you, Ms. Edna, you did good job, Que said, "come here right quick." Ms. Edna opens the door and Que hands her a 50 dollar Bill.

"Oh, thank you baby, you didn't have to do that. Why don't one of y'all come in and keep an old lady company for a while? Ain't no need and running them streets tonight with that shootin' and stuff carryin' on, plus I cooked some turkey chops macaroni and cheese, mash potatoes and string beans. It's plenty of it too; I know one of y'all hungry. I ain't going bite nobody, I promise," Ms. Edna said with a sly grin on her face. Although the meal sounds delicious, everyone declines Ms. Edna's offer.

"Shoot cha' self then more for me," replied Ms. Edna.

Then with one last try, she said, "My door is always open for either one of you boys if you ever wanna get a way or you hungry."

"Okay, thank you, Ms. Edna," everyone replied. Then they all went back into Que's house and discussed what Ms. Edna had just told them.

"Man, them Riverside niggas gotta go; they done shot Twin all up," said Scooby.

"We goin' take care of all this shit the war has officially started. So, it's on sight with these niggas. I was going to try and leave this shit alone, but now it is what it is," said Que.

"That's all it is," said Saleem with enthusiasm.

"He loves beef. Chill out, little homie; I know how you get. Be smart how you ride out," warns Que.

"No doubt, big homie, no doubt. Yo, tomorrow Imma shoot up Chester for a minute to holler at this shorty," said Saleem.

"No, not shorty from the concert?" asked Scooby.

"Yeah, that's the one," replied Saleem.

"Damn little nigga you move fast," said Que.

"All man, I learned from the best."

"Well, be safe up there. You know them Chester niggas get messy."

"Yeah, I know, but I fuck with some of them niggas up there, so I'm good."

"Oh, okay, well, how long you plan on staying up there?" asked Que.

"Just to take her out to lunch; I should be back a little later in the day."

"Oh, okay, I think a little away time would be good for you; too much done happened lately, so you need a break from this city," said Que, "but when you come back, you need to find a Connect so you and Scooby can keep y'all business running smooth."

"Yeah, I know. I got an idea who Imma get at about that."

"Good, well Imma let cha'll go. Imma bout catch up on some sleep."

"A'ight, Peace."

Saleem and Scooby leave Que's crib.

"Yo, what chu' bout to do?" asks Scooby.

"I'm bout to take my car to the crib and fall back til tomorrow. Why, whats up?"

"Ain't chu' comin'."

"Yeah, probably later."

"I'm hungry as shit," said Scooby.

"Man, Ayonna cooked for us so its food at the house."

"Nah, I'm cool. You go head."

"A'ight nigga, don't be mad if you come home and everything gone," said Saleem laughing as he left Scooby standing in front of Que's house. Saleem walk to the back lot, jumps in his car and eases out of the back lot with his lights out back on to Que's block just in time to see Scooby creeping into Ms. Edna's house.

"Look at this nasty dirty dick ass nigga," Saleem said out loud to himself with a chuckle, *"I knew something was fishy with that nigga tryin' to lag behind,"* laughs Saleem, *"Ms. Edna going to turn his dumb ass out,"* thinks Saleem as he rides past shaking his head at his comrade.

CHAPTER 24

Kid from Delaware

"Yo son, I love Delaware Kid. You shoulda been sent for me a duke. Word to mother, these bitches can't get enough of a nigga," said Ghost.

"Nigga I bought you down here to get money son, and on occasion rock a nigga to sleep," said Dreadz, a major nigga with connections in New York and Florida but been makin' mad moves in Delaware for a few years.

Now he's the dude that was supplying Omega and his dearly departed team and a lot of niggas know that Omega and his team were dealing with him, so he wonders if the hit on Omega was a message to him and his team or just a robbery homicide. However, or whatever the situation may be, Dreadz has called on a couple of wild niggas from East New York that get busy but also, when called upon to get money, they do that too.

"No doubt, my nigga you know I'm bout that murder murder and that cream," said Ghost.

"Yeah, well, stop thinking with ya little head and use ya big one more often."

"You right, my nigga, but I'm sayin' in the process, can't a nigga get some skins?"

"Of course," replied Dreadz with a chuckle.

"Man fuck them bitches. I'm here for this bread and if my nigga needs me to toe tag a nigga, so be it."

"It ain't down here for nothin' else. I don't like these off-brand ass niggas anyway," said OX.

Given that name 'cause that's what he's built like a fucking ox which comes from doin' time upstate most of his life.

"Aww man fuck outta here wit dat shit B. you only coppin' dat shit 'cause ya ugly ass can't get no pussy you keep scaring all the bitches away from you wit cha' big stocky Shaba Ranks lookin' ass," said Ghost with a laugh.

"Man fuck you. Unlike you, I know my position, so Imma play it to the fullest," replied Ox.

"Listen, when Omega got killed, it put a slight dent in the profit I've been making down here, but as you know, one monkey don't stop no show. With that being said, let's keep getting this money," said Dreadz.

"Tonya! Tonya!" calls Dreadz and in comes one of the thickest baddest redbones a nigga ever seen. She looks like Diamond from Players Club but a little thicker and a little prettier.

"Yes, daddy," she said with a sweet angelic voice.

"Hey Beautiful, I need you to make me and my fam some of that good breakfast that you be makin'. You know that French toast, bacon, eggs with the home fries," said Dreadz.

"Okay daddy."

Dreadz gives Tonya a light smack on the ass before she walks away. She giggles, looks over her shoulder and glares at Dreadz with her sexy green eyes and puts an extra switch in her walk, driving everyone in the room crazy.

"Yo son, where her sister at?" asks Ghost.

She doesn't have one," replied Dreadz.

"Well, whats up with her mom, grandmom, aunt or somethin'? It gotta be another one like that somewhere."

Dreadz laughs, "Yeah, she is a bad bitch, ain't she."

"So whats the count from last night's take from the apartments around 25th Street the regular," replied OX.

"Ten thousand?" asked Dreadz.

"Nah son, you know we make at least 15 a night at the apartments. Why you tryin' to test us, my nigga," said Ghost catching on to Dreadz, trying to see where Ox and Ghost's loyalty was at when it came to money."

"Nah, my niggas you know I be mixing up the apartments take with the Broad Peaches crib on 23rd and Lamothe Street, which does 10 thousand a night."

"Yeah, whatever son. We know you don't get nothin' confused when it comes to this cake," B. replied.

Ghost knowin' better that Dreadz is just playing the dumb role to test him and Ox.

"Son, it's cool. I smell where you coming from with ya little test and I respect it. You taught me a long time ago you can't trust nobody in this game, not even family," said Ghost.

Remembering one of the many jewels Dreadz used to drop on him before they ever came to Delaware.

"Yo Kid, I'm glad you be paying attention when I talk son," said Dreadz.

"So, have there been any problems at the spots with the local niggas?"

"Nah Kid, these niggas been mostly exceptive. They be buying double-ups and ball games and shit."

"I guess as long as they get a good deal, they stay in they lane, but you know it's a couple hard heads that come through with the face fucking, but you know we return the looks letting them niggas know the feelings are mutual.

"Word to mother, I can't wait to send one of these niggas too good-looking," B. replied.

"Ghost, well as long niggas keep the peace, avoid unnecessary conflict Kid," said Dreadz.

"No doubt son," replied Ghost.

"Excuse me daddy, breakfast is ready. Would you like me to bring you y'all plates or set up the table?" asked Tonya.

"Could you set the table ma 'cause I don't wanna mess up ya beautiful living room that I know you love so much."

"Okay, daddy, Just give one a second and I'll have all y'all plates ready."

"Okay, ma," replied Dreadz.

"Yo Kid, I gotta get me one of those tokes Ghost."

Everybody begins laughin', waiting for Tonya to prepare their plates of food so they can eat breakfast.

CHAPTER 25

Twin Got Killed

Ring… Ring… Ring…

"Hello," answers Saleem in a groggy voice.

"Baby, is that you? Are you okay?" asked Ayonna.

"Oh yeah, babe, I'm good. Whats up? Good morning. You a'ight?" asked Saleem.

"Yeah I'm fine. What time did you get in last night? I've been trying to call you at cha' moms. Then I was callin' there and ain't get no answer."

"Yeah babe, a lot been going on."

"I know that's why I was trying to call you. I heard about Twin. They rushed him in while everybody was there for Tameka."

"Oh yeah, how is she?"

"She doing better, but she's still kinda out of it; she ain't talking to nobody. They said she's traumatized, but in time she should be good but I know you going through it right now 'cause Twin was throwing chairs and everything. The police had to put him in cuffs. He was talking about killing people and he wanna die too and all types of crazy mess."

"Whoa! Whoa! Whoa! Back up a little bit. What chu' mean he wanna die too?" asked Saleem.

"Boy, his brother died last night during surgery. Ms. Kim passed out when the doctor told her; it was crazy in there. I was crying; I didn't know if anything had happened to you 'cause I couldn't get in contact with you, so I was going through it babe."

"I'm good," replied Saleem reassuringly, "damn my fucking nigga dead this shits gettin' outta hand."

"What are you talking about Saleem; you know who did this?"

"Nah, I don't know who did shit. I'm just saying shit messy and if shit don't come to an end, it's only going to get messier."

"Baby, don't go and get yourself in no trouble; you doing something ain't going to bring Twin back and I don't wanna even think about losin' you."

"That chu' don't have to worry about. I get busy."

"Yeah, Yeah whatever. You don't have to prove you tough to me baby."

"Nah, it ain't even about that. I know if tables was turned, Twin would ride out for me, no questions asked," said Saleem. Knowing that Twin woulda painted the town red if it was Saleem that got kilt. So, he don't have a choice but to hold his fallin' comrade down.

"Baby, whatever you decide, be careful and I want you to know I love you."

"I love you too," replied Saleem, "I'll talk to you baby girl, bye."

"Ok bye."

They both hang up the phone. Saleem gets up, goes to the bathroom, and takes a shower, never hearing Scooby enter the apartment.

"Yo Leem, where you at nigga?!" calls out Scooby.

As he walks towards the bedroom, he hears the shower running, so he goes back into the living room, turns on the TV, and rolls up a blunt 'cause he's full. Ms. Edna made him breakfast right after she woke him up with some of the best head he had ever had in his young life. Then they fucked until half an hour ago, ate, then Scooby decided it was time to go 'cause he found himself liking Ms. Edna's company too much, but he did promise her that it wouldn't be their last time together 'cause she not only gave good head but that pussy worth something too. Not noticing Saleem staring at him while he's still in thought, he unconsciously rubs his dick.

"A nigga, I know you ain't rubbing ya dick at Michael Jordan," Saleem jokes, breaking Scooby out of his thoughts.

"Man fuck outta here with that bullshit. I was watching Sports Center and got to thinking about this bitch I fucked last night," said Scooby.

"Is that right," said Saleem with a smirk, knowing he was over Ms. Edna's.

"Damn, it must've been all that for you to lay up with her all night," said Saleem, continuing to keep fucking with Scooby.

"Yeah man, that pussy was all that and don't even get one started on what the head like," exclaims Scooby, getting excited.

"Damn nigga you sharin'?" asked Saleem with a big grin on his face.

"Nah nigga not this one dog. I mean, you probably wouldn't want her anyway; she ain't cha type," said Scooby trying to turn Saleem off.

But Saleem presses with, "Man, if she's ya type, then I know she's mines too."

"Nah man, I'm telling you I know ya style, she ain't it."

"Yeah, you right, Ms. Edna ain't my style, you nasty ass nigga," said Saleem bursting out laughing.

Scooby's eyes get wide as saucers.

"Man, what the fuck? You spying on a nigga now," exclaims Scooby, embarrassed.

"Nah nigga, instead of leaving out the back way, I came out of the front and seen ya nasty ass creeping into Ms. Edna's," Saleem said, bent over, holding his stomach and laughing his ass off.

"Man fuck you dog," said Scooby throwing a couch pillow at Saleem.

"Let me find out Ms. Edna got chu' sprung nigga."

"Nah dog, that shot is good though I can't even front," said Scooby being honest.

"A you wanna order breakfast?" asked Saleem.

"Nah dog, I'm full as shit; Ms. Edna made breakfast for me before I left."

"Damn nigga, either you put work in or she trying to wife you up nigga," laughs Scooby.

"Fuck you dog, that ain't happening, but I will say this, Imma hit that pussy every now and then on the low."

"I heard that, do you a dog. Imma bout to get dressed and go make some rounds and see what that count lookin' like."

"Shit, it better be lookin' right," said Scooby.

"Yo dog, I almost forgot to tell you while you was all laid up with the misses," Scooby gives Saleem the finger, "man Twin died during surgery."

"What!" Scooby exclaims, jumping to his feet off of the couch.

"Nah dog, don't tell me that shit."

"Yeah, Ayonna was at the hospital with Tameka and her family when they bought Twin in. She said Twin started flippin' out when the doctor said Twin ain't make it. She also said Ms. Kim fainted."

"Damn, dats some crazy shit right there. Man, them niggas gotta pay," said Scooby.

"Yeah, it's on, but right now we goin' chill 'cause it's hot but best believe retaliation is a must," said Saleem.

"Man, cool go head Imma go take care of business; after that Imma shoot up Chester."

"Oh yeah, that's right, you are going to see home girl from the Biggie concert."

"Yo, you should let me come. She might got somebody for me."

"Nah, I told her it's just going to be us."

"A'ight, I respect that," said Scooby, "yo you think she goin' let you see what that shot like?"

"Man, on some real shit, it ain't even bout that. We just going to lunch, that's all, but if the opportunity presents itself, then it is what it is."

"A yo, what do you think about the bitches selling weed for us out of a junkie crib down the way?" asked Saleem.

"I don't know dog, the bitches smoke big weed," said Scooby talking about Gutlynn, Shantay and Dina.

"I know, but they be out there 24/7 they might as well get some type of money besides boostin' clothes.

"Yeah, well, we can start them off with like a pound or two just to see how they do with that," said Scooby.

"Solid, Solid," replied Saleem.

"Well, Imma holler at them and see if they trying get this money."

"Yo, make sure you go grab some sneaks for Boomer. Ms. Robin, go see him this week. I saw her and she said he asked for some Bo Jackson's, the orange, white, gray and blue ones," said Saleem.

"A'ight, I got him that's my peoples right there with his crazy ass," exclaims Scooby talking about they homie that's in Ferris school for boys. A juvenile joint for wild little niggas that can't go to big boy jail yet.

Boomer been down since last year; he caught 18 months for a gun and an ounce of weed. He's a cold-blooded canon who loves the drama. If he was home right now, he would probably try to go down Riverside by himself and start poppin' everything in sight. The Twins, Hakeem and Khalif, are like his brothers, so I know he feels some type of way about Twin getting killed. Saleem said his goodbyes to Scooby, jumped in his car and goes through tapes to find something to ride to while he did his pickups around the city. As he fumbles with the tapes, he finally settles for one and pops it into his tape deck and Tupac's familiar voice comes through the speakers. *"I'm up before the sunrise/first to hit/the block little bad Mafucka, wit a pocket full rock."* Raps Tupac.

Saleem begins making his rounds, vibing to the music. His first stop is Eastside to holler at Che' Ball and Bell-Bell. As he pulls up, he sees Bell-Bell, so he hops out and walks over to him.

"Hey player, whats up?" asked Bell-Bell.

"All man maintainin' not complainin'," replied Saleem.

"Yo, you alright? I heard the boy Twin got hit up last night."

"Yeah, some coward ass nigga creeped up on 'em, but you know it'll get handled in due time."

"Man, you ain't gotta tell me. I know how you do," said Bell-Bell, "yo Imma go grab whatever Che' Ball got in the spot. Wait right here," said Bell-Bell before going into a house across the street.

Seconds later, Bell-Bell comes out of the house with a bookbag strapped over his shoulder and Che' Ball stands in the doorway and gives

Saleem the thumbs up and a head nod; Saleem nods his head back.

Bell-Bell said, "Yo, let's go sit in ya car," they got in the car and Bell-Bell said, "we only got like 7 ounces left on the brick left and two pounds left on the trees. All that should be gone in no time, so we should be ready for you soon. This is what we got now."

Saleem opens the bookbag and peeks in, nods his head, gives Bell-Bell dap, then tells him, "Imma get at cha'll when y'all done."

"Okay, just come through."

"A'ight," replied Saleem.

After Bell-Bell hops out, Saleem pulls off, continuing to make his rounds. He hits Westside and collects what Cheese and Tiz got, and then he shoots over south bridge al collects what Adismal and Shame have for him, which is everything except for their money from the 10 rounds. They still got 2 pounds left. Before he leaves them, he lets them know that he'll give them a whole brick apiece the next time. His next stop is back on the Northside up Concord Ave. Clark Bar and Bucko knocked off everything except 5 ounces of coke. Saleem lets them know that he'll hit them with more work on the next go-round.

After making all of his rounds except for Buck-Jones and his crew 'cause he knows he'll see them later. So, he shoots to the apartment to put up the money. After he and Scooby split the profit down the middle like they planned fifty-fifty. See, it ain't no big I's or no little U's. That way it won't be any conflict; everybody got the same thing when things go like that, there's no need to be jealous of your homeboy 'cause you feel like he got more than you. Yeah, it sounds suckerish, but that's usually how best friends that been cool all their life become total strangers. It's always over some money or some bitch. If you take the time out to look back in a lane or even in the present niggas that were once cool ain't cool no more. I bet 100 to 1 that it has to do with some money or some bitch that don't give a fuck about either one of them niggas. As we speak, she probably gets the next nigga dick in her mouth while both of her hands are rummaging through his pockets. So, if you are going to partner up with a nigga make sure you are able to satisfy each other's hunger and don't never let no whore come in between true friendship.

CHAPTER 26

Pookie Came Back

"Yeah, I took Little B. on a caper with me last night and he got shot in the leg. I almost left his ass and said," Gangstar talking to his two of his young boys.

"Man, this nigga has blood all over my truck. You know I had to take that nigga up Crozer Hospital in Chester so the police down here couldn't link the shootin' back to him."

"Man, you should've took us," said one of the young boys.

"I would've, but it was spear of the moment and y'all wasn't around at the time."

"Yo, they said that nigga died last night too," said the other young boy.

"Man fuck that nigga. That was the point; that was for Kurt and B.G. and then it was time for one of them niggas to die. We Ride 187 Style if we didn't put nobody to rest after all our homies been getting killed. How was that going to box on us," Gangstar asked heatedly.

"You right, Big Homie," replied the young boys, not trying to make Gangstar flip on them, "I know that ain't Pookie over there," said Gangstar referring to one of the young boys he banned from the projects for not following directions which resulted in little Kurt getting killed. The two young boys look across the street and see Pookie making a sale in between two houses.

"Yeah, that's him," replied one of the young boys.

"And this nigga got a nerve to be hustlin'. A Yo y'all go over there and distract him while I go around the other side of the house and catch 'em from behind 'cause you know if he see me he gone run," said

Gangstar.

Gangstar heads across the street so he can walk around the side of the house so Pookie can't see him when they call out his name.

"Pookie!" calls out one of the young boys.

He looked up quickly, trying to see who spotted him as he called his name.

"Over here!" yells the other young boy.

Pookie sees them and relaxes, then says, "Yo chill, what you tryin' to get me killed calling my name out all loud. Y'all know I ain't suppose to be down here. Now what if Star would've heard y'all," he said nervously.

"All man, Star ain't worrying about chu'," said one of the young boys pulling him in for a hug.

Then the other young boy does the same. Just as Gangstar appears from behind the house, the young boy tenses up a little and he ain't even the target. If Pookie could've seen the young boy's eyes or would've paid attention to his body language, he would've known something wasn't right. The young boy backs away from Pookie.

"Whats up dog? You look like you seen a ghost or somethin'," said Pookie as he turned around BAM!

Everything goes black and Pookie hits the ground asleep from the right hook to the side of his head that Gangstar threw. Gangstar then kicks Pookie in his ribs.

"Wake up Pussy." Pookie moans but lies stiff on the ground

"Oh, you don't wanna get up nigga! Let's see if this'll help you."

Gangstar pulls out his dick and begins pissing right in Pookie's face. Pookie starts to come to; he feels the wetness but doesn't immediately know what it is. He focuses his eyes and tries to block the wetness as best as he can. When he sees it's Gangstar pissing on him, he tries to scramble away, but Star steps on his chest.

"Nah nigga, didn't I tell you not to come back down these projects nigga, huh?" asked Gangstar as he stomps Pookie until he began to piss on himself.

"Star chill! Star, chill out! You gone kill 'em!" Shouts one of the young boys.

"Fuck this nigga. If he would've followed directions, Kurt would be alive!" exclaims Gangstar, then spits on Pookie and tells him to "get the fuck up and get out of the projects the next time catch you down here. The coroner going to have to come get cha' body," said Gangstar, "come on y'all!"

He calls out to his young boys as he walks away, heads back across the street, and takes his position on the green box. When the young boys cross the street, he tells them to, "Let everybody now to be on point 'cause he knows that beings though that nigga Twin died last night them Jessup Street niggas might try to come through and catch us slippin'. So go grab all the guns and make sure they in reach so everybody can get to them easily. If they get the urge to come through with that being said, they go alert everyone and strategically place the guns in separate places where they can be reached, just in case. Gangstar feels better safe than sorry. Now the only thing to do is sit back and see it the Jessup Street niggas going to have the balls to come through or fallback and try to catch him and his squad out of bounds." He doesn't know, but whatever it is he plans to be prepared for whatever.

CHAPTER 27

Saleem and Simone

Saleem gets off of the Kerlin Street exit and heads to 9th Street to meet Simone at the A-plus gas station in Chester, PA. As he rides, he zones out to the music coming through the sound system. *"As soon as I get home, I'll make it up to you Baby I'll do what I gotta do,"* sings Faith Evans. Saleem pulls up into the gas station, all eyes on him. Simone is standing by the entrance staring at the car briefly, then turns her head in the opposite direction as if she's looking for someone.

Saleem got out of the car and said, "Hey beautiful, you looking for me?" Simone turns around and sees Saleem standing by the car with a big grin on his face.

She covered her mouth with both hands and blushed, then said, "Oh My God! Boy, I didn't even know that was you. Is this ya car?"

"Yup."

"It's nice," said Simone admiringly.

"Thank you baby," said Saleem as he walked around her side of the car and opened the door for her. She smiles, that lovely white teeth smile, then get in. Saleem closes the door, then walks around to his side of the car and walks past a couple.

A woman said to her man, "You need to get some manners from that young man. He opens doors and everything," she said giving Saleem a smile. Saleem smiles back, then gets in the car with Simone, who is into the song.

When Saleem gets in, she turns the music down and says, "I didn't know you liked Faith Evans."

"Yeah, its a lotta things you don't know about me."

"Oh yeah, like what?" asked Simone.

"Well, for starters, did you know I was going to do this?" Saleem leans over and kisses Simone with a deep passionate kiss, then laughs 'cause he can see she's dazed a little.

"Wow, what was that about?" gushes Simone.

"Well, that was my way of saying I like you."

"Oh, in that case, come here," she leaned in and gave Saleem a deep kiss, then said, "the feelings are mutual."

Now it's Saleem's turn to look dazed, then he pulls himself together and asks, "So you ready to eat?"

"Yup," replied Simone.

"A'ight, let's go, boy, you act like Farillos in Mexico."

"Girl, I know it's only across the street," laughs Saleem.

He pulls off and parks right across the street in a bar parking lot called City Grill when he pulls up. Several guys are eyeing the car beings though it's unfamiliar.

Simone said, "I don't think you shoulda parked right here. Those dudes is all on this car." Saleem reaches under his seat and tucks his pistol in his wristband.

"Oh My God, Saleem you got a gun!" exclaims Simone.

"Yup, never leave home without, but you don't have to worry about nothing going down, though. You see the dark skin dude right there?"

"Yeah," said Simone.

"That's my "H" and the light skin nigga with the big nose, that's my peoples Jay both real cool peoples. They ain't never seen me before in this car; the only time I use to come up here was usually with Jay in his whip.”

“Oh,” said Simone with a sigh of relief ‘cause she knows all too well that dudes from Chester can get messy real quick.

She’s from the Metcalf Projects and if you know Chester, you know about the Calf. Saleem hops out of the car, walks around to the passenger side and lets Simone out of the car. Jay recognizes Saleem first.

“Aw man, “H” that’s Saleem,” he said with a laugh, “you Saleem who you think you are Billy D. Williams or somebody opening doors and shit,” cracks Jay making everybody around him laugh.

Saleem grabs Simone’s hand and pulls her with him toward the crowd.

“Whats up Gonzo? I see you got jokes.” Everybody burst out laughing, pointing at Jay’s nose.

“You got that, you got that,” said Jay.

“So, what brings you up here?” asked “H.”

“Aw man, I came to take my lady friend out to lunch.”

“Aw ain’t that sweet,” cracks Jay.

“Yeah, you know, can’t be a Gangstar all the time.”

“I feel you on that said, “H.”

“Well, this is Simone, Simone, this is “H” and this chip tooth, flat nose fool is Jay,” cracks Saleem.

“Nice to meet you,” said “H.”

“You too,” replied Simone.

“I’m very pleased to meet you Ms. Pretty and when you get tired of this chump I’ll be right here waiting for you,” said Jay jokingly.

“Well, I’m sorry to inform you Mr. Nose.”

“Oh my bag, Mr. Whatever, I’m taken and even if I wasn’t you wouldn't have a shot any way everybody instigates."

"Excuse me," said Jay, slightly offended 'cause he swears he's gods gift to women.

"I was just joking."

"Oh well, I was just stating facts."

"Easy baby girl, take it easy on him," said Saleem.

"That's how them Delaware girls act?"

"Yeah, but worst but she ain't from Delaware though; she from the Calf."

"Oh yeah," said "H," "who ya mom and dad?"

"That's too much information."

"Oh Nah, I was trying to see who ya people was 'cause I know a lot of people in the Calf," said "H."

"Well, anyway, where y'all going to eat?" asked Jay.

"Right across the street."

"Where?" asked "H."

"Man Farillos!" exclaims Saleem.

"Oh yeah, they do got some good food," said "H."

"Hey baby, hang tight for a second."

"Okay," replied Simone.

"A y'all let me holler at cha'll for a second," Saleem said to Jay and "H," "man, I got things poppin' in my city right now, but the thing is, I don't have a steady supplier, so I was wondering if y'all new somebody with grade A shit that can cover whatever order I ask for?"

"Well, I know a couple dudes, but they be having good stuff every now and then but not all the time. I mean, you know we be doing our one-two up here. What you looking for halves or wholes?" asked "H."

"I'm looking for wholes family."

"So, you done came up down there, huh?" asked Jay.

"A little bit," replied Saleem.

"Now you wanna be modest and shit," said Jay.

"Nah, I just need a Connect, bottom line."

"Well, Imma shop around for you, but in the meantime, I got a couple of wholes for the low," said "H."

"Nah cousin, I need more than a couple yum!"

"It's like that?" asked Jay.

"Nah, not really. I just need something consistent."

"Yeah, I hear you," said Jay, "but If you need to dump some of that work once you get rollin' holler at us, we might be able to help you expand said," Jay.

"I heard that," said Saleem, "look Imma holler at cha'll peace."

"A'ight nigga, be safe."

"Y'all too," said Saleem as he walked away, "hey sweetheart, I apologize for keeping you waiting; you ready."

"Yeah, I'm ready," replied Simone.

Saleem grabs her hand and heads up the street toward Farillos. As they go inside, Saleem takes Simone to a table in the back. A waiter comes to them and immediately asks them if they are ready to order. Saleem looks at Simone to see if she's ready.

She said, "I'll have whatever he's having." So, the waiter waits for Saleem to give the order.

"Well, in that case, have turkey paninis and some potato salad and two bags of BBQ Potato chips.

"And anything to drink?"

"Yes, two large Sprites."

"Will that be all?" asked the waiter.

"Yes, for right now," said Saleem.

"Okay, your meal will be ready shortly," said the waiter before leaving.

"Then so beautiful, why did you give my peoples such a hard time."

"'Cause I don't know them; wasn't trying to get to know them, I'm with you, so no one else matters right now."

"Wow, I respect that."

"You know you're one of the special ones. I can feel it in my heart. I really like you," said Saleem.

"Oh yeah, well, I really like you also and I know your one of the special ones," Simone said with a smile.

"Oh yeah, what makes you think I'm so special," asked Saleem.

"Well, some…" Simone stops because their food and drinks have arrived at their table.

After the food is placed in its proper places, Saleem thanks the waiter and turns his attention back to Simone.

"Well, as I was saying."

"Nah baby girl, we'll get back to that enjoy your meal."

They begin eating both in their own thoughts.

Saleem breaks Simone out of her thoughts when he says, "See you like paninis," noticing how Simone handled hers.

"Oh My God! I am so embarrassed I haven't eaten all day and this pineeki is so good." Saleem burst out laughing.

"Stop laughing at me punk," said Simone.

"Nah, you called it a pineeki it's a paninis."

"Oh, whatever its name is, it's delicious."

"I knew you'd like it; my mom turned me on to them a while ago. I've been on them ever since." They both finished up their meals and the waiter appeared.

"Is there anything else I could help you all with?"

"Yes, could you please give us a refill on the sodas?"

"Sure can," replied the waiter cleaning off their table and walking away to get their sodas.

Saleem asked Simone what she was getting ready to say earlier before they started eating.

Simone blushed a little, then said, "I was just going to say some people try too hard to be someone their not, but that's not you your naturally cool and you don't have a facade and my heart also tells me that your decent and I know your very mature for your age. Look at chu' got a car, your own money and you know how to make a girl feel special, safe and secure. I have no worries with you; I feel so at ease. Then you got the nerve to be handsome with sexy deep dimples. Boy, you just don't know what you do to me when you smile I just...."

Simone stops, "let me stop. I don't wanna scare you off like I'm some type of groupie or something."

"Nah sweetheart, never that I was enjoying every word. I dig your honesty. What was you about to say," asked Saleem.

Simone looked Saleem in the eyes and said, "You know I'm leaving and I don't know if I'll ever see you again, so I was wondering if never mind."

Saleem grabbed her hands, held them, and he looked her in the eyes and said, "Baby, never be afraid to speak your mind around me. Whatever you feel, say it." The waiter appears with their sodas and then disappears.

Simone cleared her throat and took a sip of soda, then said, "Saleem, I'm very attracted to you and I don't want you to think I'm some type of whore, but I would love if you and I got together before you leave today."

Saleem smiled and said, "Girl, I could never look at you like a whore and I would love to get together with you."

He leans over the table to give her a Kiss. Saleem pulls out $25 and leaves it on the table, not caring if it's too much 'cause he knows it's definitely enough. They set up and head back to the car. As they reach the parking lot, Jay and "H" comes over to say their goodbyes.

"H" said, "Yo Imma let you know if l come across something."

"A'ight," replied Saleem.

"Yeah, and Imma look after ya little girlfriend while you in Delaware," said Jay.

"Boy if…"

"Chill baby," said Saleem cutting Simone off before she goes on.

Saleem opens the door and lets Simone in, then walks around to his side of the car then says, "If things go my way, I'll get at cha'll and Jay, tell ya sister I said when I come back up here make sure she wears that see through bra and party set I bought her for her birthday. "H" bursts out laughin' while Jay stands there with the I don't play the sister jokes look.

Jay shook his head and said, "You got that one."

Saleem gets in the car Simone asked, "What did you just say to that smart ass big nose boy 'cause he looked like he was heated.

"Oh, I told him to tell his sister the next time I come up here; tell her I said wear the see-through panty and bra set I bought her on the birthday."

"Oh My God! Is it true?"

"Nah, but I knew he wouldn't like that, so I said it to get under his skin."

"Oh boy, you are crazy," exclaims Simone.

"So do you have some where specific you would like to go?" asks Saleem.

"No, not really," replied Simone, "anywhere with you would be nice."

Saleem smiles and thinks about taking her to his apartment but quickly puts that thought out of his mind 'cause Ayonna has a key and all hell would break lose if she caught them in the act, so Saleem finds the nearest hotel. As they pull into the parking lot, Saleem observes the parking lot bingo. He Jumps out of the car and approaches a slender, well-dressed Black man. The two speak briefly; Saleem hands him some money. The guy walks into the hotel, then after 10- 15 minutes, comes out of a side entrance, hands Saleem a key card to a room then walks back towards the hotel. Saleem waves Simone out of the car. She hurries towards Saleem, he grabs her hand and they enter through the side entrance. Saleem looks at the key card. Room 112 is embroidered on it with white numbers. As they reach the room, Saleem sticks the key card into the slot. The light flashes green, then a clicking sound lets him know the door is unlocked. As they enter the room, it's plush with thick fluffy beige carpet, a nice sofa King size bed, nice big TV, and a mini bar.

"This is nice," said Simone

"Yeah, it is," replied Saleem as he walked to the bathroom, "yeah, I like this shit," exclaimed Saleem, "hey babe, come look at the bathroom."

Saleem steps out of the way so she can see.

"Oh My God!" gasps Simone when she sees the Jacuzzi-style bathtub, "Oh My God! Saleem, thank you, this is so beautiful I'll never forget this day," exclaimed Simone with glee.

"All baby, its nothing. I wanted our first time to be somewhere decent. Take your clothes off and get in the Jacuzzi and I'll be right with you in a minute," said Saleem as he headed back into the room. Once inside, he heads straight to the mini bar, searching for something to help calm his and Simone's nerves and put them both at ease. He remembers that he had some weed in the car. He goes to the bathroom just in time to see Simone stepping out of her parties.

"Damn sweetheart, you look amazing."

"Oh My God! You scared me boy," squealed Simone, covering herself as best she could with her hands.

"Baby, you don't have to hide yourself from me."

"Nah, I was just caught off guard a little but still slightly covering herself.

"Babe, I was about to tell you I was going to the car and grab some weed right quick. Would you like a drink or something til I come back?"

"Yes, that would be nice."

"Do you like Hennessey?"

"Yeah."

"A'ight, I'll be right back."

He grabs the little bottle of Henny out of the mini bar, passes It to Simone, looks at her hungrily, shakes his head, then heads out to the car as if he was Flash Gordon; he was back in the room in record-breaking time. He takes off all his clothes, sits on the bed, rolls a blunt, then walks into the bathroom, dick swinging scaring Simone.

"Once again, boy you need to start announcing ya' self," said a startled Simone, "Oh My God!" Simone exclaims, got meaning to actually say it out loud, looking at Saleem's dick.

Saleem smirks at her reaction, then climbs in the Jacuzzi and sparks the blunt, takes a few tokes, then passes it to Simone, who coughs instantly at the first toke of the potent weed.

"Damn boy, what kind of weed is this?" asked Simone.

"I call it Jamaican funk. Why it's too strong for you?" laughs Saleem.

"A little," replied Simone, "honestly, It's good though. Just gotta get use to it," she said, taking another toke, this time holding in the smoke a little longer before blowing it out and passing it back to Saleem. He graciously excepted the blunt and began blowing like a chimney.

He can see that the weed and Henny are taking their effect on Simone, so he says, "You a'ight over there?"

"Yeah, I'm good. I was wondering why you all the way over there," said Simone seductively.

"Oh, my bad," said Saleem moving over closer to where Simone is.

"You think you can handle some more of this Kill Kill?

"Yeah, sure," replied Simone.

"Have you ever had a shot gun?"

"A what boy, I don't mess with no guns," Simone said seriously.

Saleem begins laughing hysterically.

"Boy, whats so funny I don't mess with guns," exclaimed Simone, not understanding the humor.

"Girl, I'm not talking about no real gun. I'm thinking about when I put the fire part of the blunt in my mouth and you put the part you pull from in your mouth and I blow on my and filling your mouth with smoke."

"Oh," said Simone.

"Do you want try it?"

"Yeah why not."

"Well, come on."

Saleem puts the blunt in his mouth and then blows hard as he can, instantly filling Simone's mouth with smoke. She tries to inhale it, but it's too much smoke, so once again, she begins choking. Saleem burst out laughing again. Simone climbs out of the Jacuzzi, soaking wet to, trying to catch her breath. Saleem hops out and comes to her aid, but she pushes him away from her.

"Aww baby, I apologize," said Saleem trying to contain his laughter.

Simone walks into the bedroom and starts gathering her clothes.

"All baby, where you going?" Saleem grabs her arm and pulls her in close.

"Let me go; you play to much you tried to kill me and thought it was funny."

"Girl, stop it with that. I'd never try to kill you."

"Well, why you do that for then?" replied Simone in her baby voice with a pout.

"I was trying to get chu' a little higher, that's all."

"Well, I'm high you succeeded now what?"

"Now put those clothes down so I can suck that pretty pussy."

"Boy, you nasty," giggles Simone as she drops her clothes.

Saleem leads her to the bed; she climbs on it and lays back. Saleem stopped and stared at her beautiful naked body, then said, "Girl, you are so gorgeous. I can't wait to feel you."

Simone blushes, Saleem climbs between her legs and goes straight for her clitoris, making her gasp a little and her legs spread open.

"On My God! Saleem, that feel so good."

What is that referring to? The way Saleem is working his tongue on her, it feels like he has something down there besides his tongue. Saleem continues to work the clit and pussy lips back and forth, occasionally tongue fucking her, making her squirm. Simone keeps trying to close her legs, but Saleem has his arms and hand holding them up in the air.

"Oh My God! Oh My God! exclaims Simone as she begins cumming and shaking uncontrollably. Saleem smiles as Simone lies there, convulsing, knowing he has done his job. A single tear runs out of Simone's eye-catching Saleem off guard. So, he asked her if she's okay, thinking maybe he had done something.

Simone wiped the single tear from her eye, embarrassed and replied, "I'm fine. I just never had nobody make me feel like this before."

"Oh," said Saleem, still wondering why a tear fell from her eye so he asked, "so you still wanna keep going?"

"Boy yeah, I'm good; it's a girl thing now, come on," she said, spreading her legs so Saleem could get a full view of her soaking wet pussy.

"That's all it is then," said Saleem as he climbed on top of Simone and put the tip of his dick head in her.

"Tss hisles," Simone was trying to adjust to the size of Saleem's dick. Saleem continues to work his way inside.

Simone slowly, "Ahhh!" exclaims Simone.

"You okay?" asked Saleem.

"Yeah," replied Simone, "it's just that I never been with no one your size before I only been with one other guy before and he wasn't this big, but I'm fine, don't stop."

"Okay, baby," said Saleem.

He begins to work up a rhythm and Simone begins to relax a little allowing him to fill her completely.

"Yeah baby, that's right, grind that dick," said Saleem encouraging her to fuck back, "yeah, put cha' legs on my shoulders."

Simone complies, and when she does, Saleem goes deeper, making her scream out.

"Oh shit! Oh shit!"

"Yeah, unh hunh, take this dick baby," said Saleem speeding up the pace.

Within minutes Simone begins cumming, digging her nails into Saleem's back. Saleem continues to pound her tight pussy, on the verge of cumming himself.

"Oh Shit, um, bout to cum!" exclaims Simone, "Saleem take it out! Take it out!" yells Simone.

Reluctantly Saleem pulls out, shooting cum all over Simone's stomach.

"Ahh shit!" exclaims Saleem jerking the rest of the cum out of his dick.

"Eww! Boy, you had a lot built up in you," said Simone and you goin' put it all on me, ill boy."

"Girl, you said don't cum in you. Lucky, I pulled out good as that pussy is," replied Saleem.

"Boy, you better had pulled out. I'm not trying to have no babies yet."

"I feel you, but I want kids."

"That's cool, but they won't be with me, at least not no time soon and I'm bout to move. I may never see you again."

"Girl with shot like yours, I might move with you," jokes Saleem.

"Boy, you are crazy," replied Simone.

"Yeah, crazy about chu'."

"Saleem."

"Whats up baby?"

"I'm going to miss you. I'm really starting to fall for you. Like I said, I'm always going to remember this day; this is the day I can truly say I became a woman. This day is special. I'll also never forget you baby."

"I'll never forget you. Who knows, one day I might see you again."

"Hopefully," replied Simone. "Come on, let's take a shower."

They head to the shower so they can get themselves together. They each take turns washing each other, cherishing what may be their last time together.

CHAPTER 28

Jerome Boomer Green, aka Holifield

"48, 49, 50," counts Jerome Boomer Green, aka Holifield, 'cause he's known for his hands in the hood. He's been knocking niggas out his age and older for the longest and he busts his gun, which is why he's down right now for a gun and some need that he got caught with last year, so he's in Ferris School for Boys.

"Yo," Boomer calls another juvie name Smoke.

"What up?" replied Boomer.

"Bout to do another set of fifty."

"Man, I Just got off the phone with my peoples and they said that ya peoples got hit up last night."

"What nigga who ma people?"

"One of the Twins from over ya way."

"What? Which one?" replied Boomer angrily.

"They said it was Hakeem."

"Nah man, not my baby," exclaims Boomer, "you know who they said done it?"

"My peoples was saying nobody really knows for sure, but everybody said Jessup St. been beefing with Riverside ever since ya peoples cousin Wayne knocked out the dude Gangstar at a dice game around y'all way."

"Yeah, my mom had said something about that when I talked to her on the phone. So, it's on with them, River niggas Boomer," said out loud to no one in particular, then looked at the dude that gave him the heirs on what going on, "yo good looking family," Boomer said, giving him a dap.

"Yo, if you need me, I got cha' back; you know a couple of them

Riverside niggas is on the block."

"Yeah, I know. I'm about to see whats up with them right now."

"Yo, you should chill 'cause you ain't got that long left, so be easy, but if you wanna ride on them niggas I'm with you man."

"It's on with these niggas dog, fuck that shit!"

"Well, it's on then," replied the young juvie. Boomer approaches the two niggas from Riverside.

"Yo, which one of y'all niggas wanna lock in the cell with me?"

"What nigga?" replied one of the two, "fuck you talking bout."

"I'm talking about beating the shit outta one of you niggas," replied Boomer.

"Man, you on some bullshit; we ain't got no beef with you, but if you keep talking crazy, its whatever."

"Oh yeah, well, suck my dick. Is that crazy enough for you bitch ass niggas?"

One of the two niggas from Riverside said, "We can fight right here fuck a cell."

With that being said, Boomer swings and connects with a hook to the dude's jaw, breaking it on contact. The young dude hits the ground and the other one jumps up and rushes Boomer and tries to wrestle. Boomer backs up and catches him with an upper cut and a right hook knocking him out cold before the staff can see what is going on. Boomer backs up and walks away, blending into the crowd that has begun to form around both of the dudes from Riverside.

"Hey, watch out!" yells the staff as they bust through the ground to see whats going on.

When they see the two young guys on the ground, one grabs his walkie-talkie and calls back up and medical while the other one checks the kid's pulse that's out cold and asks the other with the broken jaw what happened, but he doesn't respond due to the fact his jaw is crooked. Boomer stares at him the whole time, seeing if him or anyone else tries to snitch on him, but nobody does. The other staff member rushes to the block and makes everyone lock in their cells. Medical comes shortly after with a stretcher and a wheelchair taking both the young juvies to the infirmary.

Supervisor Henderson yells at the top of his lungs, "Somebody better say something, or y'all going to be locked down for the rest of the day. So, speak up now!" Nobody said anything.

"Okay, y'all wanna play hardball? Let's see how hard y'all are when I run the tape back on the camera and see what happened. Whoever was involved will be charged. So, speak up so we can work all this out!" Still, nobody said a word.

"Okay, have it y'all way then." Then exits the block. Then everybody starts yelling and talking through the door.

"Yo, you see that shit? Man, I think he killed Richie."

"Nah man, that nigga just counting sheep!" yells another. Everybody burst out laughing.

"Yo Boomer! Boomer! You good!" yells out one of the juvies on the block.

"Yeah nigga, I'm good but don't nobody call my name no more. You know these Mafuckas be trying listen in so fallback on saying too much." "Oh, my bad, I got chu' cousin," replied the juvie.

Everybody continues to talk through the doors but not so much about the incident that took place on the tier. Boomer lays back on his bunk, looking through his pictures of him and the Twins.

"Damn dog, I can't believe you gone," thinks Boomer to himself, *"don't worry dog, I'm on my way up outta this bitch soon and if niggas ain't handle what needed to be handled, Imma handle it,"* Contemplates Boomer ready to put work in already for his falling comrade that he grew up with.

"Damn, I know Ms. Kim going through it right now. Imma have to call her later and send my condolences."

Boomer puts his pictures up and gets back to his sets of pushups he was doing before the incident with Riverside niggas. He usually works out to relieve stress. So he hits the ground "1, 2, 3, 4, 5."

CHAPTER 29

Cousin Wayne Sees Sheema and Gangstar

"Ahh!!" yawns and stretches Cousin Wayne.

"Damn, what time is it?" he said out loud to no one in particular.

He looks over at the clock on the wall, "Damn, 1:30. I been knocked out in this Mafucka." He goes into the bathroom and takes a piss.

"Ahh!" exclaims Cousin Wayne enjoying that early morning piss.

He finishes, washes his hand and looks in the mirror at himself and says, *"you a pretty Mafucka, even when you wake up, even with cole in my eyes,"* He laughs to himself, then he does the breath test with his hand.

"Oowl, that ain't right. Damn, ain't no toothpaste in this Bitch."

So, he rinses his mouth out with water, gargles, and spits it into the sink. Then he grabs the complimentary soap, turns on the shower and hops in. After the shower, he steps out, feeling a little better about himself. He grabs a towel, dries off and goes and sits on the bed. He picks up the phone and calls Que's house to see if he's still in. Ring Ring.

"Hello, who dis?" asked Que.

"It's the nigga you wish you could've been instead of ya' self," cracks Cousin Wayne.

"All nigga fuck you. Whats up wit chu'."

"I'm a'ight fam, just now getting myself together."

"Oh yeah, make sure you hit that mouth nigga."

"All fuck you nigga," replied Cousin Wayne, "a-yo, I'm bout to go home and take care of that 'cause this dumb ass hotel don't got none."

"Oh, you still there?" asked Que.

"Yeah."

"Damn nigga it's 1:30; thought you might've gone home and slept in ya own bed by now."

"Nah nigga I wasn't staying there after that shit last night. Plus, I gotta get somebody to come clean my shit up and get my door fixed, but I'm bout to take care of all that."

"Yeah, I feel you my nigga, but yo, am I the first person you talked to today?" asks Que.

"Yeah why?"

"'Cause I know you haven't heard about what went down last night."

"Man, what the fuck happen besides the shit with me."

"Man, I don't really wanna go into detail over the phone, but shit got messy in the hood and one of the Twins got kilt."

"Nigga go head with that shit."

"Nah cousin, that's on the real."

"Oh Shit! who was it ?"

"Man, we put it together, homeboy that couldn't take a punch and one of his youngins."

"Oh word, yo Imma handle my shit with the house, then I'll be in the hood later."

"A'ight," replied Que. Then they hang up.

"Man, Imma kill this pussy ass nigga!" exclaims Cousin Wayne heated, *"damn, they done kilt one of the youngins this shit crazy,"* Cousin Wayne thinks to himself.

He then gets dressed, grabs his keys and heads to his car so he can go home and have his house cleaned up and his door replaced. He gets in his car and turns on some music, "Scarface from the Ghetto Boys" comes through the speakers, but he takes out that tape and puts in Tupac's album "Thug Life" and plays, pouring out a little liquor while the music plays. He begins to think about Twin and all the shit that's been going on. As he rides down Concord Pike, he sees a familiar truck it has R.I.P. Kurt. Cousin can't see who's driving, so he follows close behind so he can get a visual. He turns down his music and rolls up all his windows so no one can see inside of his car. He puts on his left blinker so he can switch lanes so he can see who's driving the truck. As he gets closer, he can barely see through the window of the truck, but he can tell that the person driving is a female. As he gets closer, he sees another figure on the passenger side which appears to be a male. The truck makes a right into a gas station. Cousin Wayne keeps driving down a little further, then makes a U-turn so he can go all the way back around so he can see who is in the truck. As he nears the gas station, he sees the truck is still there, but to his surprise, he recognizes the female pumping the gas.

"Oh, you dirty bitch!" exclaims Cousin Wayne when he recognizes the female to be Sheema from the projects and standing on the other side of the truck smoking a cigarette is Gangstar.

Cousin Wayne rides past without being recognized. As he continues down the road, he begins to contemplate his next move. He turns up the radio and his song Pressure by Tupac if coming through the speakers *"When the Pressure On it's a hit ski-mask extra get bring ya clips/don't nobody move when we walk the street/We stay silent/ 'cause talk is cheap,"* Cousin Wayne raps with Tupac word for word thinking about doing both Sheema and Gangstar dirty the first chance he gets but first he heads home so he can take care of everything that was damaged.

CHAPTER 30

The New York Kid

"A yo ma whats poppin'!" yells someone with a New York accent, but Ayonna just keeps on walking 'cause she doesn't know nobody from New York and it's getting dark outside.

She has an arm full of Chinese food. She has been at the recovery center all day with her girl Tameka, so she's tired, hungry and really doesn't have time. Plus, She knows if Saleem hears she stops to talk to somebody, he'll snap. So, she just acts as if she can't hear him.

"Oh, you don't hear nobody calling out to you! Ma hold up, let me help you with those bags shorty," said the guy with the New York accent approaching Ayonna from behind.

Finally revealing himself, they make eye contact, and for a second, she blushes 'cause the guy kinda favors her favorite rapper from the Wu-Tang Clan, Ghost Face Killah, but then she pulls herself together and says, "I'm alright; I can carry my own bags. Thank you though."

"Sweetheart, your too fly to be carrying your own bags ma. If you was my lady, you wouldn't have to lift a finger for nothing and that's word on my two dead goldfishes," the New York boy said, kissing his fingers and raising them to the sky for emphasis.

Ayonna giggled a little and said, "Your two dead what?"

The New York boy said, "Yo ma, that ain't suppose to be funny."

"Well, it was," said Ayonna, still giggling.

"Well, do you even know what he meant by two dead gold fishes mean?" questions the New York Kid.

"Well, honestly, I don't know what it means but the way you said it sounded funny," replied Ayonna.

"Well, would it be funny if I told you I was referring to my dead relatives?"

"Oh My God, are you serious!" gasps Ayonna, not wanting to believe that's what he meant by two deal goldfishes.

"Yeah, it's true ma," replied the New York Kid.

"Oh, well, I apologize."

"Nah, you good shorty, but you know what will make me feel better?" asked the New York boy.

"What?" said Ayonna with attitude, thinking the New York boy was about to ask her for sex.

"Whoa! ma easy wit the neck rollin' calm ya' self. I know what you probably think I was going to say, but it ain't even like that. I'm feeling your whole being and I was going to ask if I could take you out to eat nothing more, nothing less." Ayonna's attitude softens a little but thinking to herself, *"Maybe she should give him a chance."* But at the same time, she knows Saleem would lose his mind if he found out that she was talking to a guy, let alone take her out.

So, without further thought, she said, "That's nice, but I'll have to decline 'cause like I said, I have a man and he wouldn't appreciate me going out with you and I have to ask you to respect that," exclaims Ayonna.

"Yeah, ma, I respect that, but maybe I'll see you around or something."

"Yeah, maybe," Ayonna said with a smile on her face.

She can't help but feel attracted to the Ghost Face Killah look alike; he seems so different and aggressive.

"You a'ight ma?" asked the New York Kid breaking Ayonna from out of her reverie.

"Oh, I apologize; I zoned out for a second there," she replied with a giggle.

"I see. I hope whatever you were thinkin' about involved me," said the New York Kid with a smile.

"Maybe, maybe not," said Ayonna starting to walk away, leaving the New York Kid standing there with admiration written all over his face.

"Yo Ghost, come on, you fake ass Rico Sauve ass nigga!" shouts Ox from off of the porch.

"Nah, fuck you, you ugly Mafucka."

"Yeah, whatever, ya moms love the dick nigga," replied Ox. They both began laughing.

Ghost heads back up on the porch and walks into the house so they can begin cooking up some work for the night to sell out of Peaches' spot. Ayonna continues walking down the street in thought about the New York Kid when the sound of a car horn breaks her thoughts. When she looks, she sees it's Scooby; she wonders if he saw her talking to the New York Kid.

"Whats up Ayonna, you need a ride? asks Scooby.

"Nah, I'm good, thanks though," replied Ayonna.

"Okay and stay out of niggas faces before you get somebody kilt," exclaims Scooby catching Ayonna off guard.

But she quickly recovered and replied, "If you were paying attention, you would know I shot him down and kept it moving."

"Yeah a'ight 'cause you don't want me to tell my nigga you out here trickin'."

"Boy, you better not start no bullshit 'cause I kept it moving and where is your nigga at anyway?"

"He had to take care of some business."

"Well, tell him to call me."

"A'ight," Scooby said, rolling up his window and pulling off before she got to trying to interrogate a nigga.

Scooby is on his way to Shontay's crib, where he told her and the crew to meet him so he can give them some weed to move for him and Saleem. Scooby began dreaming of being his own boss for as long as he can remember. Way back when Uncle L. and B. had the park on smash back in tha eighties and nineties. He could remember watching them dudes clock big money on the regular and they used to always look out wit dollars and tell Saleem and me to get away from the park 'cause we were too young to be around. But if you were young coming up, you loved being down the park. It was like a party every day; car systems were playing all the latest music, LL Cool J., Rakim, Big Daddy Kane, MC Lyte, Krs 1, I mean everything. They even would slow it down and go old school with the O'Jays, Marvin Gaye and Al "Grits" Green. I mean chics, weed, beer, liquor food, craps games, basketball tournaments, splash parties at the pool, and park parties. I mean, shit was live, and at that time, Uncle L. B. niggas like John Jackson and others were hood superstars with all the gold chains, four finger rings, gold teeth, scabs boomers, Volvos with the rags 1.8's hooked up to the tee. I mean, being a little kid growing up with less and seeing all the glitz and glamor of street life made you feel like school was secondary. Them Crackers in school were trying to make little Black kids wanna grow up to be doctors, firemen, plumbers, fast food workers and police officers. The same police officers that we would see beat our people down like dogs in the street. And how were we going to be doctors when we could barely pay the rent? So, where were we going to get the tuition money from? Scooby and Saleem had to watch their mothers struggle to make ends meet. Yeah, we had the raggedy clothes, holey shoes, mayonnaise sandwiches, that block of government cheese that came in a brown box, powdered milk, and off-brand cereal. The stove was the heat 'cause we couldn't afford any gas. We know about no cable. You could only get three, six and ten on the black and white TV with the missing knobs, so you have to turn the channel with a pair of pliers. Yeah, I can write a whole book about me and my comrades' poverish lives, but growing up under these conditions and seeing how easy it was to make money right outside your doorstep had Saleem and me thinking, *"Fuck school the hood looking like a meal ticket and it may sound ignorant, but Its kids til this day feeling like the hood is there only option to get money. So, don't judge if you ain't never liked it."*

As Scooby pulls up in front of Shontay's house, he sees Gutlynn talking to some nigga he doesn't know on the porch, so he falls back until they finish their conversation. She sees Scooby ain't trying to get out of the car, so she puts two and two together and tells her little friend that she'll talk to him later. Unaware of Scooby pulling up, the guy never pays attention to the unspoken understanding between Gutlynn and Scooby. As he comes off the porch, he then recognizes the car, but if he was a target, he would've been dead caught slippin' worryin' about a bitch instead of his surroundings. He stops, admires the five stars on the car, then turns to Gutlynn and says, "I'm bout to cop somethin' just like this, so if you play ya cards right, I might let you push it from time to time. Gutlynn starts to say something slick because she knows he ain't getting it like that, but he ain't stingy with his money and her girl Dina said he eat pussy like he starvin', so for now, she decides to hold her tongue and let the lame be a lame. Scooby, on the other hand, hears everything the dude just said and laughs at the dude 'cause Ray Charles can see he's a boss lame as the guy bands the corner out of sight, Scooby hops out of the car with a book bag on his shoulder one strap on one strap off. Gutlynn opens the door for him as he walks into a cloud full of smoke and music coming from a nearby stereos Gutlynn closes the door and locks it behind them.

"Scooobbie!!!!" Shanty and Dina scream in unison.

"You wanna hit the weed?" asked Dina.

"Nah, I'm good. I step my game up. I don't smoke dirt, no more," Scooby said with a chuckle.

"Boy, we don't smoke dirt either."

"Well, why does it smell like burnt tree bark in here, then?"

"Boy, stop hatin'," exclaims Shontay.

"Yo, turn that music down some so we can talk."

Gutlynn walks over and turns the music down. Scooby takes a seat on the couch, and Dina sashays over, flops down beside him and scoots extra close. Scooby looks over at her and smirks.

Gutlynn said, "Damn bitch let him breathe."

"Bitch fuck you," responds Dina.

"Bitch, you wish you could fuck me good as this pussy is," retorts Gutlynn looking Scooby in the eyes while she said every word and rubs her hand between her legs and then pretended to lick her fingers as if she just tasted her pussy and goes Ummm.

"Y'all bitches is too much," exclaims Shontay.

Scooby freak ass loves the attention, but he can hear Saleem in his mind, business before pleasure. We do whatever after we get money. With that in mind, he takes the book bag off of his shoulders and unzips it even though its weed already lit up; the smell from the book bag is so potent that you can smell it over the weed that's already lit.

"Dayuum, that shit is strong and I ain't never seen that much weed before," said Dina.

"How much is it?" asked Shontay coming closer to get a better look this is.

"Five pounds of the best weed in the city. I want y'all to break two down into nickels, another into dimes and one into quarters. Me and Saleem want back is $1000 off of each pound and y'all keep the rest. We can go from there," said Scooby pulling out a pre-rolled blunt, "now that that's out of the way, let's smoke some real weed," he said, lighting It up, taking a few tokes and passing it to Dina, who pulls on it greatly then begins choking half the death causing Scooby to laugh. Shontay and Gutlynn to rush over to her and start patting her on the back.

"Oh My God! Bitch is you okay?" asked Gutlynn and reaching for the blunt.

"Yeah cough! Cough! Hold up bitch let me get myself together so I can hit it again," exclaims Dina.

"Bitch, you just almost died and you wanna hit it again?" said Shontay laughing her as off at her home girl.

"Yeah, it's good, just strong. I gotta take my time with this."

They all begin smoking and get used to the weed. Dina starts rubbing on Scooby's thigh, making his dick hard instantly.

"Boy, what Kinda weed is this? My pussy starting to jump," says Gutlynn, who sits down on the other side of Scooby and grabs his dick through his jeans.

"Uhmm, I ain't know you was holding like this bitch feel this."

Dina reaches over and rubs Scooby's dick.

"Oh yeah, It is big."

"Where Saleem at?" asked Shontay.

"He on a mission; he'll be through the block later," said Scooby.

"Hey, what this?" asked Gutlynn, feeling a budge in Scooby's pocket.

Scooby smacked her hand away and said, "The next best thing besides my dick."

"Boy, you think you all that 'cause you getting money now."

"Nah, I've been all that; it's just now that I'm shinin' you can see me."

"Boy, it ain't like that," exclaims Gutlynn trying not to get on Scooby's bad side.

Dina squeezes her hand down Scooby's pants and starts playin' with his dick. Scooby grabbed her hand out of his pants and said, "I ain't with all this touchy-feely shit."

"Y'all trying to see a nigga or what?"

"It's whatever with me," said Gutlynn.

Dina said, "Me too, but I want It to be just me and you."

"Damn, you's a greedy Bitch," said Gutlynn.

"Both of y'all ain't bout to do nothing but help me break all this week up and bag it."

"Ahh! exclaims Gutlynn Ahh!!"

What retorts Shontay you Just made 'cause Saleem ain't here."

"Bitch I'm not worrin' about no Saleem. I want this money."

"You right," said Dina, who gets up off of the couch. Gutlynn then grabs the book bag, walks into the kitchen, puts it on the table, and comes back into the front room.

"Well, come in so we can bag up."

Scooby grabbed his dick and said, "Nah fuck that, somebody better take care of this dick. What type games y'all playin'?"

"Maybe next time," said Dina.

"Yeah, next time," said Gutlynn.

"All it's like that!" exclaims Scooby getting up off of the couch and heading for the door."

"Don't be mad, we got chu'!" shouts Dina as the door closes. They all can be heard laughing as the door shuts.

Scooby looks around, steps off the porch and says, *"Fuck this, I gotta get my shit off. I hope Ms. Edna home,"* he thinks, heading to her house.

CHAPTER 31

Sheema

Three days later, Saleem and Scooby are at their apartment smoking a blunt and discussing their next move so they continue to keep their business running smoothly. Everybody on every side of town is feeling the work, and it's moving fast, so they need to connect fast with somebody that keeps A-1 coke.

"So what do you suggest about who we should choose for a Connect," asked Scooby.

"Well, I was thinkin' about that New York nigga."

"What New York nigga?" asks Scooby, already not liking where this is headed.

"I'm talking about that nigga Dreadz cousin."

"Nah man, this our city. I ain't trying to cop no weight from no out of town nigga that's gettin' money in our city he the competition. Why should we help that nigga get rich off us for real? For real, that nigga can get it just like Omega and them," said Scooby heatedly.

"Calm down family, before you bust a gasket in this ma'fucker," jokes Saleem, "but nah listen, tell me whats the difference than a nigga going up top out of his way risking himself to go cop from a out of town nigga then having the luxury of saving yourself a trip and less risk by scoring from a nigga in your own backyard."

"I mean, when you put it like that, you sound right; it makes sense," said Scooby.

"My nigga it wouldn't make dollars if it didn't make sense, dig me?"

"Yeah, I dig you like a shovel brother, but I just don't like helping the competition win."

"And I feel you on that, but he's the best option for right now unless you get somebody else."

"Nah, I'm with you on this, but that dread head nigga get shady; he gotta go."

"I feel you homie. Well, you know how we do when shit need to get handed but right now, let me see if I can connect with cousin."

"A'ight handle ya B.I. family."

"Nah cousin, our B.I. solid."

"Solid Solid," replied Saleem as he rose from the couch and headed for the door. He steps outside and hops into his car, and heads over to the broad Peaches crib to see if she can get him In touch with Dreadz 'cause he knows that one of his main spots where Dreadz moves work from.

"Yo Peaches come here ma," calls Ghost.

"No, 'cause I know what chu' want," smiles Peaches switching her phat yellow ass into the living room where Ghost and Ox are. Peaches is a high yellow phat as shit, bowlegged and big country titties.

"What boy?" exclaims Peaches as she stands bowlegged in front of Ghost with her tight-ass daisy duke-style shorts on.

"Damn shorty, why you gotta what a nigga?" asks Ghost.

"'Cause you only want one of two things and that's some pussy or your dick sucked."

Ox and Ghost both start laughing, and Peaches too. She's a freak broad. Ain't too many dudes ain't have Peaches freak ass. They said she be turnin' niggas out with that mouth on some old. If a nigga lets her, she'll eat a niggas ass all type shit the bitch is a boss freak.

"Well, which one is it?" asks Peaches knowing that if she could turn this nigga out, she'll have a steady piece of money. Truth be told, Peaches is one of these broads in the hood. Has she not been a whore a nigga would wife her 'cause she bad as shit; just a stone cold whore.

"Ma, I was trying to feel that warm mouth."

"Well, come on then," Peaches said, grabbing Ghost by the hand and leading him into the back room.

"Yo Ox, hold It down baby pa."

"Nigga don't I always," replied Ox.

Ox turns the TV from Threes Company to Good Times, that Lil show. He always had a crush on the sister."

"Whats her name?"

"Thelma."

"Yeah, that's It with her sexy ass self."

Boomp! Boomp! Boomp!

"Yo Ox, who the fuck is that bangin' like the Police?"

"I'll don't Know son, but I'm bout to find out."

Ox grabs his gun and peeks out the peephole, only to see Saleem standing there.

"Who the fuck is this nigga?" Ox thinks to himself.

"Who is it Ox?" A voice booms through the door.

"It's Saleem, Peaches here?"

"She busy, come back later."

"Yeah, a'ight," said Saleem starting to walk down the steps to his car when the door opened up.

"Yo, what up Kid, what chu' want with Peaches?" asked Ghost, standing at the door with his shirt off, his pants halfway up and his belt buckle dangling from his Jeans.

"Whats it to you? What you her man or something?" asked Saleem, turning back around to face the questioner, who he knows is one of them New York dudes that he heard be around here hustlin', probably one of Dreadz flunkies.

"Nah, I'm not her man. I just lay dick when ever I'm bored son," replied Ghost.

"Boy, move hey, Saleem," Peaches said, pushing Ghost out of the way and wiping her mouth.

"Whats up, Peaches? Let me holler at chu' right quick."

"Boy, I ain't even dressed," she said, looking down at herself.

"Damn this bitch Phat, " thinks Saleem to himself

"It's only going to take a minute; come sit in the car."

"Boy, that's ya car?" asks Peaches.

"Yeah," replied Saleem.

"Things must be picking up for you around the corner." Peaches smile with her mind already scheming on trying to get in his pockets.

"A Lil' something," replied Saleem as he opened the doors to his car so they could get in before they got in the car.

Ghost yells from the door, "Don't kiss her Kid!" Then burst out laughing.

"Peaches give him the finger and get in the car."

"Yo, whats up with that nigga. What he don't like breathin' or something?"

"Saleem, don't pay him no attention; Sweetie, what can I do you for?"

asks Peaches looking at Saleem with lust and hunger in her eyes.

"Nah, baby girl, it ain't that type of party. I just want to know if you could introduce me to the nigga Dreadz. I'm trying to do business with him."

"Oh yeah, you done stepped ya game up," exclaims Peaches.

"Listen, I'm just trying to have a convo with the man. Can you set it up or what?"

"I'll see what I can do, but whats in it for me?" asked Peaches.

"I got a couple dollars for you."

"And?" asked Peaches licking her lips.

"And that's it," said Saleem.

"Oh, its like that?" asks Peaches.

"Like what," replied Saleem.

"A bitch gots needs and wants to."

"I can dig it. I mean, I offered you some. Look, what else could you want?"

Peaches smiled and said, "You can let a bitch Jaffe that dick."

"Oh shit, girl you crazy."

"So, whats up?" Peaches ask seriously.

"You mean right now?"

"Nah, next year, yeah, right now nigga."

"Hold up, let me pull around the corner."

Saleem pulls around the corner and pulls into Gordon St. alleyway, parks his car, leans his seat back, and lets Peaches do what she does best. Eat a fat dick up til she hick up.

"So, I'm sayin' whats up with you. What chu' been hidin' from a nigga or something?" asks Cousin Wayne to Sheema, who he saw at the gas station on 36th and Market St.

"Nah baby, I've just been chillin', that's all."

"I heard about what happened at cha' crib; that's crazy 'cause that coulda been us in there."

"Yeah, anybody talking about who put them niggas up to it?" asked Cousin Wayne.

"Nah, I ain't heard nothing, but If I did, I would of been told you," exclaims Sheema.

So, what chu' bout to get into asked Cousin Wayne.

"Nothing bout to go home and chill, take a shower and find something on TV."

"You can come do that with me. I can go rent us a room at the Marriott, order room service and lay up."

"For real?"

"Yeah it ain't bout nothing."

"Well, shit, that's all it is. Let's go get some weed and something to drink."

"Come on, hop in."

They go and grab some weed and liquor. Cousin Wayne puts in one of his slow jams tapes, sparks a blunt, and passes it to Sheema, who takes it and starts blowing like a chimney Cousin pulls over, cracks a bottle of Henny, and takes a swig, tucks it in his pocket and starts to get out.

"Where you goin'?" asked Sheema.

"I gotta piss like a Russian Racehorse; I can't hold it," said Cousin Wayne before running into an alleyway out of sight.

"That boy is so crazy," thinks Sheema.

Cousin pulls out the bottle of Henney and some crushed-up pills G.H.B., better Known as roofies, the date rape drug. He puts the powdery substance into the bottle of Henney and shakes it up well until the pills dissolve. Then jogs back to the truck.

"Damn, what? You piss a river back there?"

"Yeah, let's get outta here before it start floodin'." They both crack up laughin'.

"Boy, you are a mess," said Sheema passing Cousin Wayne the rest of the blunt, then said, "Damn, what you going personal on the Henney?"

"Oh My Bad! Nah, here you go' do' ya thing," Cousin Wayne said, passing her the bottle.

She takes several strong swigs of the liquor, half-emptying it.

"Damn greedy," said Cousin Wayne.

"My Bad, a bitch trying to get right before we get to where we going 'cause I know you love to try and kill a bitch with that horse dick," said Sheema cracking up.

"Girl, you crazy as shit," replied Cousin Wayne, who fakes like he is sipping the Henney, then passes it back to Sheema, who graciously excepts and begins guzzling the liquor like Woody the Wino from Sanford and Son. Not too long after, Sheema begins to feel dizzy and can barely keep her eyes open.

"Yoooo I'mmm feelin it," said Sheema in a groggy state.

Cousin Wayne just keeps on driving, headed toward his destination, which is not the hotel. Instead, he takes her to a wooded location on the outskirts of Wilmington where it's an old shed where he and Que used to go hide the work when they were a little younger and were still living with their moms and ain't want them to find. If they found it in these particular woods when they were younger play'n hide and seek. About a mile away from the shed lives Que's grandparents, who used to let Que and Cousin Wayne stay the weekend as they got older. They also used to sneak girls from Que's grandparent's neighborhood and have sex on an old mattress that they found on the side of the road in some bodies trash that was throwing it out. Cousin pulls into the wooded area wit his lights out. Before long, he's in front of the shed. He gets out and inspects the area. He doesn't see nor does he hear anything unusual. He walks over to the shed and cautiously opens the door. Creeek! is the sound of the old shed door. As it opens, Cousin Wayne steps inside.

"Hiss! Hiss! What the fuck," exclaims Cousin Wayne as he looks closer. He can see two shiny eyes. So, he backs out of the shed with the door open to shed a little light inside. He can see something furry inside the left corner. So, Cousin Wayne picks up a stick and throws it in the corner and runs and holds the shed door open. When the stick lands, the creature makes another hissing noise but doesn't move. Cousin Wayne goes to his truck, where Sheema is sound asleep snoring. He reaches into the back and grabs a bat, walks into the shed and walks up on the creature in the corner, which he realizes now is an Opossum, so he swings away Wack! Wack! The Opossum attempts to run, but it's too late Wack! Wack!

Cousin Wayne continues to swing like a madman, then stops and kicks it a couple times to make sure the Opossum ain't playin' possum. He then looks around and sees that the mattress from all these years is still laying on the ground, which looks old and rotted, but Cousin Wayne ain't here to make a bitch feel comfortable; he here to terrorize a bitch. So he goes to his truck, opens the passenger side door and begins to undress Sheema until she's butt butter ball naked.

"Damn, this bitch gotta nice body too. I'm bout to torture this bitch. He lifts her out of the truck, carries her into the shed, and throws her onto the old dirty mattress. He then heads back to the truck and grabs his hunting knife out of his glove box, some gloves and some lighter fluid and goes back into the shed, then walks over to Sheema and kicks her viciously in the ribs.

"Uhmm!!!" groans Sheema, still under the drugs and liquor.

"You dirty ass bitch, you thought I wasn't going to find out that you was playing both sides of the fence bitch, hunh!" Cousin Wayne viciously kicks her in the head, making Sheema's eyes slightly open and then roll up in her head and groan again.

Cousin Wayne kneels beside her and slaps her viciously across the face. He grabs her by her cheeks and squeezes them, making her lips resemble a fish. He then traces the hunting knife over her face. Then he said cocks the knife back and stabs her in the stomach while still gripping her face. So, when she opens her eyes, they'll meet his, which is exactly what happens, but Sheema wears a confused expression on her face.

"That's right bitch wake up! Wake up your silly ass!"

But she can barely keep her eyes open. Cousin Wayne begins carving the word whore into her flesh. He then flips her over on her now bleeding stomach, drops his pants, puts on a condom, gets down behind Sheema and positions his big dick directly to go into Sheema's ass hole with no lubrication whatsoever. He forces his dick into her asshole, ripping open her rectum. As he continues to work all of his dick inside her Sheema, she begins to whimper into the dirty mattress.

"Yeah, you two-faced bitch take all this dick," said Cousin Wayne, whose dick is now covered in shit and blood, but he continues to fuck Sheema like a man possessed by the devil. Sheema goes in and out. Cousin Wayne feels his nut building in his balls. With a few more strokes, Cousin Wayne grabs the back of her hair and rides her like a prize-winning thoroughbred horse.

"Ahh!!! Yeah, you funky bitch," growls Cousin as he releases into the condom still inside Sheena's asshole.

He then flips an unconscious Sheema over on her back, she's barely breathin', but Cousin Wayne could care less. He takes the knife and shoves it viciously inside her pussy. Sheema doesn't even have the strength to moan. In and out, in and out, the knife plunges Cousin, then stands up, takes off the condom a puts it in his pocket. He then pours the lighter fluid all over her body.

He kneeled down beside her and whispered in her ear and said, "I'm the last nigga you'll over cross bitch."

Then he stands up, makes sure he has everything he came with, steps back, lights an old cloth he found in the shed, then throws it on Sheema's body. Immediately she bursts into flames, and what little life she has in her screams a low painful scream. Cousin Wayne jogs to his truck, hops in and heads home so he can shower and get himself together. All the way home, he rides in silence.

CHAPTER 32

My Moms House

Two days later, Saleem and Scooby just came from uptown on the Market St. Mall from a little shopping and buying a couple of pagers. They exchange numbers and then head to their cars. Saleem gets into his car and takes a ride by Peaches spot to see what's up with Dreadz and if not, just give her his pager number so when she does contact Dreadz, she can get in touch. As he's driving, his song comes on the radio, "Sugar Hill" by A. Z. he loves this song 'cause he was all the stuff the New York rapper is talking about. As he pulls up in front of Peaches spot, he feels like coming there is a headache 'cause he doesn't really wanna go through it with Peaches thirsty ass and that fake ass nigga that was there the last time, but he's got bigger fish to fry and if this is what he has to go through to plug in it is what it is. So, he parks, turns off his car and gets out and heads towards Peaches spot. Before he can even knock on the door, it opens a crack, and there stands Peaches in a bathrobe wide open, butt naked.

"Hey daddy," Peaches said seductively.

Saleem tries to concentrate on why he's there, but he can't deny how bad this bitch is.

"A whats up Peaches? Did you make the move for?"

"Yeah, I talked to him last night said he think he know who you is already. Something bout your name been buzzin' lately in the streets."

"Oh yeah?" replied Saleem.

"Yeah," shoots back Peaches, "so what, you just going to stand there or you going come see what this pussy hittin'."

"For I would if I could, but I gotta go check on my moms," said Saleem.

"Boy stop lyin'."

"Nah, I'm serious baby girl; you think I would turn something as fine as you down," said Saleem, gasping Peaches head.

"Oh boy, come through some time 'cause this pussy be here waiting for you daddy."

"I heard that but look, give Dreadz my pager number. Tell him to use the code #212 and I'll know it's him."

"Okay sexy, but you sure you can't stay a little while longer?" asked Peaches backing away from the door and opening up her robe, exposing her beautiful body while doing a little dance.

"Girl, you crazy, I gotta go, but I'm a definitely see you another time, though."

Peaches pouts a little, then says, "Don't be lying." Then walks back to the door and tries to kiss Saleem on the lips.

"Whoa!" said Saleem pushing her back a little, "chill with all that."

"What, boy, don't act like that."

"Nah, I'm a holler at you," said Saleem backing away and then turning to walk down the steps to his car.

"Damn that bitch a freak," thinks Saleem as he pulls away from her spot headed to his moms' house to see how she's doin'.

When he pulls up in front of the house, he doesn't see her car, but he still parks and goes into the house anyway. When he enters, he hears Teddy Pendergrass playing in the background, *"Turn off the lights and light a candle,"* sings Teddy.

"Damn, it smells good as shit in here," said Saleem out loud as he nears the kitchen only to see his mom throwin' down in the kitchen cooking and singing along with Teddy P. then, out of nowhere, she said, "If I hear you curse in my damn house again like you grown it's going to be too good for your ass." Saleem stands there baffled 'cause it never seems to amaze him that she always can hear him cuss like she got bionic ears or something.

"Yeah, you ain't think I heard ya ass, did you? One day you goin' come in here, and I'ma have my gun, and I'm a shoot ya ass for trying to sneak up on somebody; you ain't slick."

Saleem started laughing, "Mom, you crazy," said Saleem as he walked over to her and gave her a hug, then said, "mom, where ya car at?"

"I let Tommy see it to go somewhere."

"Mom, what I tell you about letting that nigga use ya car? He don't pay no bills."

"Boy, I'm the fuck grown. You'd tell me who I can date and can't!"

Tommy is some ol' head from Philly she deals with from time to time and he a'ight, but I just don't like feeling like a nigga using my mom.

"Boy, you think you my damn dad."

"Mom, I ain't come here to argue with you. I just came to see how you was doing."

"Well, I'm okay, just fixing some dinner. You hungry?"

"Nah, but I can eat, though."

"I bet you can with ya greedy self," they both share a laugh, "well if you want a plate, it's going to be a little while longer. The roast ain't done yet, and as you can see, I'm still cutting potatoes and bout to make this macaroni from scratch."

"My favorite."

"Yeah."

"Well, I'll probably be back later and grab a plate. Could you put me one up in the fridge?"

"Okay baby."

Then out of nowhere, "smack!" right in the head.

"Yo, mom what was that for?"

"I've been meaning to put my foot in for ya ass. What I tell you about drinking my damn Kool-Aid and leaving a swallow."

"Mom it wasn't me."

"Boy, you's a damn lie ain't nobody been here to touch my Kool-Aid but chu'."

"Dag ma, I'll buy you a hundred Kool-Aids," said Saleem pulling out some money and putting it on the table.

"Boy, take that. I ain't ask you for no money."

"I know and you shouldn't have to," replied Saleem.

He loves taking care of his mom. It makes him feel like a man, and even though he's a young boy, he handles his business like a man.

"Boy, be careful out there and stop walking around with all that money and somebody bust you over your head and won't think twice."

Even though Saleem does what he does, his mother still doesn't approve, but she knows he's going to do it anyway, so she tries to remind him to be careful and not get too comfortable out there in the streets.

"Baby, I just want you to be safe. It'll kill me if I have to get a call like Kim got." Referring to the Twins' mother about when Hakeem got killed.

"Mom, I ain't God, but that's one thing you don't have to worry about. I mean, I'm not going to sit here and go into detail but know that your baby is good out there in them streets, and I don't plan on being in them forever. I got big plans to own a lot of stuff, but it takes money to make money. Well, mom, I'm bout to be out," Saleem said, giving his mom a hug and a kiss.

"I love you mom."

"I love you too baby; you be careful out there."

"I will," replied Saleem.

CHAPTER 33

Page "212"

Two weeks later, Saleem and Scooby are sitting in their apartment playing NBA Jams for the Money when Saleem's pager starts buzzin' on the coffee table.

"Yo, hold up dog, my pager buzzin'," said Saleem.

"Man fuck that pager. I'm losing my money nigga!" exclaims Scooby.

"Man, calm down about losing pennies. This page could be about thousands," states Saleem, then pauses the game so he can take a look at his pager.

As he reads the digits that appear on the screen, he says them loud, "212," not quite remembering whose code it is, then like a ton of bricks, it hits.

"Oh shit! Oh shit!" he exclaims, now realizing who's paging him.

Scooby looks at him awkwardly, then says, "Damn nigga you all excited. I hope no bitches ain't gotchu' like that," cracks Scooby.

"Nah nigga, this the page we've been waiting for. This that nigga Dreadz this the code I gave Peaches to give him."

"Well, nigga pick up the phone and call the nigga," said Scooby.

"Nah, not from this phone Imma run across the street to the pay phone. I don't wanna conduct no business on the house phone. You can never be too careful," states Saleem.

"Yeah, you right," replied Scooby.

Saleem heads out the door to the pay phone when his pager buzzes again with what appears to be Dreadz phone number. So, he puts in the digits after putting twenty-five cents into the phone and half a second later, the phone begins to ring.

"Hello," said the voice on the other end.

"Yo, somebody page me?" asked Saleem.

"Yeah, is this Saleem?" asked the voice.

"Yeah, this him, whats up?" asked Saleem.

"Yeah, I was just making sure this Dreadz. Son got your math from Peaches meaning Saleem's number to his pager. She told me you wanted to Polly wit me, meaning speak to him."

"Yeah, I do," said Saleem, "you got a place where we can meet? I don't do phones," states Saleem.

"Me either Kid," replied Dreadz, "yo check it. Meet me at Peaches spot in like 15 minutes," said Dreadz.

"Okay," replied Saleem then hung up the phone.

Saleem runs back into the house and tells Scooby what was said on the phone. Scooby ask does Saleem need him to come with him.

Saleem replied, "Nah," he said that he'd let him know all the details afterward.

Scooby said, "A'ight," then stood up off the couch, gave Saleem a dap and a hug, then said, "this what we've been waiting for."

"Yeah," said Saleem, then grabbed his car keys and headed for the door in pursuit to Peaches crib to see what this nigga Dreadz talkin' bout.

CHAPTER 34

A Cold Case

"Early this morning, police are still investigating the brutal rape and murder of a woman found burning in a shed a couple of weeks ago, whose identity wasn't revealed at the time because her body was burned beyond recognition; through dental records, the woman later identified as one Sheema Brooks 24 years old from 26th and Claymont St. in the Riverside Projects. Eastlake section of the city has now been labeled a cold case. Police have no motive and no suspects at this time. Governor Goldsberg had this to say this crime is just one of many heinous crimes that have plaques our state. The individuals behind this case and others will be prosecuted no matter how long it takes that was the governor. Ladies and gentlemen, if there is anyone out there with information about this case or any other, please call Crime Stoppers at 555-2400. Signing off, I am Gloria Clark from Channel 6 Action News."

Cousin Wayne cuts down the news with the remote control he's been laying low the last couple of weeks since the incident with Sheema. He was sure he dotted his eyes and crossed his tee's, but you could never really be safe. That's why after he got his house in Delaware at once, he disappeared without telling nobody. Stewart Ave., where he has been going for the past couple of weeks. Cousin Wayne has been in an apartment he purchased in West Philly on Preston St., right off 40th and Lancaster.

"Damn, this shit won't go away. Here I am up in Philly and this shit all on TV, but hey, it ain't like I went to Mexico or something. I'm still in the tri-state area," Cousin Wayne thinks to himself.

"I sure am glad to hear it's a cold case. Now I gotta handle this nigga Gangstar. This pussy nigga think its sweet," Cousin Wayne thinks.

BZZ! BZZ! Cousin Wayne's pager sounds off, taking him out of his reverie.

"Who the fuck is this?" wonders Cousin Wayne as he picks up his pager, "ma nigga Que."

Cousin Wayne grabs the phone and calls.

"Que?" Que Answered on the first ring.

"Whats happening, player?" asked Cousin Wayne as soon as Que picked up.

"I'm coolin'. I was bout to ask you the same Shit."

"All man, everything; just seen the news," said Cousin Wayne.

"Yeah, me too," replied Que, "that's why I was calling you to see if you was up watching it."

"Yeah, you know I was turned in," replied Cousin Wayne, "shit happens when you do dirt you get dirt," said Cousin Wayne.

"You already know, I know," replied Que, "so when you coming back down the way, I miss my nigga said," Que.

"Aww! Don't worry daddy, I'll be home soon. Did my baby cook dinner," said Cousin Wayne, bustin' Que's balls and referring to his mom.

"Nigga fuck outta here wit that nonsense," responds Que with a chuckle.

"Nah, on some real shit, I'll probably be back down there tonight. I'm bored as shit up here. It's bitches galore, though, but I was trying to keep a low profile, but now that shit dying down Imma come up here more often so I can sow my royal oats on some ol' Coming to America shit."

"Nigga you crazy," replied Que.

They both share a laugh and then say their goodbyes.

Cousin Wayne sparks a blunt, lays back on his bed and contemplates killing Gangstar.

CHAPTER 35

The Connect

"Thinkin' back reminiscin' on ma team a young & getting' paid off of dope fiends, Fuckin' off cash that I make. Nigga whats the since working hard if you never get to play" sings Saleem along with Tupac as "Bury Me G" comes booming out of his sound system.

"Leemer! Burmp! Burmp!" yells some niggas from up top of 23rd and Market St. standing on the corner by Milton's Liquor Store.

Saleem sees them and hits the horn just to show love back. On his way down the street, this continues. Everybody knows his car now when they see it; his and Scooby's names have been buzzin' lately. Everybody can see the young niggas from Jessup St. is on the rise. Saleem reads the end of the block, looking for a parking spot to his left on the side of Peaches crib. He sees a gold LS 400 automatically, and Saleem knows who it is. Saleem finds a parking spot across the street from Peaches crib. As he gets out, Lil' Vae, Bushwick and Gotti come over to him and dap him up.

"Whats up dog? I hear you bumpin' that Pac shit," said Gotti.

"Yeah, that's my shit," replied Lil' Vae.

"Yo, I see you coming up in the world," said Bushwick.

"Yeah, a Lil' somethin'," replied Saleem.

"So, what brings you around here?"

"All the money obviously on Jessup St.," cracks Gotti.

"I heard that," said Saleem, "Nah, Imma bout to go over Peaches," replied Saleem.

"AW! SHIT!" laughs Bushwick.

"Nah nigga, not for that," laughs Saleem.

"A-Yo, you know them New York niggas up in there? You need us to come witchu'?" asked Lil' Vae.

"Nah, I'm good."

"Cause you know we strapped up," said Gotti.

"Yeah, I know it, but if you think for a second I move around these streets with my waist naked, you must be higher than you look," replied Saleem, while discreetly lifting up his shirt showing a .38 Special all-black with a black pistol grip."

"I know that's right," replied Bushwick with a smile likin' what he sees. He's known to carry guns bigger than him.

"Well, Imma holler at cha'll."

"A'ight," they all replied in unison.

Saleem crosses the street and heads to Peaches house. As he begins to knock on the door, he can smell the familiar smell of weed. Not Just any weed, it's definitely that Omega shit; within seconds, the door opens up and a cloud of smoke hits Saleem in the face.

"What up?" Duke asks Ghost.

"Yo, where Dreadz at?"

"He in here Kid, come on in son, we don't bite," cracks Ghost.

"On the real, it wouldn't matter if y'all did. Last time I checked, all dogs have teeth."

"Yeah, I hear you B.," Ghost said with a devilish smile on his face when Saleem walked into the dining room. Dreadz and some short husky nigga smoking blunts; no doubt in Saleem's mind the weed they blowin' is definitely that Omega.

"Yo what up son?" greets Dreadz standing to his feet coming to shake

Saleem's hand. Saleem shakes his hand.

"Yo son, these my niggas right here. The one that answered the door, that's my manz Ghost."

"What up! What up!" shouts Ghost, extra animated.

"And this here is my manz Ox." Ox just gives a nod; on some brah man from the fifth floor Shit.

"So, what do you need to see me about?"

"Do you smoke? We got plenty," said Dreadz.

"I do, but I'm good night now. I just wanted to discuss some business," said Saleem.

"Oh yeah, and what kind of business might that be?" asked Dreadz.

"Well, I've been looking for a Connect with some grade-A shit and can stay consistent and cover my order no matter what it is."

Dreadz nods his head up and down, takes a huge pull off his blunt then asks, "What type of order are we talking about? A brick or two maybe?"

Saleem looked Dreadz square in the eyes and said, "I was thinking more like 10 at a time. I also need at least a hundred pounds of weed." Dreadz and his boys look at each other, then back at Saleem.

Dreadz said, "I heard you and your team was getting money, but damn Kid, I ain't know y'all was playing like that. What cha'll caught a nigga shipping or somethin' son?"

Immediately Saleem knows what Dreadz is trying to inquire but it seems on point.

"Nah, not at all. Me and squad just know how to get money; that's it, that's all," states Saleem with a straight face, not showing any signs that he could be possibly living.

"Yo, let me polly with my fam right quick," said Dreadz. Saleem nods his head as to say go ahead.

"Yo son, you thinkin' what I'm thinkin'?" asked Ghost.

"Yeah, but I don't see that Lil' nigga pullin' off that caper and livin' to tell about it," said Dreadz.

"Yeah, me either," replied Ox.

"Yo, at the end of the day, this kid trying to spend that paper with us, we need somebody to fill that void that's been hauntin' us since Omega and his team got murdered."

"Yeah, you right B., but if I find out that nigga or anybody he run wit had something to do with Omega's death Imma personally send them niggas to good lookin'," states Ghost.

"Word as born duke," replied Ox giving Saleem the evil eye.

"No doubt, no doubt," said Dreadz.

Saleem notices that them niggas keep cutting their eyes at him, which is starting to make him uncomfortable.

"If these niggas get on some ol' funny shit Imma go out blastin' fuck that," thinks Saleem.

"Yo Kid, we gave everything you said some thought as we decided that we accept your business. Now let's talk numbers," said Dreadz.

"Okay," replied Saleem.

"So what was you paying a brick and a pound?" asked Dreadz.

"Twenty-five a brick and five hundred a pound."

Dreadz nodded his head up and down them and said, "Those are good numbers, but here's what Imma do for you; give me twenty-three a brick and we goin' keep the price the same for the pound. That sound fair to you?" asked Dreadz.

"Yeah, that's beautiful," said Saleem.

"So, we got a deal?" asked Dreadz.

"Yeah, we got a deal."

Dreadz sticks his hand out, Saleem shakes it, and then the other two dudes' hands as well.

Dreadz said, "When do you think you'll be ready to cop?"

"In a couple of days, I'll let chu know said," Saleem.

Dreadz gives Saleem his pager number and they decide to keep their code 212.

Saleem decides to shoot past the hood and then back to the crib to let Scooby know what's up.

CHAPTER 36

The Guy in the Hoodie

"Yo Gangstar, that's fucked up about Sheema, ain't it?" asked one of Gangstar's flunkies.

"Yeah, Lil' homie that's fucked up. Somebody done killed that good pussy like that," replied Gangstar, "remember how good Sheema pussy was?"

"Yo Gang, you got any idea who could've done some shit like that?" asked the young flunky.

"Not really, it could've been my hustler in the city that could've had that done. Sheema stayed on some scheming type shit," said Gangstar, "shit, I had her on plenty of missions myself, so ain't no tellin' who could've kilt her."

"Yo, if you find out, you gone handle it?" asked the young boy.

"Fuck no!" exclaims Gangstar, "I mean the shot was good, but I ain't goin' all out for no bitch. I got my own problems," said Gangstar.

"I heard that," replied the young boy.

"Yo, I'm hungry as shit. Go across the street to the Chinese store and grab me two pints of Egg Fried Rice and twenty wings and five pizza rolls and a pack of Newport's and a Kiwi Mystique and make sure they put extra suey sauce packs in the bag 'cause them chinks tight with the suey sauce you know that's like they ketchup and hot sauce," laughs Gangstar.

The young boy said, "Yo Gang, I'm hungry too. Can you buy me a shrimp roll or somethin'."

"Nigga fuck, I look like ya dad or something! Get the fuck outta ma face and go get my shit. You Lil' niggas hustle all day and can't never afford to buy y'all selves nothing, exclaims Gangstar.

The young boy puts his head down and walks off to go get Gangstar's food from the Chinese store.

"A Yo Mecca, come here for a second!" calls Gangstar to a female that's pretty decent looking but likes to smoke laced-up joints consisting of crack mixed with cigarettes.

"Whats up Star ?" asked Mecca.

"You," replied Star.

"Oh yeah?" asked Mecca.

Mecca is like 5'6" with thick brown skin and is a freak.

"Yeah, you," replied Gangstar.

"Well, whats up? You got something for me?" asked Mecca.

"Of Course," replied Star and "whats that hard dick and bubble gum?" cracks Star with a laugh.

"See, you always playin' Star," said Mecca in a whiny voice.

"Nah, you know I got chu'," replied Gangstar.

"So, where we goin' go?"

"In my truck across the street."

"Oh," said Mecca.

"Here, take my keys, go get in there. I'll be over there in a second," said Gangstar.

"Yo Scooter, come here right quick."

"Yo Imma bout to get my dick sucked."

"Stay on point. You got ya gun on you?"

"Yeah Star."

"Okay, hold me down."

"Okay, I get chu'," said Scooter.

Gangstar goes over to his truck and gets in.

"I was getting ready to say what type games is Star playin'."

"Bitch you know I don't play no games," said Star while unzipping his pants and pulling out his dick.

"Damn Star, I ain't know you was holding like that," said Mecca.

"Yeah, Yeah, Fuck all that. Let me see you try to swallow this Mafucka," said Gangstar grabbing Mecca by the back of her head and forcing her head in his lap so she could suck his dick.

"Ewwwl yeah, that's it!" exclaims Gangstar while starting to relax in his seat, enjoying the way Mecca is handling her business.

Meanwhile, Scooter is busy making sale after sale. In the distance, he sees somebody riding a bike coming down the block but doesn't recognize who it could be in the distance. Plus, whoever it is their wearing a hoodie concealing their face. Scooter is distracted when he hears his name called from the other direction.

"Yo Scooter!" calls the young flunky that Gangstar sent to the Chinese store.

"Yo, come help me with these bags. I'm bout to drop this Shit; it's too heavy!" exclaims the young flunky struggling with the bags in his arms.

"Man, you better not drop that Shit. Star a kill ya ass out here," replied Scooter with a laugh.

"Well, come help me then nigga."

Scooter walks over to help the young flunky disregarding the fact that his instincts were telling him that the guy on the bike looks shady.

"Yo nigga gimme some of those bags," exclaims Scooter.

"Yo good lookin' those things was heavy as shit," states the young flunky.

"A Scooter where Star at?" asked the young flunky.

"That nigga in the truck getting his dick sucked," replied Scooter.

"Oh yeah, by who?" asked the young flunky enthusiastically.

"Man that bitch Mecca."

"Oh word, damn, I wonder if she'll do me next?" asked the young flunky.

"Nigga that's why you don't never have no doe 'cause all you wanna do is trick ya whole pack away all the time," states Scooter while looking through the bags trying to see what Gangstar ordered.

"Yo Scooter, who that right there?" asked the young flunky.

Before Scooter could turn around and see who he was talking about, shots go off. Boom! Boom! Scooter and the young flunky drop the bags and hit the ground, trying to take cover from the shooter.

CHAPTER 37

A Smokers Nightmare

"A drug dealer's dream is to stash cream keys on a triple Beam 500 SL gleam 95 triple beam condominium this dressed like a gentleman...." Raps Nas through Saleem's money-green Honda Accord as he cruises through the block on his way home to tell Scooby about the meeting he had with Dreadz. As he rides through the block, he notices a guy coming out of the alleyway, walking swiftly followed by one of the young boys that pump coke for him and Scooby. As he gets closer, he sees the guy getting into a blue Chevy Caprice.

"I know that ain't my mom car," Saleem said out loud to himself.

Saleem slows down and mutes his radio and calls the young worker over to the car. The young boy rushes over immediately.

"Yo Leem, I ain't done yet, but…" Saleem cuts him off before he can finish talkin'.

"Nah, I ain't call you for that," exclaims Saleem.

"Oh, whats up then?" replied the youngin'.

"That dude you just came out of the alleyway with, did he cop off you?"

"Yeah, he bought two for fifteen; why that one of your customers? He owe you money as somethin' 'cause the next time I see him, I'll handle that for you," exclaims the young boy.

"Nah, it ain't nothing like that good lookin' though; be careful out here keep getting that money. Imma holler at chu'," said Saleem.

"A'ight," replied the youngin'.

"I know that nigga wasn't shit trying to play my mom. I should kill

that junkie Mafucka,," thinks Saleem, *"gotta tell my mom about this shit,"* as he continues down the block headed straight to his mom's house to let her know what he just saw.

"Tommy is that you?" asked Saleem's mom, Ms. Betty.

"Yeah baby, it's me," replied Tommy, her boyfriend from Philly.

"Come here for a second!" calls out Ms. Betty.

"Hold on baby, I'll be right back. I gotta use the bathroom," replied Tommy as he ran up the steps straight to the bathroom, closed the door and locked it. He then opens up the bathroom window then he turns on the sink to help drown out any noise. He reaches into his pocket, pulls out two dime bags of crack cocaine, then goes into his jacket pocket and pulls out some chore boy and a glass pipe that's burnt up from prior usage. He then pats his pockets.

"Where the fuck is my lighter?"

He's beginning to sweat; every junkie knows that not having no fire to smoke their crack is called a smokers nightmare. Tommy picks up his coat and frantically starts searching through all of the pockets. Unable to locate his lighter, he screams, "fuck!" throws his jacket on the bathroom floor, unlocks the bathroom door and heads to the bedroom where he believes there are some matches, a lighter or something that 'causes fire.

At this point, he'll take two pieces of pencil lead and stick 'em in a socket on some jailhouse shit. That's how desperate he is to smoke right now. He finally finds some matches on Ms. Betty's nightstand. He rushes back into the bathroom, locks the door and begins stuffing his pipe with chore boy to substitute as a filter. Then he takes one of the black rocks out and stuffs it inside of the pipe and begins to place the pipe in his mouth. Then strikes three matches to make as big a flame; he can then places the fire to the tip of the pipe. He then pulls deep and hard on the pipe. You can hear the crackling of the coke as it burns and sizzles inside of the crack pipe. Instantly the bathroom is filled with that familiar bitter smell that hustlers and junkies know all too well. Tommy lets out the smoke in his lungs and a fart out of his ass. For the life of me, I don't know why every time a junkie gets around some coke or smell it, they start farting and all type of crazy shit. Don't you love it when they start geeking? You know all junkies have their own geek; some wanna start cleaning every damn thing in sight. Some wanna start dancin' and singing. Then you got the ones that wanna get butt ass naked talkin' bout its hot, or if they take their clothes off, they'll be invisible. The most famous geek of all time all across the world, the paranoid junkie, that everybody shushes! Did you hear that junkie; every five minutes looking out the window junkie, that shit be all-time funny, right?

Saleem pulls on the corner of his mom's block; he sees her car parked right in front of the house, so he knows that Tommy's in there.

"I'll kill this Mafucka, if he got my mom hooked on that shit," thinks Saleem as he reaches into the glove compartment and grabs his .38, checks the cylinder to make sure he's fully loaded just in case he has to put the same hot shit up in Tommy.

CHAPTER 38

Ayonna Schools Ericka

"Ayonna! Ayonna! Hold up girl, wait for me!" yells Ericka, one of Ayonna's friends in school.

She's from the Northside too, but she lives on 17th St., that's right off of Vandever Ave. by where Omega and his team were killed.

"Damn girl, you be walkin' all fast," said Ericka.

"Girl, I be trying to get where I gotta go," replied Ayonna.

"What up with my girl Tameka?" asked Ericka.

"Oh, she doing better; she home now. They got her on bed rest. I was over her house the other day," replied Ayonna.

"Oh, okay, that's whats up. I need to go see her myself; bring her a get-well card or something. You know, just out of common decency," states Erica.

"Yeah, that would be nice of you," replied Ayonna.

"So girl, what bus you riding' home?" asked Ericka.

"The one I ride every day, why?" asked Ayonna.

"Cause I was going to see if you was ridin' a bus at all," replied Ericka.

"Girl, what are you getting at?" questions Ayonna.

"Everybody know ya man got that fly ass car. If he was mines, I'll be driving it whenever I want and that nigga would have his ass right outside every day after school waiting to pick me up," said Ericka with a snap of the neck and fingers.

"Girl, I don't sweat Saleem like that and trust, if I wanted him to come pick me up, that's nothin'," states Ayonna.

"I hear you, girl," replied Ericka, "girl can you hook me up with his boy Scooby with his fine ass self?" asked Ericka.

"Girl, you don't want him. He's a whore, he'll stick his dick in anything," replied Ayonna.

"I hear you, but word is Saleem and Scooby got the city on smash," states Ericka.

"Girl don't believe everything you hear; people see they cars and automatically think somebody doin' same thing major. My mom been schooled me to that niggas may stay geared up and got a car, but that's all they worth. These fake ballers don't be havin' nothin' saved up; all they got is re-up money," exclaims Ayonna.

"Damn girl, you just ran that shit like a Mafucka,," replied Ericka, in awe of the knowledge that Ayonna has to be so young.

"Any way girl,` if you really wanna holler at Scooby, I'll let Saleem know and he'll tell 'em, but Imma tell you this, don't let your heart get involved 'cause you'll only be setting yourself up for hurt. I mean, maybe you got something the other thousand girls he dates don't. All I'm saying is guard your heart," states Ayonna.

"Girl, that is some real Shit; that's why you my girl," replied Ericka.

"What are friends for," exclaims Ayonna.

CHAPTER 39

Gangstar is Shot

Inside of Gangstar's truck, Mecca has been going hard on him and he's on the verge of bustin' off. Mecca can feel Star's dick starting to swell in her mouth, so she knows her job is almost done. With the thought of getting high afterward motivates her to finish up. So, she begins to quicken her pace. Gangstar is so focused on Mecca's head that he's oblivious to what's going on around him.

"Ahh, yeah Bitch I want you to catch all this shit!" exclaims Gangstar knowing he's about to cum.

Rights as he's about to fill Mecca's mouth up with cum shots rang out, Boom! Boom! Shattering the truck's front window.

"Oh Shit!" exclaims Gangstar as he desperately tries to take cover, but there's nowhere to go. Mecca's head is in his lap, so he can't lift up and try to crouch down in the seat. So, he grabs Mecca by the hair in an attempt to pull her over top of his body as a shield. Only to let her go.

"Oh, Shit!" screams Gangstar like a bitch looking at the blood on his hand and now all over his lap and stomach area. One of the bullets that burst through the window hit Mecca in the head, killing her instantly.

"Fuck!" shouted Gangstar as two more shots went off.

Boom! Boom!

One just missed his head by inches, but the other ripped straight through his shoulder.

"Ahh! Shit!" screams Gangstar from the burning, painful sensation that's shooting through his shoulder.

Gangstar grabs his shoulder, closing his eyes in agony. When he opens them, he's staring down the barrel of a black Glock nine-millimeter. Gangstar begins begging for his life.

"Please don't kill me. I'll give you anything you want."

But the figure in front of him said, "Good, then you won't mind giving me ya life," but before the figure could squeeze the trigger, a single shot went off, hitting the figure in his left triceps.

"Argh!" grunts the figure turning around and firing a wilding Boom! Boom! Boom! with no target in sight.

Scooter hits the ground hard, taking cover.

"I got that nigga! I got that nigga!" exclaims Scooter excitedly to the young flunky lying on the ground next to 'em, scared to death.

The figure runs towards Governor Printz, gun in hand, looking back the whole time, holding his gun wound to the arm. Gangstar peeks his head out the truck window wondering why the shooting stopped and to see if the close was clear to get out of the truck. As he looks around, he sees the nigga with the hoodie that almost took his life from him disappearing in the distance.

"Whoever that nigga was, he's a fucking dead man," thinks Gangstar to himself.

Scooter peeks his head up and sees Gangstar standing in the middle of the street.

"Star! Star! You alright?" exclaims Scooter.

"Fuck no, I ain't alright nigga! Where the fuck was you at when a nigga just came through here head hunting!" yells Gangstar.

"I...I... was helping the young bo..y carry you fo...od," stammers Scooter nervously.

"Fuck that food! A nigga almost took my fuckin' life and you worrin' about helpin' a nigga carry some food! If my shoulder wasn't in the shape it's in, I'll whip ya ass out here!"

"But Star, when I realized what was going on, I did what I could," exclaims Scooter, "that was me that shot 'em when he was about to hit chu' up."

Again, Gangstar softens a little bit, but a crowd has formed, so he still has to remain hard in front of the people, but at the same time, he really is thankful that the young boy came through when he did.

So, he responds with, "Nigga you should've kilt that Mafucka. Matter of fact, gimme ya gun!" demands Gangstar.

"Aww man Star," wines Scooter, thinking Gangstar is about to shoot him. Reluctantly he hands Gangstar the gun.

"All of you mafuckas out here eat 'cause I let cha'll. Where the fuck was y'all at when a nigga came through here like shit was sweet, huh!" yells Gangstar. Nobody responds.

"Oh, now everybody, deaf, dumb and blind. Yo Scooter, which way did he come from?"

"Down bottom," points Scooter.

"Everybody that was just down bottom, come line up! Hurry up!" yells Gangstar, "mafuckin' shoulder killin' me!"

Three young boys line up with terror in their young eyes.

"Now, who the fuck had look out down that end?"

Two of the young boys immediately point to the only other remaining young boy next to them. Star raises the gun at the young boy's face and then tells the other two to move out of the way. The remaining young boy begins shedding tears but is too terrified to move.

Gangstar said, "I should close ya casket!" but instead, Gangstar lowered the gun Boca!

"Ahhh!" the young boy screams, falling to the ground and grabbing his leg.

Gangstar looked down at the young boy and said, "Next time ya life is mines pussy; now somebody go get my other car and take me and this little Mafucka, to the hospital!" shouts Gangstar to his young flunkies.

CHAPTER 40

Tommy Exposed

Saleem enters his mom's house with a gun tucked in his waistband.

"Mom, Mom, where you at?!" yelled Saleem.

"I'm in here boy, in the kitchen! Why the hell you yelling like you done lost ya damn mind or somethin'!" exclaims Ms. Betty.

"Where Tommy at mom?" asked Saleem.

"Why? Whats going on?" questions Ms. Betty.

"Mom, are you getting high? Be honest don't lie," demands Saleem.

"Boy, you really done lost ya damn mind now. Coming in here talking stupid," replied Ms. Betty heatedly, "why in the hell would you ask me some shit like that any damn way?" asked Ms. Betty.

"Cause I just seen ya junkie ass boyfriend come out of a alleyway with one of my young boys who told me that Tommy just bought some crack off of him."

"Boy, I understand your upset, but you better watch ya damn mouth in here. You ain't grown, I don't care how much money you got you're still my child, and you're going to respect me," replied Ms. Betty.

"Mom, where's Tommy?" Saleem says calmly.

"He upstairs. He come in here not too long ago and said he had to use the bathroom," said Ms. Betty.

"Yeah, so he can get high," replied Saleem.

"Are you sure it was him?" asked Ms. Betty.

"Yes, I'm sure mom. He had ya car and everything."

"Oh no, he didn't buy no drugs in my car," exclaims Ms. Betty, clearly pissed off, "Tommy! Tommy! I need to talk to you right now come down here!" shouts Ms. Betty up the stairs.

Tommy damn near jumps out of his skin when he hears Ms. Betty scream his name. He begins to clean up as fast as he can. He is sweating profusely. He flushes the toilet and runs some water on his face as if that's going to stop him from looking high. He gathers up anything that looks like he's been getting high, tucks the pipe, matches and box of Chore boy in his jacket pocket and puts the other dime piece of coke inside the little pocket on his jeans, opens the bathroom door, eyes bugging out of his head and unbeknownst to him his mouth keeps twitching from side to side. All tales tell signs he's high.

As he makes it to the steps, he sees Saleem standing next to his mother and pauses at the top of the staircase and asks, "Whats up baby, everything alright?"

"Nah nigga everything ain't...." Ms. Betty cuts Saleem off and tells him she got this.

"Betty, what the hell's going on?" exclaims Tommy.

"You tell me, are you getting high Tommy?" asked Ms. Betty with her arms folded across her chest.

"What?" asks a confused Tommy thinking to himself, *"damn, how the fuck she find out I'm getting high?"* not knowing the block he just copped from is run by Saleem.

"Well, are you?" asked Ms. Betty.

"Baby, I don't wanna talk about this in front of your son," replies Tommy.

Ms. Betty looks at Saleem and says, "Baby, let me handle this. If I need you, I'll let chu' know."

Saleem stares at his mom for a second, then he stares at Tommy and says, "Imma respect ya wishes and let chu' handle it your way but if I catch 'em around the way copping again, you ain't going have to worry about talking to 'em. If anything, you goin' have to worry about what church you goin' have his funeral in says, "Saleem." Never taking his eyes off of Tommy.

Tommy started to pop fly but decided against it. At least now he knows where his mom got her information; from now he has to talk his way out of this situation.

"Yo Dreadz, you think that kid really can handle all that work he asking for?" asked Ox.

"It's a tall order for someone his age, but nowadays, kids his age are more advanced, plus he got a whole block backin' 'em, so yeah, I can see him being able to handle the order," replied Dreadz.

"I ain't know them niggas was eatin' like that around the corner or I woulda been made a move son, word to mother," says Ghost grimily hating the fact that a nigga not too much younger than him grabbing big weight like that and he's just one of Dreadz soldiers/hustlers.

Secretly he thinks Dreadz is soft and be taking it easy on these soft-ass Delaware niggas. He wants his own empire and he knows one sure way to get it is to take shit over and rule with an iron fist.

CHAPTER 41

Twin is Hit

Saleem gets in his car and begins to think before starting it. He's still clearly upset that his mom is dealing with a smoker.

"If it wasn't for his mom, he would've shot Tommy and made him leave town, and if he saw him around his mom again, he'd kill 'em dead, but off the strength of his mom, he decides to let her handle it her way but if one thing for sure and two things for certain if she don't dump Tommy or he doesn't get his shit together Tommy goin' to come up missin' 'cause he'll be damned if he let some junkie nigga turn his mom onto that shit," thinks Saleem.

As Saleem stares into the distance, he sees a figure dressed in all black, wearing a hoodie running up the hill through Prices Park, holding his arm as if he's been shot or something. He can't really tell who it is, so he starts up his car and drives slowly down the street so he can try to get a better look at the dude in the hoodie. As he gets closer, his eyes widen because he recognizes the dude in the hoodie. It's Twin, Khalif, the brother of the twin Hakeem that got hit up on the block and died. Saleem pulls up and beeps the horn; as soon as Twin reaches the top of the hill, the sound of the horn startles Twin making him reach for his gun. Saleem jumps out of the car, so Twin can see that it's him.

"Yo Twin, it's me!" shouts Saleem.

Twin recognizes Saleem and shouts, "Yo dog, I'm hit! I'm hit!" exclaim Twin.

"Get in!" exclaims Saleem.

Twin rushes over to the car and hops in. Saleem does the same pulling off like regular so as to not draw any unnecessary attention. A few blocks away, Saleem pulls over.

"Yo dog, why you stoppin'?" exclaims Twin, wondering why all of sudden Saleem just out of the blue pulls over, knowing that he's been hit in the arm.

"I got chu' dog," says Saleem, poppin' the trunk, hopping out of the car and running around to the trunk.

Saleem reaches into a gym bag, grabs a white T-shirt and begins to rip it. Grabs a bottle of spring water and pours it on the ripped shirt to moisten it. He then tosses the bottle, runs back around the car, and gets in.

Twin looked over at him with the ripped t-shirt in his hand and asked, "Whats that for?"

"Take ya hoodie off so I can wrap it around ya gun wound to slow the bleeding down. Imma bout to take you up Chester to Crozer Medical Center so the police can't trace you to whatever just happened with you," says Saleem while tying the damp T-shirt around Twins gun wound.

"Ahh! shit dog!" exclaims Twin, "that shit hurt cousin."

"You alright dog? That shit went through and through you good. We just gotta get chu' cleaned and sewed up," replies Saleem on his way to Chester.

"Yo dog, I really appreciate chu' doin' this for me. Where you learn how to do what chu' did with the shirt and shit?" asked Twin.

"On some real, between me and you, I saw that shit on New York City Undercover," says Saleem with a slight chuckle.

"Are you serious dog?" exclaims Twin in disbelief.

"Yeah dog, on everything," replied Saleem.

"Seriously man, that was some Doogie Houser M.D. shit," laughs Twin. Also causing Saleem to burst out with laughter.

"Yo dog, you crazy as shit," exclaims Saleem, "nigga you bout to make me kill both of us. You feel like blowing asked Saleem.

"Yeah nigga, where its at?" replied Twin.

Saleem reaches into the armrest and pulls out a Phillies blunt and some of that Omega.

"Yo dog, you think you can crack this blunt," asked Saleem.

"Mafuckin' right I can," replied Twin, "ma shit hurt, but it ain't paralyzed," cracks Twin with a laugh as he cracks and roll the blunt.

He looks over at Saleem and says, "you a real ass nigga."

"Dog, why you say that?" asked Saleem.

"Cause dog you seen me hit ain't ask no questions about what happened. Where I just came from? Did I kill somebody? Did somebody try to kill me? Nothin' you just jumped into action and started holding a nigga down. If that ain't a real nigga, I don't know what is," stated Twin.

"Man, you my nigga right or wrong, Imma ride for you or any nigga I fuck with that goes without sayin'. I seen my comrade in need of assistance and I did what a real nigga was supposed to do," replies Saleem, "matter of factly, true?"

"True," replies Twin, "well since I know you ain't no rat or nothing dog Imma let chu' know whats up," said Twin.

"Man, you ain't gotta explain shit cousin," responds Saleem.

"Nah dog, I wanna tell you," replied Twin.

"Well, if you gotta get it off ya chest, by all means, do so," said Saleem, looking over at Twin, who takes another toke of the refer before passing it to Saleem and then going into the story about what happened. A few minutes later, Twin finishes up his story.

Saleem stares out the window as if deep in thought, then begins to speak, "Dog, I feel you on everything you just said and that was some honorable shit how you code out or ya brother, but you got to be easy with the not lead spear of the moment shit. We a team in our hood; you know niggas wasn't going to let Hakeem die in vain. It's a time and place for everything; by you going down there like that by yourself, you could got more than just a shot in the arm. Instead of one Twin funeral, we could've been done had to have two and just think how Mom Kim would be feeling right now if she found you done got cha' self murdered. Dog, you get two teams to use. Your (I) before the (E)."

"Whats that?" asked Twin tentatively.

"Man, that's Intellect before Emotion basically, think before you react, dog, too many niggas done got murdered by reacting before thinking or caught for whatever they done because they were impulsive."

"That's some real shit," replied Twin.

"Man, it ain't bout nothing. We learn something new every day," said Saleem, "a yo pass the (Gonk) nigga; over there letting me run my mouth while you smoke like a chimney," laughs Saleem.

"I just wasn't trying to interrupt you," replied Twin, "but yo this some killer weed, though."

"Yeah, I know," replied Saleem, "and its plenty more where that came from. I got about a half on me now. Imma give you half of it when we get you taken care of, but if you want more, the bitches got it for sale in the hood," said Saleem.

"Which ones?" asked Twin.

"Gutlynn and them."

"Oh yeah, which one of them you fuckin'?" asked Twin.

"None all of them, but I probably can fuck all of 'em on some real shit," replied Saleem.

"I heard that player."

"Nah, that's you nigga, everybody know you be fuckin' (Dime) nigga," cracks Saleem.

Twin looks at him with the damn how you know that face.

"Yeah nigga you ain't think I knew that did you?" said Saleem.

"Damn nigga what chu' been stalkin' me or something?" cracks Twin.

"Never that cousin, but the hood talk its only but so big," states Saleem.

"True, true," replied Twin, "yo dog turn some music on. I know you got that Pac shit in here."

"Better believe," responded Saleem, popping in his Me Against the World by Tupac and outcomes Pac's raspy voice, *"It ain't easy being me, will I see the penitentiary or will I stay free"* as the music plays Saleem and Twin lay back in their seats and listen to the music both deep in their thoughts.

CHAPTER 42

The Visit

"Heey baby!!!" shouts Mrs. Robin excitedly to Boomer, grabbing him, hugging him, and kissing him with a bag in her hand, "you got so big you must be eatin' the whole kitchen," cracks Mrs. Robin with a big smile on her face.

"Take it easy mom, with all that lovey-dovey shit before these nigga think is sweet or somethin'," replied Boomer.

"You are my son; I don't care what none of these knucklehead boys think," replied Mrs. Robin seriously as she took the seat at the visiting table.

"What you chu' got in the bag mom?" inquired Boomer; noticing the bag, she sat on the floor.

"Oh yeah, here boy Saleem and Scooby gave me these to give to you," handing Boomer the bag, "do you know Scooby had the nerve to try and give me some weed to sneak in here to you," said Mrs. Robin with a distasteful shake of the head.

"You ain't take it?" asked Boomer seriously.

"Hell no! Boy, what I look like smugglin' some damn drugs in here?" asked Mrs. Robin heatedly.

"Yo, keep it down mom," stressed Boomer, looking around to see if anybody was listening.

"They told me to tell you to look underneath the soles of the sneakers when you get a chance."

Boomer opens the box and smiles when he sees the BO Jacksons inside. He takes one out and starts to reach inside to pull the sole out, but his mom stops him.

"Boy, don't do that shit right here."

"Chill mom, the staff cool he ain't goin' say nothing," replied Boomer.

"I don't know why you just can't wait til you go back to your unit. It ain't nothing but money in there anyway," replied Mrs. Robin.

"Damn mom, what you looked in there already?" asked Boomer.

"I sure did. I told you I wasn't smugglin' no drugs in here," said Mrs. Robin.

"Well, how much in them?" asked Boomer curiously.

"Two hundred dollars, a hundred underneath each sole," replied Mrs. Robin.

Boomer cracks a smile, *"My niggas out there playin'. I remember we use to have to put our money together to buy a quarter of coke and bust it down. Now my niggas throwing two hundred around like it ain't nothing,"* thinks Boomer.

His mom breaks his thoughts saying, "They said to tell you things is going good and you don't have to want for nothing when you get out of here. They got pretty cars and always got pockets full of money. Everybody saying they got the city on lock. I don't want you to come home and get caught up in that baby. You should take this as a lesson. I want you home for good. I hate having to see you in here," replied Mrs. Robin.

"Mom, I feel you, but I don't know nothing but the streets, getting money and holding my hood down is all I know. I mean, one day, I hope to get my life on a better track, but right now, all I know is the streets," said Boomer honestly, looking his mom in her hurt eyes.

"Baby, I'll pray for you and hope that God changes your heart before it's too late."

Mrs. Robin rises to her feet, as do the other family members of the other juveniles that came to see. The light flicker on and off, indicating that the visits have come to an end. Boomer and his mom embrace.

"Hopefully, the next time I see you, it'll be on the outside," stated Mrs. Robin knowing Boomer was on his way out the door.

"Yeah, me too mom, me too," replied Boomer.

CHAPTER 43

Met at the Store

"A yo let me get a large cheese steak with everything on it and don't be stingy with the meat either 'cause I'm mad starvin'!" shouts Ghost to the Korean lady in the Qualities Sub Shop located on 23rd and Market Street.

"Yo Ox, what chu' getting' son? I know ya big Arnold Schwarzenegger ass hungry," says Ghost with a chuckle.

"Nigga fuck you son, move out ma way said," Ox, with a light shove pushing Ghost from in front of the counter so he could place his order.

In comes Ayonna and Ericka, her friend from school. As soon as she comes into the store, she and Ghost make eye contact, and she looks the other way and says, "Oh My God," under her breath.

"Bitch whats wrong with you?" asked Ericka.

"That's the New York boy from 23rd Street that tried to talk to me not to long ago."

"Umm girl, he cute," replied Ericka, "girl, if you don't want him, I do," said Ericka, all thirsty.

"Girl, you can have him," replied Ayonna.

"Girl, don't he kinda look like Ghost Face Killah from Wu- Tang- Clan?" asked Ericka.

"Girl, I said the same thing to myself when I saw him."

"Damn ma, whats up? No hi, hello or nothin'?" asked Ghost as he swaggers over to where Ayonna and Ericka are standing.

"Nah, it ain't like that. I just wasn't trying to lead you on in any kind of way. I told you I'm with someone," replied Ayonna.

"Yeah, I dis all that ma, but I was just saying hi. I know you allowed to speak to a nigga, right? Or do you be on some abusive shit 'cause if he does, that can be taken care of if you want it to," stated Ghost, lifting up his shirt and showing Ayonna his Chrome 44 with the black handle.

"Oh My God, girl, he got a big ass gun on him," said Erika covering her mouth slightly in fear. Ayonna, on the other hand, sees guns all the time because Saleem keeps his on him at all times.

"Oh Nah, I'm good. My man does not put his hands on me, so you can cover that back up," replied Ayonna with and unimpressed tone of voice.

"Why you got that big gun on you are you in trouble, somebody lookin' for you or somethin'?" asked Erika outta curiosity.

"And who might you be shorty?"

"Oh, I apologize; this is my friend Erika and she's available," said Ayonna.

"Is that right?" replied Ghost picking up on Ayonna, trying to push her friend off on him.

"I hear you ma," in response to Ayonna, "so Miss Ericka, how are you?"

"I'm good, but I could be better."

"Yeah, we all can," replied Ghost looking at Ayonna with a sly grin on his face.

"So whats up with that big ass gun?" asked Erika again.

"Damn ma, what chu' work for the boys in blue?" asked Ghost with a chuckle.

"Oh Nah, I was just askin'," replied Erika, kinda embarrassed.

"I'm just messing with you ma. I keeps my heat on me at all times;

you never know when drama might come ya way, so it's best to be caught with it than without it. Smell me ma?"

"Actually, I can. You smell like Egyptian Musk or somethin' replied Ericka seriously. Ox and Ghost and even Ayonna all fall out laughing.

"What? Whats so funny?" asked Erika, not understanding whats so funny.

"My bad ma, I forgot I was in square Delaware," replied Ghost.

"Oh, ain't nothing slow about Delaware," replied Ayonna with a slight attitude, "she might not of caught your slang, but I did. It wasn't really that hard to pick up on," said Ayonna.

"Oh my bad ma, no disrespect," replied Ghost.

"I'm still lost," said Erika.

"Well, I am wearing Egyptian Musk, but when I said smell me, I meant it like, do you understand me?"

"Oh, I feel so stupid," said Erika.

"Nah ma, you good, you just ain't no. Pardon me for being so ignorant. This big nigga over here is my man, his name is Ox."

"Oh hey."

"Hi, you doin'?" asked Erika.

With a wave in true Ox fashion, he just nods his head up and down.

"Yo ma don't mind him he get anti-social when he hungry," says Ghost with a laugh.

Ayonna walks up to the counter and places her order, and so does Erika.

"Yo Kid, shorty mad fly."

"Son um diggin' her whole ora B.," says Ghost to an uninterested Ox, "yo son, she acting like the ain't feelin' the god, but I see through her like a empty glass son," continues Ghost.

"A yo Kid, why don't you just stop sweatin' shorty so hard didn't she say she wit a nigga?" asked Ox.

"Son, since when do that matter?" asked Ghost seriously.

"All I'm getting at Kid is we don't need no unnecessary focus if her nigga finds out you keep trying to get at his lady," replied Ox.

"Once again son, when do that matter?" said Ghost cockily.

"Listen B., you know and I know that burying a niggas ain't nuffin', that's the easy part, but we here to get money! Understand, get money! And on occasion, let the blicka burn," said Ox getting angry.

"Yo easy son not so loud, Kid you right I smell you B., but if opportunity presents itself, Imma do what it do," replies Ghost looking at Ayonna devilishly.

CHAPTER 44

Scooby Learns About the Intruders

BZZ! BZZ! BZZ! BZZ!

Buzzes Scooby's pager, he hears it and pauses his game to see who it is, hoping it's Saleem so he can know how things went with Dreadz. As he eyes the number on the pager, another page buzzes in 911. He jumps up off the couch, grabs his pistol off of the coffee table, puts on his sneakers and rushes across the street to the pay phone and dials the first number that comes through his pager. The receiver picks up on the first ring.

"Scooby is that you?" asked a shaken Shontay.

"Yeah, whats up?" asked a concerned Scooby, hoping she ain't bout to tell him something happened to his ace boom coon Saleem.

"We just got robbed; come through here; we at the spot," said Shontay.

"What robbed?" asked a confused Scooby, not fully believing the news Shontay just laid on him 'cause he can't believe somebody's that stupid to rob their spot.

"Yeah, robbed," replied Shontay.

"A'ight, I'm on my way," replied Scooby.

Scooby debates for a second on whether to call Saleem but then decides against it because, for one, he knows Saleem is supposed to be at a meeting with Dreadz and two, this is his operation too, and it's a chance to show Saleem that he can handle these type situations without him. So, he jogs across the street to the parking lot, hops in his car and heads to the spot, thinking who would be stupid enough to rob one of their spots, beings though the hood is only a hop, skip and a jump from Scooby and Saleem's apartment. Scooby reaches the spot in no time. As he comes through, all eyes are on him. He sees Shontay on the porch; she flags him down and he stops in front of the house. Shontay approaches the car; Scooby lowers the window just a crack and tells Shontay to go open the back door. She nods, then walks back into the house. Scooby parks around the corner, observing the scene. As he rides down 23rd and Lamotte Street, he notices Dreadz gold LS 400. He scans the rest of the block but doesn't see Saleem's green Honda nowhere.

"Where the fuck is this nigga at? He was suppose to call me when the meeting was over fuck it, I'll catch up with him later," thinks Scooby as he makes a left on 23rd and Lamotte, then makes another left on 23rd and Canter Street. He parks, get out, then proceeds to walk through an alleyway, opens a fence, and then walks into the back door of the spot where the girls are waiting in the living Room.

"Whats good?" asked Saleem.

"Oh shit!" exclaims Dina, caught off guard, "you scared the shit out of me." Everybody laughs, lighting the most

"A little bitch, I told you he was coming in through the back way," says Shontay.

"I know, but a bitch on point right now," replies Dina, dead serious.

"So what happened?" asked Scooby to Shontay.

She began to explain everything in detail. Just as Shontay was finishing her story, Tosh came down the stairs and sat on the last two steps.

Scooby notices her and says, "Whats up Tosh? Where were you at?"

"I was upstairs smoking, then I heard what was going on, so I hid and was listening."

"Oh yeah, did you recognize any voices, or did you set this shit up?" asked Scooby catching everybody off guard 'cause nobody was even thinking like that.

"Hell No, I ain't crazy!" exclaims Tosh with fear in her eyes.

Gutlynn jumps up off the couch and tries to rush Tosh screaming, "Bitch, if you had something to do with it Imma beat cha' ass!" Scooby grabs her around the waist holding her back.

"Chill, Chill," said Scooby in Gutlynn's ear.

"No fuck that I got pistol-whipped! If she had something to do with it, I'm a fuck her up."

"I hear you but right now, just chill til we find out whats really going on," says Scooby, walking Gutlynn back over to the couch to sit her down.

"Now, back to you, did you recognize any of the voices?" asked Scooby through clinched teeth, visibly angry.

"I'm not sure I think so."

"Bitch I will break your fucking face in here. Did you or didn't you recognize anybody voice?" asked Scooby pulling out his nine millimeters and turning it around as if he's about to gun butt Tosh, but before he reached her, she screamed out, "Jerse!"

"Who bitch?!" exclaims Scooby.

"Jerse! one of them sounded like it could've been Jerse!" shouts out Tosh scared to death.

"Are you sure?" asked Scooby.

"It sounded like he was trying to disguise his voice, but I'm sure it was him, though," replied Tosh.

"You better not be lying and if you was in on it, you a dead bitch," stated Scooby.

Meaning every word, he can't wait to tell Saleem this fuckin' Jerse must got a fuckin' death wish. If that's the case, his wish is my command.

Scooby turns to the girls and says, "Don't worry about shit; everything's going to get handled. Did they get everything?"

"No, they got bout a half pound and fifteen hundred from us."

"A'ight finish what cha'll got. Imma send my young boy over here to hold y'all down from now on; is everybody okay?"

"Yeah," replies everybody in unison.

"Gutlynn, you can chill for the night if you want days if it's with you."

"Yeah," replied Gutlynn. Everybody started laughin'.

"Girl, you just got ya head cracked and still want some dick?" says Scooby with a chuckle.

"Shid dick is all the medication I need," said Gutlynn causing everybody to burst out laughing.

"Imma see you, but right now, I gotta take care of this shit at hand, but Imma definitely give you what you looking for," replied Scooby as he walked toward the back door leaving the same way he came in.

Upon leaving, he could hear Gutlynn crazy ass saying, "Don't threatin' me with a good time." Followed once again by everybody bursting out laughing.

Scooby shakes his head, smiling and heading back to his car, thinking, *"That bitch Gutlynn is a freak."*

He sees one of his young boys, calls him over and tells him from now on play Tosh crib. Pump and hold the bitches down."

The young boy nods in agreement. Scooby gets in his car and puts on his Ready to Die C.D. By Biggie Smalls. He finds his song *"Damn niggas wanna stick me for ma paper/damn nigga wanna stick for ma paper,"* and those words couldn't be truer, thinks Scooby.

CHAPTER 45

Tommy, Whats Going On?

"Would you like to tell me what the hell is going on Tommy?" asked Ms. Betty.

"Baby ain't nothing going on," replied Tommy, sweating bullets, mouth twitchin'.

"Oh, something going on, ya damn eyes popping out ya head looking like mini golf balls," said Ms. Betty.

"Baby, you got it all wrong. You keep listening to your son. He don't know what the hell he talking about," replied Tommy unconvincingly.

"See, you think um some kinda damn fool that fell off the turnip truck or think I was born last night," says Ms. Betty heatedly.

"Baby, um, be real with you. I've been smoking weed that's it, I promise. Come here," says Tommy reaching out to pull Ms. Betty in close.

"Get off of me, Tommy I ain't trying to hear it," says Ms. Betty.

"Damn it Betty, I'm sick of this shit; I told you I ain't getting high off nothing but weed. Now, if you don't believe me, I don't know what else to tell you!" says Tommy becoming upset because Ms. Betty ain't falling for his bullshit.

"All that raisin' your voice at me in my house ain't goin' cut it. I'll don't know what type of women you use to, but I ain't them. Far as I'm concerned, you can get ya little bit of shit and get out," says Ms. Betty heatedly.

"Woman, you think I give a fuck if you put me out," replies Tommy angrily.

"There go the door right there motherfucker!" exclaimed Ms. Betty.

"Seriously Bitch I ain't going nowhere I'm tired of being nice to your ignorant ass, always running ya damn mouth."

"Unh! Unh! Mafucker you gotta go! You done fucked up callin' me outta my damn name. I know you high now Mafucker!" screams Ms. Betty beside herself, "get the fuck out now!" shoots me Betty.

Tommy walks over, grabs her by the throat, and begins to choke Ms. Betty violently, then viciously smacks her across the face to make blood come out of her mouth.

"Ahh!" screams Ms. Betty as she hits the floor gasping for air, tears running down her face.

"AWW! Baby, I'm sorry, I didn't mean it. You got me upset; I'm sorry, forgive me," pleads Tommy standing over top of Ms. Betty.

Ms. Betty glares at him from the ground with pure hatred in her eyes. She finally manages to say in a shaky voice, "Just go."

Tommy started to reply, but Ms. Betty shouted, "GO!"

And Tommy turns and walks out the door leaving Ms. Betty lying on the living room floor shakin' and disoriented in utter disbelief of what has just takin' place from the only other man besides her son Saleem whom she loves has just put his hands on her as if she was a common whore and he was her pimp being beaten 'cause she didn't have his money, how disgusting. Ms. Betty knew if Saleem found out bout this, he would go ballistic, but at the same time, she thinks about getting her own revenge.

CHAPTER 46

Catching Up On the Events

The next morning Scooby and Saleem are both catching up on the events that took place yesterday; Twin getting shot and the bitches getting robbed at the weed spot and how things went with Dreadz.

"Yo dog, shit is crazy; too much is going on at the same time. On one hand, things is beautiful but on the other hand, shit is hectic. I mean the meeting with Dreadz went according to plans. So, we straight on a Connect, but we warring with these project niggas over some bullshit. We lost cousin Twin now his brother Khalif got shot in the arm yesterday and on top of that a nigga done basically bought they own death over some weed," says Salem to an attentive Scooby.

"So, whats our next move?" asked Scooby.

"Well, finding that nigga Jerse should be easy. Ending this war with the project niggas ain't that easy, but right now, our main priority is gettin' this money. The key thing right now is to stay alert at all times and continue to flood the city," replied Saleem.

"That's all it is then dog," says Scooby.

"A yo Boomer crazy ass get out this week what you wanna do for him throw a party for him somewhere or just take him to a outta town club?" asked Saleem.

"Man, it's whatever, I would like to throw him a party, but its a lot goin' on right now, so that outta town club might be where it's at," says Scooby.

"I was thinking the same thing, but at the same time fuck the project niggas and who ever else. I was thinking of having his party down

Ambrosias or Longshoreman. Hell, get Cousin Wayne and Q to rent it out for us," said Saleem.

"Word that would be the shit dog," said Scooby excitedly.

"I don't know we'll think of something," replied Saleem, "right now, let's just focus on this money," said Saleem.

"I agree," replied Scooby.

"You know I found out that nigga Tommy my mom fuck with been getting high on the low; saw the nigga cop of off one of the Lil' niggas round the way," said Saleem.

"Word?" replied Scooby in total disbelief.

"Word on everything dog," says Saleem, "I told my mom I wanted to kill that nigga, but she wanted to handle it herself," says Saleem.

"Yo, he better not get Mom Betty on that shit. I'll kill that nigga myself," says Scooby, dead serious 'cause he really loves Saleem's mom like his own.

"You already know I asked her," said Saleem.

"You did?" asked Scooby.

"Yeah," said Saleem, "she snapped too, but I had to ask," replied Saleem.

"Yeah, I feel you dog," says Scooby.

"But on another note, you heard from Cousin Wayne and Q?" asked Saleem.

"Nah, but I was planning on goin' over Q crib when I went down the way," said Scooby.

"Me too," replied Saleem, "yo I'm bout to call Ayonna, check up on her see how she doing," said Saleem.

"Nigga don't you mean check-in, you ole' sucker for love ass nigga," cracks Scooby with a chuckle.

"Nigga fuck you; I know you ain't talkin' ole' tender dick ass nigga, not you the same nigga in love with old ass Ms. Edna," said Saleem, laughin' but serious.

"Aww nigga that's fucked up you goin' go there though," replied Scooby wiping his laugh off his face.

"Yup," replied Saleem with a smirk.

"A'ight nigga you got that," said Scooby turning back to the T.V. so he could play Sega Genesis. Saleem grabs the phone, heads to his room, flops down on his bed, and dials Ayonna's number; a couple of rings go by before a male's voice comes through the phone.

"Hello," says the voice.

"Ah hi, you doing Mr. Smallwood this Saleem. May I speak to Ayonna please?" asked Saleem recognizing the voice to be Ayonna's dad.

"Nah, she ain't here and cut that fake ass proper shit out on this phone. You know I know you out there in them streets cursing and smokin' weed and I heard you playin' a strong hand right now, Lil' nigga," said Mr. Smallwood catching Saleem totally off guard with his boldness and blatantness.

"Nah, Mr. Smallwood, somebody done told you some false information," replied Saleem.

"Yeah a'ight, Lil' nigga I ain't goin' get into it over the phone, but I might need to holler at you. I'll page or somethin' and oh yeah, whatever you in to keep my daughter safe and out of harm's way. I don't wanna have to break Betty's heart by puttin' my foot up your little ass," said Mr.

Smallwood with a chuckle.

"Yeah, you don't have to ever worry about me putting Ayonna in danger, but if a nigga did lay a hand on her, it'll be the last time he breathe this air and don't page me, I'll page you. Give me your number."

Reluctantly Mr. Smallwood gives Saleem his number.

"And oh yeah, tell Ayonna I called. (Click)

"Hello, Hello. *Lil' slick talkin' ass nigga hung up on me,*" said Mr. Smallwood to himself, but really liking how Saleem handled himself, especially on the phone about business.

"Yo Scoob Ayonna dad a trip talkin' all reckless on the phone," says Saleem walking back into the front room where Scooby was playin' NBA Jams. Scooby pauses the game so he can hear what Saleem is sayin'.

"Yo, what he say?" asked Scooby.

"Nigga was basically fishin' talkin' bout he know I know he know I'm playing with a strong hand right now and he might need to holler at me later."

"Oh yeah, so what you tell 'em?" asked Scooby.

"I ain't tell that nigga shit; we was on the phone. However, I did tell the nigga I'll page him. I'm a see whats up with him. He might be a potential customer plus, he might know some other ole' heads that might be good for business, feel me?" asked Saleem.

"Yeah, I feel you dog; now come on over here and lose some of that money nigga," said Scooby.

"Don't you mean make money? Money, you bum ass nigga always trying to bet and don't even know how to play," replied Saleem laughing as he flops down on the couch next to his road dawg.

CHAPTER 47

Two-Four Project

"Yo Star, this two-four project shit is getting outta hand player got the 'jects hot ass shit. I know you your own man and everything, but you might wanna squash that shit for a while, then maybe get at them niggas later. I mean, I could have a sit down with them niggas and dead this whole shit," said Rico, another nigga from the projects that got at a dollar and one of the only niggas that Gangstar might even look up to and take heed to what he says.

"Rico, you of all people, should know I ain't trying to hear none of that shit. My arm in a sling right now 'cause one of them niggas shot me."

"And I feel you on that player, but sometimes you have to pull the wool over niggas eyes, make them think everything is everything, then when they least expect it, then you make your move," stated Rico.

"Yeah, I hear you on that," replied Gangstar in thought, thinking about the jewels Rico just dropped on him, "yeah set that up, but if them niggas try some funny shit, all them niggas is dead, they moms, everybody," Gangstar seriously. "Alright, player, I'm a make the call."

"A'ight do your thing," replied Gangstar, still in thought.

CHAPTER 48

Fallback

"Yo, you a'ight nigga?" asked Q to Cousin, who just came over to his crib.

"Yeah, I'm straight."

"Are you sure? Want a beer or something?" asked Q.

"Nah, but you can roll some of that good shit that the youngins hit us with," replied Cousin Wayne.

"Well, I'll supply the tree but nigga you rolling it up though," replied Q with a laugh.

"Daman nigga I thought I was your guess," replied Cousin Wayne with a light laugh of his own.

"You are, and I appreciate your company, but ah, here you go," replied Q, passing Cousin Wayne the weed and a Backwoods.

"I love you too," said Cousin Wayne grabbing the wraps and weed and beginning to crack it down the middle emptying the guts into an ashtray.

BZZ! BZZ!

"Damn pimp, you over there blowing up, ain't you?" said Q to Cousin Wayne about his pager going off.

"Yo, let me see your phone Q," said Cousin Wayne.

"Here," says Q, passing Cousin Wayne the phone.

Cousin Wayne dials the number on the second ring somebody picks up.

Cousin Wayne says, "Somebody page this number?"

"Whats going on player?" said Rico.

"Yo, who this?" asked Cousin Wayne.

"Rico from the projects."

"Oh, whats up dog?" replies Cousin Wayne.

"Yeah man, I just had a conversation with the boy Gangstar. We was recapping y'all situation and we had a long talk."

Knock, Knock, Cousin Wayne looks at Q and whispers, "This the nigga Rico."

"From the projects?" asked Q.

"Yeah," replies Cousin Wayne with a nod of the head.

Q then heads to the door as he peeks through the peephole, he sees it's Saleem and Scooby then unlocks the door and lets them in, putting a finger to his lips and letting them know to be quiet 'cause Cousin Wayne is on the phone with Rico from the projects. Saleem and Scooby both look at each other with the what look but decide to say nothing and grab a seat on the couch.

"So what are you getting at family?" asked Cousin Wayne.

"Listen, I hollered at the nigga Gangstar and I told him that y'all beef is bad for business and that y'all need to squash it 'cause it's not benefitting neither one of y'all and I ain't going to lie. He was reluctant at first, but after some thought, he agreed to let bygones be bygones. Now I'm not saying to completely let y'all guard down 'cause y'all know what type nigga y'all crew dealing with, so what I'm asking you is can you squash the beef at least for a little while?"

"Family, I feel you got love for you, but a lot of bloodshed has already took place and niggas is on go right now and I wish we could've had this conversation long time ago. I ain't going to promise you nothing, but I'm a holler at my folks and get back to you," replied Cousin Wayne.

"That's all I ask player, but like I said, Gangstar agreed to peace, so you don't have to worry about him," replied Rico.

"Never was worried family," replied Cousin Wayne, "but like I said, I'll talk to my folks and get back to you."

"A'ight player hit me when you ready," replied Rico.

"A'ight," said Cousin Wayne, then hung up.

"Whats good?" asked Saleem.

"That was the nigga Rico from the 'jects; he said that the nigga Gangstar agreed to a truce if we willing to fallback as well," replied Cousin Wayne.

"I don't know about that Cousin Wayne shit real right now," said Scooby.

"Yeah, I feel you on a that," replied Cousin Wayne.

"On some real shit, a truce would be good for right now because It's too much going on. We need to sit back and refocus and in the process, get this money, but if that nigga play his self then off with his head," said Saleem, dead serious.

"Yeah, I'm with that," said Q.

"So, we all agree to fallback for now?" asked Cousin Wayne.

"Yeah." Everybody agreed.

"But always stay alert and aware because to be aware is to be alive," said Cousin Wayne.

"Pass the weed y'all in here smelling real good; smelt that funk through the door," said Scooby with a laugh.

"Hold up youngin'," said Q as he reached for the blunt from Cousin Wayne.

"This nigga been baby sittin' like a Mafucka, while he was on the phone," said Q laughing; everybody laughed with him.

"Man fuck that," said Scooby pulling out his own weed and blunt. Everybody starts laughing again.

"Yo, don't that nigga Boomer come home next week?" asked Q.

"Yeah," Saleem and Scooby said.

"That's why we here. We came to get y'all to rent out the Longshoreman Hall or Ambrosias for us so we can throw Boomer a Welcome Home Party," said Saleem.

"Yeah, that's whats up," said Q.

"Yo y'all should rent out the Crystal Ballroom on Philadelphia Pike and instead of making it a everybody party, it should be a hood party but let bitches from anywhere come in, maybe some niggas from other sides we deal with but fuck everybody else because we still at war in my book. So, we don't wanna make it easy for the enemy, feel me?" said Cousin Wayne.

"Yeah, that sound like a good idea," said Saleem.

"That's all it is then; set it up for us," said Scooby.

"A'ight," replied Cousin Wayne, "let me call Rico and tell him whats going on but remember, stay on point," replied Cousin Wayne.

"You already know ol' head," replied Scooby and Saleem.

CHAPTER 49

The Shoe Box

"This boy must think I'm his own damn personal maid or something; clothes every damn where," said Ms. Betty, discussing how Saleem leaves his sneakers and clothes all over his bedroom floor.

As she continues cleaning, she notices a shoe box underneath his bed which puzzles her 'cause all of his other shoe boxes are in the closet. So, her being nosey, she reaches under the bed and grabs the box; it's kind of heavy.

"What the hell this boy got in here," thinks Ms. Betty as she sits on Saleem's bed and opens the box up.

"I'm a kill this damn boy!" shouts Ms. Betty out loud because she has just found one of Saleem's thirty-eight specials.

This is the one he keeps in his room at all times, fully loaded and a box of shells in the box, some weed, a couple of Phillies blunts and a few hundred dollars.

"I'm a whoop this boy's ass as soon as I see him. I told him I don't want no drugs and guns in my damn house!" exclaims Ms. Betty.

Boomp! Boomp! Boomp!

"Now, who the fuck is this banging on my got damn door like they done lost their mind," said Ms. Betty agitatedly, *"I hope it ain't the cops,"* thinks Ms. Betty, *"let me hide this shit downstairs in the kitchen. If they ain't got no warrant, I ain't lettin' they asses in; they can forget about that."* Boomp! Boomp! Somebody begins banging again.

"Who is it!" screams Ms. Betty coming out of the kitchen after putting the shoe box in the oven.

Ms. Betty snatches open the door with much attitude, only to see that it's not the police but Tommy's sorry ass. Her face is still bruised from the other night. She can't believe this nigga has the audacity to show his face after he done put his hands on her. Anger in her eyes and heart, without saying a word, she turns around, leaving the door open and Tommy standing on the porch looking confused and wondering where she's going. Her leaving the door open, does that mean to come in? With that in mind, Tommy decides to come in, but before he can make it all the way across the threshold, Ms. Betty reappears from the kitchen, squeezing off Saleem's thirty-eight special. Pow! Pow! Pow!

"I told you I was going to kill you motherfucker, didn't I!" screams Ms. Betty with tears coming down her face. Pow! Pow!

Goes the gun as Ms. Betty continues to squeeze off shot after shot with total reckless abandon.

"Oh Shit!" screams Tommy.

One bullet fly past his head, the other hit him in the shoulder, and another in the stomach as the others fly by, just missing him. Tommy takes off running down the steps. Pow! Goes the last shot from the thirty-eight special, but Ms. Betty keeps on squeezing. Click Click Click, goes the empty sound of the thirty-eight. Ms. Betty drops to her knees, drops the gun by her side and watches Tommy disappear. Stuck in a daze, she never notices people forming around the house. She doesn't snap out of her trance until Mr. Pee-Wee across the street touches her on her shoulder to see if she's alright.

"Betty! Betty!" calls Mr. Pee-Wee.

"Huh?" Ms. Betty asked, coming out of her trance.

"You alright?" Mr. Pee-Wee asked again, noticing it was a man in front of her.

Ms. Betty grabs for the gun again, screaming, "I'm a kill you motherfucker!" not realizing its Pee-Wee from across the street, not Tommy. Pee-Wee grabs the gun and grabs Betty in his arms.

"It's me Pee-Wee. Calm down. I got you. It's Pee-Wee. Calm down," consoles Pee-Wee. Ms. Betty begins to relax.

"Get the fuck out my way! Watch out!" somebody outside is saying.

Then Saleem and Scooby emerge through the door, guns drawn.

"What the fuck happened!" exclaims Saleem.

Pee-Wee turns and tells Saleem what happened. Saleem is visibly pissed off and shouts, "I'm a kill that nigga! Mom, you okay?" asked Saleem, grabbing his mom and hugging her tight.

"Ms. Betty, I'm a kill that nigga myself," said Scooby heatedly. Saleem notices the thirty-eight picks it up and tells Scooby to take it and get rid of it. Scooby grabs it tucks it and disappears out the door.

"Mom, get up. Get yourself together before the cops come." Saleem grabs her chin so she can make eye contact to see if she comprehends him. When he does, he notices the swelling and bruises on her face.

She notices that he notices and turns away and whispers, "I got 'em; he paid for it."

But Saleem doesn't give a fuck 'cause as far as he's concerned, got 'em ain't got' em until he died. He helps his mom up, thanks Pee-Wee, pass him a few dollars and tells him to close and lock the door and to dispense all those people from in front of the house. Pee-Wee nods his head and leaves. Saleem helps his mom up the steps, takes her to her room, runs some bath water and grabs two Advil outta the medicine cabinet. He runs downstairs and grabs a glass of Kool-Aid for his mom, then shoots back upstairs and goes into his mom's bedroom and tells her to take the pills and let her know he's running her a bath. He goes into her closet and grabs his mom's favorite bubble bath called Skin So Soft; that shit smells good she loves that shit. Saleem goes to the bathroom and pours it into the tub, smelling up the whole house. Saleem goes in and checks on his mom, whose now sitting up, sipping her Kool-Aid.

"You okay now?" asked Saleem.

"Yeah baby, I'm fine. Can you look under my bed and grab that brown bottle?" asked Ms. Betty.

Saleem kneeled down and reached under the bed and grabbed a big brown bottle, which he knew exactly what it was because he used to sneak in his mom's room when he was little, searching around for stuff all in his mom's everything. His mom used to call what he was doing plundering. He smiles as he passes her the bottle that he used to stay sippin' on getting a little buzz and he used to tear it up 'cause it tasted good.

"Mom, whats this?" asked Saleem playing dumb.

"Why you ain't gettin' none of it," replied Ms. Betty.

"I ain't want none anyway; it ain't strong enough. I drink Hennessy," said Saleem.

"Boy, your ass shouldn't be drinking nothing," replies Ms. Betty seriously.

"Mom it smell like it got fruit in it," said Saleem playing dumb as Ms. Betty poured some in her Kool-Aid.

"It do got fruit in it. That's why it's called Peachtree Schnapps," replied Ms. Betty with a smirk.

Saleem goes into the bathroom to turn off the water in the tub and yells, "Mom, your bath ready!"

"Okay, I'll be in there in a minute!" shouts Ms. Betty.

Boom!! Boom!! Boom!!

"Damn, that's probably the police," thinks Saleem.

So, he goes back into his mom's room so he can peek out her window. Sure, enough, it's a cop car sitting across the street, but it's still two cops in it.

"Is it the cops?" asked Ms. Betty.

"I'm not sure mom. It's a police car across the street, but both police are still sitting in the car looking over," he replied Saleem, "you want me to answer it? The gun is gone. I got mine on me. I can run it out back right quick."

"Boy, how many damn guns you got?"

Boomp! Boomp! Goes the door again.

"Mom, get in the tub; hurry up and take your clothes off. I'm a take them out back just in case the cops try to take them and test them for gunpowder residue."

"Saleem, you been watching Matlock too damn much with me," said Ms. Betty laughing, "pass me my robe."

Ms. Betty disrobes and heads for the shower. Saleem rushes downstairs and peeks out the back window making sure the close is clear them he goes outback and drops his mom's clothes in the neighbor's trash can then, hides his gun then proceeds to go to the front door.

"Who is it?" asked Saleem in a disguised deep voice.

"It's me nigga, with your fake ass deep voice," clowns Scooby.

Saleem opens the door and lets Scooby in, then closes the door slowly not to appear in a rush so as not to look suspicious to the cops.

"Yo, Ms. Betty okay?" asked Scooby, concerned.

"Yeah, she good, she taking a bath."

"Oh word, I'm up there," says Scooby faking like he is on his way up the steps, but Saleem steps in front of him.

"Yo stop playin' before I fuck Ms. Cheryl," replied Saleem with a big smile on his face knowing Scooby ain't like that snappy comeback about his mom.

"Yo, chill with that dumb shit Leem," says Scooby, not smiling at all.

"See, you don't like it when the shoe on the other foot nigga. So, whats up out there?" asked Saleem.

"I got rid of the pistol and came straight back, played the crowd to see what people saying, then the cops pulled up and parked. People started movin' out. I walked down the street and sat on the steps with a couple bitches basically waiting to see what the cops was going to do. Ain't nobody approaches 'em and say shit. They did call a couple Lil' kids over to the car, but it was Lil' bad ass Darryl-Darryl and Tone-Tone. I saw Tone-Tone grab his Lil' dick and run down the street. Everybody started laughing, but other than that, that's it. I think they got a shots fired call but don't really know where the shots came from. They said Ms. Betty hit that nigga up, so if he a sucker he goin' rat, but if not, she should be cool," said Scooby, "but yo, you know what else I was thinking," says Scooby.

"What?" asked Saleem.

"Man, them Mafuckas could be waiting for a warrant to come search this Mafucka. You don't got nothing in here do you?" asked Scooby.

"Man, a Lil' bit of weed and some money, you know I moved that heavy shit up outta here like a week ago."

"Okay, that was smart," replied Scooby, "now you have to get that weed up out of here."

"Yeah, you right; let me go grab it," says Saleem.

He rushes upstairs, looks under his bed, then realizes damn, his mom found the weed, too, if she had the gun. So, he knocks on the bathroom door and asks his mom where the weed is so he can get it out of there. She tells him as he laughs and rushes back down the stairs, takes it out of the oven, and then goes out back and ditches it in his neighbor's yard. Comes back to the crib.

"Yo, I stashed that shit. Yo, I was thinkin' about getting one of them cellphone joints, just be careful how we talk on them," said Saleem.

"Yeah, that would be the shit if we had those. All them big-time niggas got 'em," said Scooby.

"Yo Cousin Wayne was talking about he know where to get some burnout joints. They'll be easy to dispose of," said Saleem.

"Well, we got to get on top of that 'cause there more convenient instead of keep having to run to pay phones every time."

BZZ! BZZ! Goes Saleem's pager; he looks at the number.

"Yo, this Cousin Wayne and them right here probably calling to see what happened. I'm about to call them," said Saleem as he walked into the kitchen to use the phone.

He dials the number and Cousin Wayne picks up on the first ring.

"Yo, whats up, Mom Betty a'ight?" asked Cousin Wayne with concern in his voice.

"Yeah, she straight she got into it with her boyfriend. I'll let you know specifics later on the police out front, but they ain't making no moves. I don't think they know what happened. They just know that shots was fired in this area. Scooby said they could be waiting on a warrant," says Saleem.

"That's true, but I highly doubt it, though," said Cousin Wayne.

"Why you say that?" asked Saleem curiously.

"Because one, just to be nosey, they would've come and at least knocked on the door by now and started asking questions plus, if they knew for a fact that somebody was in danger, they wouldn't need a warrant."

"Why not?" asked Saleem.

"Because they got this law called exigent circumstances, which means without a warrant they can come up in ya crib if they believe that someone is in danger or say if they think you was destroying evidence they can come in and arrest you without a warrant," says Cousin Wayne.

"Damn nigga, what you Johnny Cochran or something," said Saleem with a laugh.

"Nah nigga, but I done been to jail enough to pick up on something though," said Cousin Wayne with a laugh of his own, "yo let me know the rest when you get a chance; tell Mom Betty I said if she need something me and Q got her," said Cousin Wayne.

"That's whats up dog, but yo, before you go me and Scooby want you to grab us two of those burnouts," said Saleem.

"A'ight," said Cousin Wayne, "I'm a get on top of that a.s.a.p."

"Okay," replied Saleem, then hung up, "yo Cousin Wayne said it's a go on the burnouts."

"That's all it is then," replied Scooby.

"Yo, look out the window and see what 5-0 doin'," said Saleem.

Scooby peeks out the living room window and looks across the street, then turns to Saleem and says, "Dog them mafuckas gone."

"Word?" asked Saleem, surprised.

"Word," replied Scooby, "yo niggas know we up right now so they know if word get out they told they lives is at stake," said Scooby.

"Yeah, you right to dog niggas ain't dumb at all," replied Saleem realizing that he and his comrade got more power than they could ever imagine and just think they were only 15 and 16 years old.

CHAPTER 50

Boomer is Home "The Party"

"Biggie, give me one more chance Biggie, Biggie, give me one more chance."

"Yeah! Yeah! Everybody put your mafuckin' hands in the air and help welcome home a real nigga. Shout out to Boomer, who just came home! You look good, baby boy!" shouts DJ Ashley, a local DJ/hustler from round the way.

The crowd goes crazy at the mention of Boomer's name. Saleem, Scooby, Boomer and the crew are in V.I.P., each with their own bottle of Moet champagne, looking like a million bucks bitches everywhere looking their best, a couple of niggas that the team fuck with from everywhere.

"Welcome home baby," said Saleem, "a toast to my nigga Boomer. I love you like a brother; fuck that, you are my brother. We all family, it's money out here to be made and it's ours for the taken. We up right now and the plan is to stay up. Don't ever let nothing or nobody ever come between us, not no money, not no nigga and damn sure not no scandalous ass bitch. United we stand, United we fall," Saleem raises his bottle and stretches his arm out so everyone can clink bottles in agreement.

He then turns to Boomer and hugs him tightly then everyone follows suit. Scooby, Saleem and Boomer take a seat at their own private table in the V.I.P. section and begin conversing amongst each other.

"How you feeling dog?" Scooby to Boomer.

"Man, I feel like royalty right now. I can't even lie; I wasn't expecting all of this. This some boss-type shit. Y'all fuckin' it up out here obviously whats really good?" questions Boomer.

"Listen dog, yo boys done came up on some ole lick of a lifetime type shit, but here's the thing, you family, so you know if we up you up. We going to set you up with everything you need. We going to get you a apartment set you up with your own block and later on, we got a surprise for you right now. Just enjoy yourself," said Saleem.

"Man, that's love," replied Boomer, "I got some questions, though."

"What?" replied Saleem.

"Man, whats up with these project niggas?" Saleem and Scooby look at each other because they know that that was coming.

"Well, as of right now, that's on pause per Cousin Wayne, but at the same time, the word is stay on point and if them niggas get outta pocket lights out," said Saleem seriously.

"Man fuck that pause shit dog them pussy ass niggas kilt my boy Twin," said Boomer heatedly.

Just as Cousin Wayne and Q walk over to the table and sit down, they say their whats up and pass Boomer a yellow manilla envelope filled with money in it.

Boomer graciously excepts it, but then he says, "Whats up with this pause on getting at them project niggas." Cousin Wayne sees the anger in Boomer's face, so he proceeds with caution, not no bitch shit on some ole he knows that Boomer is hot-headed, especially when he's been drinking and he knows how close he was to Twin.

So, in a calm voice, Cousin Wayne says, "Since you've been gone a lot has happened, a lot of blood has been shed, a lot of moves has been made for the good and to be able to benefit off of those moves we putting that beef shit on pause. At the same time, always stay on point but also know that shit ain't over with; it's still on. Just right now, it's about this money," said Cousin Wayne.

Boomer nods his head in agreement, then says, "If them niggas do anything outta pocket, I mean anything with or without niggas, I'm a get at them niggas," said Boomer dead serious, meaning every word.

"I feel you, Lil' brother," replied Cousin Wayne, "now with that out the way, let's enjoy this party, said Cousin Wayne. Boomer looks into the envelope and sees all the hundred-dollar bills.

"Yo, thank y'all man," said Boomer reaching out to shake Cousin Wayne and Q's hand. "That ain't about nothing," replies Cousin Wayne.

As the night progresses, everybody is feeling good. The party is starting to fade and all the squad is leaving with bitches. Cousin Wayne and Q say their goodbyes leaving with their bitches.

"Yo dog, remember I told you we got a surprise for you," said Saleem to Boomer.

"Yeah, where it's at nigga? I've been waiting to see it all night. What, you got some butt-naked bitches hiding somewhere?" asked Boomer.

"Nah nigga come with us," said Saleem leading Boomer out the back of the club into the back lot.

As soon as Boomer steps outside, he sees a black-on-black Honda Accord with a ribbon on it.

"Oh shit! Is that mines?!" exclaims Boomer excitedly.

"Yeah nigga that's all you; come get the keys and open the door," said Saleem smiling.

Boomer grabs the keys, opens up the door and jumps back a little and says, "What the fuck!" as he bends down and looks into the car, "oh shit!"

exclaims Boomer again, not believing his eyes sitting on the passenger side is a badass yellow bone stripper phat as shit just smiling with nothing but a thong on, titties out and a pair of them clear type-high heels they be wearing.

"Oh yeah, it's on," said Boomer excitedly.

The stripper says, "Are you going to get in daddy? I've been waiting on you all night."

Boomer looks at Saleem and Scooby, who are both smiling. Boomer looks back at the stripper and says, "Hell yeah, I'm coming. You will too, as soon as I get this dick up in you," replies Boomer.

The stripper smiles and says, "Don't threaten me with a good time."

CHAPTER 51

Time for New Management

"I grew up on the crime side, the New York time side. Stayin' alive no jive..." C.R.E.A.M. by Wu-Tang Clan played in the background while OX, Ghost, and Dreadz counted the money up.

"Yo God, dis da most money I ever seen at one time," said Ox.

"Yeah, well, it's plenty more where that a came from Kid," replied Dreadz.

"Yeah, well, it looks like maybe for you," said Ghost with a distasteful look on his face.

"Fuck you mean by dat son?" asked Dreadz heatedly.

"You know exactly what I mean, Duke da only nigga really seein' this paper properly is you," replied Ghost looking Dreadz directly in the eyes.

"On word, that's how you feelin' after all the love I showed you and show you?" asked Dreadz with visible hurt in his eyes.

"Yo Kid, you outta line right now the God, the reason why we down here eatin' at all when we was up top shit was mad difficult; Kid and you know that," states Ox seriously.

"And I feel all that, but we should and could be eatin' a whole lot better. Its Lil' niggas around the corner movin' bricks of they own shit and we around here pitchin' pebbles fuck that shit son; it's time for bigger and better things. It's time for new management," replied Ghost pulling out his 9mm pistol.

"Yo son, what da fuck!" said Ox stepping in front of Ghost.

"Nah Ox, we deserve to be on top. This nigga done came to Delaware and got soft lettin' these slow ass niggas eat while we starve. Me and you both know that kid Saleem had something to do with Omega and his team getting killed. Them young niggas wasn't just making this kinda noise before," said Ghost.

"So, what I'm suppose to be scared 'cause you pulled your gun son?" asked Dreadz.

"I wouldn't give a fuck whether you was scared or not. The time has come for you to step down and let a real nigga take over. A nigga with heart that won't let these pussy ass Delaware niggas get away with murder, literally," replied Ghost.

"So, you think I don't know that them niggas around the corner possibly has something to do with Omega's death? You think I didn't have love for that nigga? Me and Omega go back like car seats and five-star (besties) that was ma man. He bought a lot of product off of me, but in this business and in this life, people die and when they die, that don't mean you stop livin'. Yeah, we can handle them Lil' niggas around the corner easily, but we'll be ridin' off of emotion. Never put your 'E' before your 'I' which means your intellect over your emotions. Always I before E. Now when Omega died, he left a void that needed to be filled and them Lil' niggas around the corner is filling that void," said Dreadz dropping knowledge and making plenty of sense, "but when your young and a hot head, the voice of reason is irrelevant to you to it goes in one ear and out the other."

"Oh, so now you agree that them niggas around the corner had something to do with Omega's death, but it's okay 'cause they fillin' a void?" asked Ghost in discuss without hesitation in one swift motion he pushed Ox out of his way raised his pistol and squeezed off hitting Dreadz high in the center of his chest knocking him backwards up against the wall. Clutching his chest in disbelief, looking at Ghost shocked, "Yo, what the fuck Kid! Why you do that?" asked Ox, also in shock and disbelief, "yo son, you buggin' out!" exclaims Ox.

"Nah fuck this nigga. He lost his way, he soft; like I said its time for new management either you wit me or against me ma nigga," states Ghost staring Ox in the eyes but also keeping a steady eye on Dreadz, who is now sitting on the floor bleeding profusely from the hole in his chest.

"Son, this ain't right; it was a better way to handle this," said Ox.

"Fuck all that son. I asked you a question; is you wit me or against me?" asked Ghost harshly, now aiming the gun directly at Ox.

"You got that son. I'm with you Kid," replied Ox.

As soon as Ghost lowers his gun, Ox bull rushes him to the floor, making Ghost drop the gun and slide across the floor. Dreadz losing lots of blood wants to get up and go for the pistol but is too weak to do so. He's also starting to slip in and out of consciousness rendering him useless as well as helpless. Ox climbs on top of Ghost and tries to punch holes through him, but Ghost blocks most of the punches. Ox tries to get up and go for the gun, but Ghost half forcefully kicks Ox in the balls, making him fall face first, clutching his balls to the floor. Ghost pushes Ox out of the way and then tries to crawl to the gun, but Ox grabs his leg and rolls him back toward him. Then he takes to go after the gun but instead is tripped right before he can reach it. Ghost Jumps up and (dikes) overtop of Ox for the gun. He grabs it and turns to shoot Ox, but Ox is on him like flies on shit. They both tussle and struggle for the gun. Boom! a loud echo from the gun goes off. Everything is silent for a moment, no one is moving.

CHAPTER 52

Loyalty to Gangstar

"Yo Bucket, I know you better not scratch ma muthafuckin' car nigga!" yells Gangstar to a junkie that he's payin' in drugs to wash his navy-blue Beamer with light navy-blue tints factory rims on it.

"Baby boy, you know I know better than to fuck ya shit up hell, I'll slap ma own self first," says the junkie with a chuckle but probably meant every word because, like most, Gangstar got the fear of God in 'em.

"Yeah, well, yo better do a good job if you tryin' to get paid Mafucka,," replied Gangstar.

"I got chu' baby!! Baby, I got chu'," says the junkie quickly, not wanting to piss Gangstar off 'cause he knows Gangstar is probably looking for my excuse not to pay 'em anyway.

Everybody usually pays him up of front but not Gangstar, but he puts up with it 'cause he knows he doesn't have a choice in the matter, no how.

"Yo Star whats up, big homie?" asked one of Gangstar's youngins."

"Ain't shit up but this money. What, you out of work or somethin'?" asked Gangstar.

"Nah, big homie, I was just sayin' whats up and tryin' to see if you know that the nigga Boomer from two-four came home and they threw a party for 'em last night."

"Yeah, I heard nigga, so the fuck what," replied Gangstar harshly.

"My bad Star, I was trying to fill you in just in case you didn't know," said the young boy timidly.

"I wouldn't give if the nigga was Lucifer himself. My heart don't pump no Kool-Aid. He can die just like anybody else. He come at me with that bullshit if he want to, he'll be laying next to that nigga Twin wit holes all in 'em," replied Gangstar.

"I'm wit chu' big homie, its whatever all you have to do is say when," said Star's young boy, anxious to put that work in to prove his loyalty to Gangstar.

Gangstar cracks a devilish smile then tells his Lil' homie, "In due time, in due time you can believe that, but if them niggas step out of line, sooner than later, then off with their heads."

CHAPTER 53

Taking Over the Operation

"Yo son, see what chu made me do all fuck! fuck!" exclaims Ghost, who in the midst of the struggle with Ox, squeezed the trigger hitting Ox in the stomach and knocking all the fight and wind out of him.

"All shit son, Fuck, this your fault! It could've be me and you baby!" exclaims Ghost, not wanting it to go like this.

Ghost had plans on taking over the operation a while ago and pictured Ox with 'em now with Dreadz dyin' and Ox hit. He knows for now; he is going to be all alone.

"Fuck! Fuck! Fuck! Think! Think! Think!" Ghost says out loud to himself.

He begins wiping down everything, grabbing two duffel bags and starts filling them up with cash. He runs over to Dreadz and takes his keys because they're to his house where a stash is, to the stash spots, and dope houses are where he's going to collect and set up shop and keep things going. Maybe bring some more down from NY and search around for a Connect, but he has to clean this shit up right now. So, he grabbed some gasoline in sprinkled it all over the place, even on Dreadz and Ox, who were both still alive. Ghost lit a match to a piece of paper, then dropped it to the floor, setting the house ablaze; instantly, it goes up in flames. As Ghost rushes out the back door, you can hear the screams of Ox and Dreadz screaming from the pain of being burned alive.

CHAPTER 54

Boomer and the Stripper

"Damn, something smell good as shit," said Boomer as he awakes ass naked, not remembering too much of anything from last night but no knew one thing he ain't in jail.

As he focuses his eyes around the room of the hotel and sees the sexy light bitch from last night that he does remember. As memories start flooding back in, images of the Fuck Fest they had.

"Hey sleepy head, I ordered room service," said the stripper.

"Whats up girl? I hope you ain't order no pork."

"Oh no sexy, I don't eat pork either," replied the stripper.

"I can't tell as phat as you is," said Boomer sizing the stripper up.

"Boy, you a mess," replied the stripper with a smile, "I got turkey bacon and eggs, toast butter, jelly, orange juice, grits and home fries."

"Yeah, that's what I'm talking about," replied Boomer, all hungry.

"I got chu' daddy," said the stripper in a seductive voice.

After stuffing his face, Boomer get up to take a piss.

"Damn daddy, a bitch can get use to that," said the stripper eyeing Boomer's election.

Boomer notices what she's eyein' and says, "As good as this mafucker is, what bitch wouldn't."

Then heads to the bathroom to relieve himself. He tears off a piece of toilet tissue, wets it, then wipes the tip of his dick head off, not noticing the stripper standing in the door.

She asks, "Why you do that daddy?"

"Why I do what?" asked Boomer, not understanding her question.

"Why you use that toilet paper to wipe off your dick head."

"Ha! Ha! Ha!" Boomer bust out laughin'.

"What chu' laughing at?" asked the stripper, not understandin' what's so funny.

When Boomer pulls himself together, he tells her that he's Muslim and its permissible for him to wipe off his penis after urinating.

"OOH," said the stripper kind of intrigued by what Boomer has just told her, "I never heard or seen anyone do that before that's why I asked," said the stripper.

"It ain't about nothing, that's how you learn," replied Boomer.

"Not to change the subject, but can I show you how I would clean it for you?" asked the stripper taking Boomer by the hand and leading him to the bed.

"Lay down daddy," said the stripper. Boomer complies and lies back on the bed.

The stripper says, "This how I would of cleaned it up." And begins to lick and suck just the tip of Boomer's dick.

"Tist! Shit! Damn! Girl, that it just like that," says Boomer making all types of faces enjoying the feelin' the stripper is giving him. The stripper begins to deep throat him, smack the sides of her face and mouth with his dick occasionally spitting on it and jerking him off all at the same time driving Boomer mad. He keeps squirming, trying to keep himself together, but this bitch is a fuckin' beast. Before he bust, Boomer pulls her hair, working her from out of his lap.

"Damn girl, you tryin' turn a nigga out, you ain't slick."

The stripper starts smiling because she knows he's right. Being the dirty dick nigga Boomer is, he tells the stripper to lay down on her stomach in the elephant position and gets on top of her and starts layin' pipe.

"Oh My God daddy fuck this pussy! Fuck me harder daddy fuck me!"

"You like that bitch huh! You like that dick up in you?" asked Boomer.

"Yes daddy! Yes Oh My God I'm cumming all over that dick!" screams the stripper.

"I'm bout to cum too," said Boomer, "on shit here it come! Catch it, catch it aww! Yeah!" exclaims Boomer.

"I got it daddy umm, umm!" replied the stripper catching everything and swallowing it.

"All yeah, that's what I'm talkin' bout, oh shit!" exclaimed Boomer pushing the stripper away and falling back on the bed, exhausted and drained, "damn girl, you Fucking Beast!"

Boomer gets up, grabs his jacket, pulls out some weed that Saleem gave him and told him to try it out. After cracking and rolling it up, he sparks it takes a toke and on cue, he goes into a coughin' fit.

"Got damn what da fuck is this shit!" he said out loud, passing it to the stripper who tokes a long toke herself, not knowing the potency of the weed and begins coughin' up a lung.

"That shit real ain't it?" asked Boomer laughing at the stripper bout to die.

"I got to holler at my niggas about this shit," said Boomer.

He reaches in his pants, grabs a wad of money at passes the stripper $300.

She said, "Thank you but your boys already paid me for the night."

"Well, that's for the love you showed me today and leave your info so I can hit chu' up sometime." Basically, letting the stripper know it's time to roll.

"Well, let me get myself together," replied the stripper as she gathered her stuff, called a cab, and waited.

"Yo, whats your name?"

"Precious is my stripper name, but Crystal is my real name."

"Oh okay, so what do you want me to call you?" asked Boomer.

"Either one," replied the stripper.

"A'ight," says Boomer, "don't be no stranger."

"I work up Philly at night on Broad."

"Oh okay, dats whats up? I'll check you out from time to time."

"You better. I need some more of that good-ass dick," said the stripper laughing but serious.

"Don't worry, I got chu'."

Ring! Ring! Goes the hotel phone, and the stripper picks it up.

"Hello."

"Room 112, this is the front desk. Your cab is ready," says the receptionist.

"Thank you," says the stripper, then hangs up.

"Well, hope to see you again," said the stripper.

"Ah, you will," replied Boomer with a smile.

The stripper blows him a kiss as she leaves. Boomer lays back on the bed and contemplates what's to come, which he hopes is to run the city, but little did he know his boys already got that plan in motion.

CHAPTER 55

Ayonna Spent the Night

BZZ! BZZ! Goes the sound of Saleem's pager. Saleem takes it off of his hip and reads the numbers that it displays; not recognizing them, he puts the pager back on his hip, *"Whoever it is, he'll call back later,"* he thinks to himself.

"Babe, who that, one of your other bitches you don't want me to know about?" asked Ayonna, who stayed the night over at Saleem's after Boomer's welcome home party; she told her mom she was staying over at a friend's house.

"Girl, stop trippin' early in the morning. Matter fact, here petty ass call the number back but not from here. Go across the street to the pay phone," said Saleem passing Ayonna the pager.

"Boy ain't nobody petty and you think 'cause you said use the pay phone, I won't go check," replied Ayonna thinking Saleem was just trying to deter her from calling the number.

She snatches the pager out of Saleem's hands and the pager goes off in her hand, startling her and making her drop it to the floor.

"Oh Shit!" she screeches.

"Look at chu' you so damn tough, scared of a damn pager," remarks Saleem.

"Forget chu' punk!" retorts Ayonna bending over to pick up the pager.

"Damn bitches all desperate calling back-to-back," said Ayonna sarcastically, looking at the number in confusion, then at Saleem, then back at the number.

"Ah Ahhh!! Why the fuck is my dad paging you Saleem?" asked

Ayonna with anger and tears in her eyes.

"Girl, what the fuck you talking about?" asked Saleem.

"This is my dad's number. Saleem, why is he paging and don't lie either," replied Ayonna.

Saleem takes the pager out of her hand and looks at the number, then realizes damn it is her dad's number, so the comes up with a quick lie, "Girl, to be honest with you, me and your dad been bustin' it up lately. He says that he knows we been messing around for a while and he hope that if we having sex make sure to wear protection and keep you out of harm's way. You know shit, a real father is suppose to do for his little girl. Is there anything else you want to grill me about detective?" asked Saleem with a laugh.

"Boy, forget chu' and I wasn't grilling you; I know bitches be trying holler at chu now you driving and so-called making your little bit of money," replied Ayonna.

"Girl, don't spend no more of this little bit of money then."

"Sike babe, I was just playin'," said Ayonna in her little girl voice because since Saleem been getting money he's been getting her pockets laced and her wardrobe even flyer than it was already, so she don't want to be cut off no time soon.

"So, are you going to call him back?"

"Yeah, let me put my shirt on and some sneakers right quick," said Saleem setting up off of the bed.

"Babe Imma make you and Scooby some breakfast, and you better not tell my dad I stayed the night over here," said Ayonna.

"Shid Imma tell 'em how you was calling me daddy last night when I had all this dick up in you," replied Saleem laughing hard as Shit.

"And Imma crack you to punk," replied Ayonna laughing herself.

Saleem heads out the door and across the street to the pay phone to call Ayonna's dad. The phone rings twice before Ayonna's dad picks up.

"Yo, somebody page this number?" asked Saleem.

"Yeah, whats up, young blood? This Ayonna's pop. Can we talk?"

"Yeah, meet me at the gas station on 40th and Market by the McDonalds," says Saleem, then hangs up, shoots back to the apartment and tells Ayonna her dad needs to talk to him in person, and he'll be right back.

"About what?" asked Ayonna, all nosey.

"Damn girl, you in everything but a hearse," said Saleem jokingly.

"Forget chu' punk, don't be all long," said Ayonna as Saleem shoots back out the door.

CHAPTER 56

The Fire

"As soon as I get home, I'll make it up to you, Baby I'll do what I gotta do," sings Tonya Dreadz, old lady, to her favorite song, *"Soon As I Get Home"* by Faith Evans.

As she gets closer to her street, she can see ambulances, fire trucks and tons of people in the street. As she gets closer, she can see flames and smoke shooting from houses on her side of the street.

"What the fuck!" she yells out loud, cutting down the music.

"Oh My God!" she gasps as she realizes that among the houses is her own.

Tears begin to fall as she says a silent prayer that Dreadz is not in there. She left earlier to give him and his Boys some space while they counted the money and whatever else. It didn't matter because he gave a wad of cash and told her to go shop but make sure she stopped by the Jamaican spot and grabbed his favorite platter of Ox tails, rice and cabbage, which she also got herself some jerk chicken and rice. Now, as she gets to the house as far as she can, she gets out of the car in shock. People from the neighborhood walk up to her and tell her that they thought she was in there.

"Is Dreadz in there?"

"People said they heard shots come from the house right before it caught fire and then spread to the others."

"Oh My God, did anybody see Dreadz or his boys come out of there?" asked Tonya.

"No girl, nobody came out that I saw," said one of the nosey bystanders.

As time passed, firefighters started to bring out black body bags.

"Oh My God!" screams Tonya as she rushes towards the firefighters.

"Let me see. My boyfriend might be in one of those."

Police and firemen grab her and hold her back.

One tells her, "Sorry mam, you can't see the bodies right now they're burned beyond recognition."

She breaks down in the officer's arms. Detective Cropper steps up and asks her to come with him. She tries to pull herself together as best she can. Det. Cropper walks her to his car, opens the door, and guides her in the passenger side, then walks around and gets inside.

"Listen mam, I know your upset right now but do you have any idea whats going on?"

"No, I just came home," replied Tonya.

"Well, do you know who was in the residence and is this your residence?" asked Detective Cropper.

"It's my house, me and my boyfriend," replied Tonya.

"Your boyfriend have a name mam?" asked Det. Cropper.

"Yes, his name is Curtis Freeman," says Tonya.

"Curtis Freeman, Curtis Freeman," repeats Det. Cropper to himself, *"where do I know that name?"*

Then it hits him, Dreadz, the New York guy he used to lean on when he first started out down here.

"Damn, somebody finally had the balls to kill the out-of-towner," thinks Det. Cropper.

"So, mam does this Curtis Freeman go by any nicknames?" asked Det.

Cropper.

Tonya hesitated at first but Det. Cropper reassures her that anything she says is confidential and will help find out who had anything to do with this if these fire victims turn out to be homicide victims.

So she loosens up a little, takes a breath, then relaxes and says, "Yes, his street name is Dreadz."

Det. Cropper pretends he hasn't heard of Dreadz and fakes like he's taking notes on his pad.

"So when you left the house, was there anyone else besides Mr. Freeman?" asked Det. Cropper.

"Well, just a couple of his friends," replied Tonya.

"You say a couple?" asked Det. Cropper.

"Yeah," replied Tonya.

"Well, as of right now, only two bodies have been discovered in the blaze," says Det. Cropper.

"Oh My God, so you saying that somebody's still alive?" asked Tonya.

"Yes mam, unless it's a body still in there that hasn't been detected," said Det. Cropper.

"I need to see if I can identify the bodies that did come out," said Tonya.

"Well mam, that'll be hard to do, beings though they're burned so badly," said Det. Cropper. Tears fill Tonya's eyes, mind racing a hundred miles a minute.

"Excuse me mam, could you please give me the names of the other people that were in the house when you left?" asked Det. Cropper.

"Well, one name was Ox, and the other one name was Ghost," sobs a distraught Tonya.

"I know this is probably hard for you mam, but we need all the help we can get, and you are doing a very good job," says Det. Cropper trying to muster up a comforting voice, "ah, mam do these other gentlemen have government names that you could give me?" asked Det. Cropper.

"They do sir, but I don't know them," replied Tonya.

"Well, do you have any idea where they live or where they are from or do they have any girlfriends or relatives we can contact?" asked Det. Cropper.

"Sorry sir, the only thing I know is that they're originally from New York City. I don't know what part, and I don't know of any relatives or girlfriends either," replied Tonya truthfully.

"Okay, mam, here's my card. If you find out my other information, please contact me. Also, when you have a chance, please come to the station and take a look at some photos. Maybe we can put a face and name on these other gentlemen, especially the one that may still be alive and if you run into the other guy, please contact us immediately so we can take him in for questioning," says Det. Cropper.

"Okay," replied Tonya wiping away tears, wondering who survived and what happened.

Never in her wildest dreams would she think Ghost....

CHAPTER 57

Saleem Meets Mr. Smallwood and Big Red

"A drug dealer's dream: Stash C.R.E.A.M., keys on a triple beam 500 SL green, '95 nickle gleam Condominium, thug dressed like a gentleman..." Raps Nas on Mobb Deep's Infamous Album.

Saleem cruises through the streets on his way to meet Ayonna's dad Mr. Smallwood. As he gets closer to the gas station and 40th and Market St., he turns down his music and pulls into the back of the station closest to the drive-thru car wash, right next to a blue Cadillac Sedan De Ville, which he knows to be Mr. Smallwood's.

Mr. Smallwood rolls down the window and says, "Whats up, big time? Hop in, I need to talk to you."

Saleem opens up his glove compartment, grabs a pen, then hops out of his car, locks it up, tells Mr. Smallwood to hold up, runs into the gas station, grabs a notepad, pays the cashier, and then walks back to Mr. Smallwood's car and gets in.

"Whats up, Mr. Smallwood?" asked Saleem.

"You, whats up young blood and call me Mr. Smalls, you family," said Mr. Smallwood.

"Solid," replied Saleem, "so whats up?" asked Saleem.

"Like I said big time, you whats up. Remember I told you I was going to be in contact with you; now's that time," said Mr. Smallwood starting up his car.

"So where we going?" questions Saleem.

"For a ride to one of my spots, I hang out so we can talk," replied Mr. Smallwood, "and I want you to meet some very important people that might be of value to you."

"Oh yeah," replied Saleem as they rode to their destination.

Mr. Smallwood turns on his radio and outcomes Bobby Womack, *"If you think you're lonely now, Oh, wait until tonight, girl."*

"What chu' know about that young blood?" asked Mr. Smallwood, looking over at Saleem with a smirk. Saleem surprises him and sings the song.

"When it's cold outside, tell me baby, who are you holdin'" sings Saleem.

"Aww Shit, young blood, you know a little sumptin', I see," exclaimed a surprised Mr. Smallwood.

"Yeah, I know a little bit," replied Saleem with a smirk of his own.

Mr. Smallwood pulls up on the side of an old head bar called LeRoy's. Saleem looks around he sees a cranberry Lexus LS 400 that looks kinda like Dreadz, but the color is different and the interior is milky white leather. The Lexus emblems are gold trimmed and so are the rims. They've been dipped in gold as well.

"That shit pretty," says Saleem out loud.

"You like that young blood?" asked Mr. Smallwood.

"Yeah, that shit fly," replied Saleem.

"Well, I'm about to introduce you to the owner of it," says Mr. Smallwood as he and Saleem exit his Caddy and enters the bar.

"Smalls! Hey player Smalls! What chu' got your son witchu today pimp?" inquires all the different patrons of the bar.

"Hey Smalls, you know I don't allow no kids in here man!" shouts the owner LeRoy.

"Cool out LeRoy, he good this Betty son," replied Smalls knowing that the old timer got a thing for Saleem's mom.

"Oh yeah, he sure do look like Betty now that you say that. Tell ya momma Mr. Leroy said hi," said LeRoy switching his tone of voice. Saleem gives the old man a head nod as if he's really going to relay the message. As they approach a table in the back, a heavy-set light-skinned man motions with his head to come over to his table. The man told them to have a seat when they reached the table.

"How are you gentlemen doing? Can get cha'll a drink?"

Saleem shakes his head no. Smalls, on the other hand, shouts out, "Order for a double shot of Jack Daniels and a Heineken!"

"So who do we have here Smalls?" asked the light-skinned man.

"This the kid I was telling you about that's on the come up.

Saleem, this the man I was telling you about. This is Sammy Cooper, better known to the streets as Big Red," says Smalls.

"Please to meet chu'," Saleem says to Big Red with a big out, stretched hand.

Saleem shakes his hand and then says, "So whats this all about?"

"Well, straight to the point, I like that," says Big Red, "well let me tell…."

"Hold up," says Saleem pulling out the paper and pen, "no disrespect, but I don't know you, so I don't want to talk out loud; so we can converse on paper, and before we leave, I tear it all up in front of you."

"A Smalls, I like this cat already," says Big Red, then with a serious face, says, "son, I respect what you putting down with that pen and pad Situation but dig this here I'm Samuel Dorrell Cooper and I ain't never been no rat and never will be a rat, and I don't tolerate rats so you when you in my company you never have to worry about nothing but out of good faith I'll respect your wishes and we can do this little paper thang but do your homework. I'm official as they come," says Big Red sincerely.

So Saleem and Big Red begin to converse on paper back and forth for at least an hour and a half. Big Red wants Saleem to buy weight directly from him for a better deal than Dreadz; not major, just a slight difference. Saleem tells Big Red that he's locked in with someone, but he will keep him in mind. Big Red lets him know that to be in with him is the best decision he could ever make due to the fact that he has connections. All through the city from cops, lawyers, and politicians, including the mayor.

"Listen son, you might not know it, but I run this town. Ain't too many people in power in this town I don't have in my pocket or owe me some type favor, or I got some type of dirt on," says Big Red, "so I know even though your young your smart enough to make the right decision. So go ahead and think on it and get back to me," says Big Red with an extended hand. Saleem shakes it, stands up, says his goodbyes and heads for the door.

"That's a very powerful, respected man you just met back there," says Smalls as Saleem opens the door to Smalls Caddy.

They head back to pick up Saleem's car. Saleem tells Smalls he'll let him know whats what after he contemplates everything he's heard from Big. As Smalls drops Saleem off in front of his car, he tells Saleem to make the right decision because he might not see it now, but Big Red is the missing piece to his puzzle and the answer to all of his problems. Then pulls off, leaving Saleem standing by his car in thought.

CHAPTER 58

Saleem is Schooled By Big Red

The next day, the whole city was buzzin' about Dreadz's death. Saleem and Scooby were baffled, but they had a long talk last night about the meeting Saleem had with Big Red. It's like everything that happened yesterday was right on time and the obvious decision now is to fuck with ol' head.

Several weeks have passed, and Saleem and Scooby have flooded the city. Big Red coke is good and his weed is decent, but it's nothing like what Omega had, but it's still fire and selling like crazy. Saleem and Scooby set Boomer up with his own block on 25th and Lamotte in the Junkie Special Crib. If you wonder why they call it that is because the way she sucks a dick is no other way to describe it other than "special," and she's cool with all the other junkies and they all come to her looking for the best coke. So the spot is perfect for Boomer. All he has to do is keep the spot flooded and collect. Saleem's Cousin Wayne and Q opened up a barber shop on 35th and Market Street. Scooby and Saleem opened us a soul food joint on 22nd and Market street called Mum Mum's. Saleem's mom Ms. Betty wanted her and some of her friends who can burn it in the kitchen to keep it packed. They sell all types of home cooking; everybody from all over comes to get some type of platter from Mun Mum's. Saleem and Scooby still got the apartment in Pebble Hill, but both decided they needed their own space, so Scooby went and got a condo and Saleem is renting a house for him and Ayonna. Saleem and Big Red have been having weekly meetings, usually on the progress of all of Saleem's ventures and to make sure he stays focused. Big Red has been schooling

Saleem on other things besides the streets. He knows Saleem is young, but he's smart and got a lot of potential. So every chance he gets, he schools Saleem on the future and how to transition out of the game into politics, real estate, stocks and bonds and how to hustle legitimately. Also, showing him who's crooked and who's straight as far as politicians and cops and who's palm to grease to keep the law off of his back and when the time comes, what politician you need to vote and push for your political ventures. Big Red opened Saleem's eyes up to a whole other level of the game. Right now, he's just preoccupied with everything he has going on right now, but when the time comes, he'll be prepared.

CHAPTER 59

Make an Example Out of Jerse

Ring Ring!

"Yo who dis?" asked Saleem into his cell phone.

"Yo dis Boomer. Where you at?" asked Boomer.

"I'm at the crib wit Ayonna; we just got done eating. She cooked, you want a play or something?" asked Saleem.

"Nah, dog um good."

"Well, whats up dog; talk to me," said Saleem.

"Yo dog, remember you told that the nigga Jerse suppose to have robbed the bitches?"

"Yeah, I remember," replied Saleem.

"Well, this niggas in Special's Crib right now drunk and high as shit and he by his self. Gimme the word and you know what the look is," replied Boomer, eager to handle the situation.

"Well, look here's the play; slide out and lay on him and wait for him to come out, then do 'em dirty. Make an example out of that grimy ass nigga," said Saleem.

"Say no more dog. I got it from here."

Then hangs up the phone.

CHAPTER 60

Boomer Gets His Revenge

"Damn Tss! Ah! Shit!" gasped Scooby.

"Ummm, you like dat?" asked Gutlynn as she slowly sucked Scooby's dick in the front seat of his car in the back parking lot on 25th Street.

"Yeah, deep throat dat shit!" said Scooby.

As told, Gutlynn deep throats Scooby's dick deep in her throat, real slow, then real fast, making Scooby go crazy on the verge of cumming.

Meanwhile, Boomer gives special a bag of coke containing a hundred dimes of crack cocaine, then whispers in her ear that he has to make a run and he'll be sending somebody in here later to take over. In the meantime, take five out and put the rest up until I send my peoples in here to take over.

"You think you slick, I seen you on the phone. One of them bitches done called you, now you trying to creep. I told you I can suck you and fuck you better than my of them young bitches out there. This pussy stay wet and I ain't got no gag reflexion," says Special, dead serious.

"Girl, I got business to take care of and some bitch ain't it," replies Boomer.

"Oh, but when you really let me know," says Special with a shit-eatin' grin.

"Yeah, a'ight," said Boomer, sliding and the back door into the alley.

Back in Special's house, Jerse walks up to Special and asks her why did Boomer go out the back door. Now Jerse doesn't know Boomer fuck with the niggas whose weed spot he robbed.

"Dayum nigga, you all on that," said Special.

"Nah um, just wonderin' why the nigga ain't use da front door," replied Jerse.

"Well, if you must know, he come here time to time and threat his self to this good good. And you know them young boys don't be wanting people to think they be tricking. You know how that go," said Special with a giggle throwing Jerse off.

"Girl, you crazy as shit, but I can dig it tho'," replied Jerse, "but on another note, where that good shit at? I'm trying to smoke a Wooley (which is crack and weed mixed together).

"Well, I got a little somethin' somethin'; you sharin'?" asked Special.

"Yeah, I got chu', let's go roll it up out back and smoke on the step," said Jerse.

"Okay," replies Special.

They head out back, Special passes Jerse the bag of coke. He begins to crush it so he can spread it over the weed. He begins to roll it up.

"Dayum, that's a fatty," said Special referring to the thickness of the joint.

"Yeah, this some good weed too," said Jerse.

"Well, spark it then," said Special.

Jerse rolls out his lighter and takes a deep toke and holds it in for as long as he can. Then passes the joint to Special, who takes a deep pull of the joint and coughs a couple of times, losing smoke.

"Dayum bitch you wasting it," said Jerse heatedly.

"Fuck you motherfucker," replied Special, "this shit strong as shit," said Special taking a shorter pull and then passing it back to Jerse.

They finished the joint and Jerse started grabbing his dick and asked, "Whats up Special with some of that head?"

"Shid, whats up with that money nigga," replied Special.

"Aww girl, you know I got chu'," says Jerse.

"Shid don't got me, get me," replied Special.

"I ain't got it right now but um, good for it," said Jerse.

"You know what? I am kind of horny; whats up with some of that dick," said Special.

"Yo, come here," said Jerse.

Special comes closer. Jerse pulls down his pants and pulls out his dick. "Boy, what chu' want me to do with that little ass shit," said Special with a laugh at the size of Jerse's small penis.

"Bitch, what chu' mean this dick blazing," replied Jerse.

"Boy, I'm not even going to be able to feel that little shit," said Special, seriously pissing Jerse off.

"Bitch fuck you," said Jerse pulling his pants up and leaving through the alley, calling Special all type stinking no good bitches.

Across the street, laying in the cut, is Boomer waiting for the perfect time to catch Jerse coming out of Special's crib.

"Oh shit! Ahh! Um, cumming! Catch it! All shit Burmp!! Fuck!" shouts Scooby, accidentally hitting the horn as he cums all down Gutlynn's throat.

"Umm yeah, I told you, um, a beast," said Gutlynn coming up from in between Scooby's legs.

"Oh Shit! What da fuck!" exclaimed Boomer, hearing the horn go off in the parking lot behind him, so he pulled out his gun and crept further back into the alley to see who was back there and if anybody could see him or seen him. When he gets further back, he sees Scooby's car and then the door opens and Scooby gets out, fixing his pant.

"Look at this tricking ass nigga," thinks Boomer, "he probably got a junkie in the car."

Then the passenger's side door opens up and out pops Gutlynn. Boomer holds back his laugh. Pulls out his phone and calls Scooby. Ring Ring!

"Yo who dis?"

"Yo, this Boomer. Get rid of that bitch and keep the car running. I'm bout to get at that nigga Jerse," says Boomer in a whisper.

"Yo, where you at dog?" asked Scooby looking around.

"Just get rid of the bitch," says Boomer.

"A'ight," replied Scooby.

Boomer heads back down the alley just in time to see Jerse coming out of Special's alley way cussing.

Scooby tells Gutlynn he is going to holler at her and hands her a couple of dollars. She smiles and heads out the other side of the parking lot, switching her little ass, knowing Scooby is probably watching. She makes a left and heads toward Market Street. Scooby calls Boomer's phone. Ring Ring!

"Oh shit," said Boomer dipping back into a back yard cutting his phone off.

"Fuck, I hope that nigga ain't heard that shit."

Scooby hangs up his phone and gets in the car to wait for Boomer. Boomer peeks his head out the back, only to see Jerse crossing the street and entering the parking lot.

"Yo! Who back here!" yells Jerse, "I know somebody back here. I heard your phone."

Boomer's ready as Jerse gets closer, he says, "If somebody back here, you better show yourself I got a gun."

As soon Jerse reaches the back yard where Boomer is, all you hear is Boom! Hitting Jerse in the side of the head, dropping him to the ground. Boomer steps out of the backyard and kicks Jerse over on his back, arms laying side by side, then shoots Jerse three times in the face making him um recognizable. Then once in each hand. Boomer then jogs to Scooby's car getting in the back seat.

"Go dog, go!" says Boomer.

Scooby backs out of the parking lot on the same side Gutlynn left out but makes a right because it's only a one-way street, so he can't head up Market Street.

"Yo dog, you good?" asked Scooby.

"Yeah, um, straight, take me home," said Boomer, "I'll holler at you and Leem tomorrow."

"A'ight," says Scooby riding in silence all the way to Boomer's apartment.

The End

Stay Tuned for Part 2

ABOUT THE AUTHOR

Andre McDougal

Andre Dreskeez McDougal is an excellent storyteller who grew up on the Northside of Wilmington, Delaware, well known in the streets and the prison system.

See, most authors tell crafty stories of lives they never actually lived; however, that's a different story when it comes to Andre McDougal. His life has been an open book, so to speak; he is the son of Betty J. McDougal and Booker T. Washington, not the wrestler, lol. His life hasn't been easy, but he's been doing everything in his power to make a right out of the wrongs in his life.

www.ingramcontent.com/pod-product-compliance
Lightning Source LLC
Chambersburg PA
CBHW040520170726
48295CB00012B/275